CHILD OF THE
SOUTH

JOANNA CATHERINE SCOTT

BERKLEY BOOKS, NEW YORK

THE BERKLEY PUBLISHING GROUP
Published by the Penguin Group
Penguin Group (USA) Inc.
375 Hudson Street, New York, New York 10014, USA
Penguin Group (Canada), 90 Eglinton Avenue East, Suite 700, Toronto, Ontario M4P 2Y3, Canada
(a division of Pearson Penguin Canada Inc.)
Penguin Books Ltd., 80 Strand, London WC2R 0RL, England
Penguin Group Ireland, 25 St. Stephen's Green, Dublin 2, Ireland (a division of Penguin Books Ltd.)
Penguin Group (Australia), 250 Camberwell Road, Camberwell, Victoria 3124, Australia
(a division of Pearson Australia Group Pty. Ltd.)
Penguin Books India Pvt. Ltd., 11 Community Centre, Panchsheel Park, New Delhi—110 017, India
Penguin Group (NZ), 67 Apollo Drive, Rosedale, North Shore 0632, New Zealand
(a division of Pearson New Zealand Ltd.)
Penguin Books (South Africa) (Pty.) Ltd., 24 Sturdee Avenue, Rosebank, Johannesburg 2196,
South Africa

Penguin Books Ltd., Registered Offices: 80 Strand, London WC2R 0RL, England

CHILD OF THE SOUTH

This book is an original publication of The Berkley Publishing Group.

Copyright © 2009 by Joanna Catherine Scott.
"Readers Guide" copyright © 2009 by Penguin Group (USA) Inc.
Cover design by Judith Lagerman.
Cover photograph of Woman copyright © Gaetano Puccini / Alinari Archives / Corbis; photograph of Mountains and Train copyright © agefotostock / SuperStock.
Text design by Tiffany Estreicher.

PRINTING HISTORY
Berkley trade paperback edition / April 2009

Library of Congress Cataloging-in-Publication Data

Scott, Joanna C., (date)
   Child of the South / Joanna Catherine Scott. — Berkley trade pbk. ed.
      p. cm.
   Sequel to: The road from Chapel Hill.
   ISBN 978-0-425-22602-5
  1. Women, White—Southern States—Fiction.   2. North Carolina—History—1865—Fiction.
3. African American politicians—North Carolina—Fiction.   4. Freedmen—North Carolina—
Fiction.   5. Southern States—Social conditions—19th century—Fiction.   6. Southern
States—Race relations—Fiction.   I. Title
   PS3569.C638C49   2009
   813'.54—dc22   2008039390

PRINTED IN THE UNITED STATES OF AMERICA

10   9   8   7   6   5   4   3   2   1

Praise for *The Road*

"A rich and rewarding journey into the Civil War era, full of historical detail, surprising characters, and all the complexity of the time."   —Thomas Dyja, author of *Play for a Kingdom*

"Joanna Catherine Scott demonstrates great ambition in her new novel, *The Road from Chapel Hill*. Here she tackles the dual subjects any writer on the American South must eventually face: the region's history of race relations and the legacy of the Civil War. Each is tangled with the other in a web of pain, misunderstanding, heartache, loss, and occasionally, redemptive love. And so they are in Scott's novel . . . She is to be commended for her adept skill with language (especially in her creation of mood), for her ability to enter fully into another historic era and into the minds of three dissimilar characters facing heartrending circumstances."

—*The Raleigh News & Observer*

"A story at times disturbing, at times uplifting, *The Road from Chapel Hill* is at once heart-wrenching and heartwarming. But most of all, it is a story of humanity at its very worst and very best . . . Scott uses three characters to tell a fascinating tale of love, war, valor, wickedness, and the cost we must all pay for what we believe in and hold most dear."   —*The (Roxboro, NC) Courier-Times*

"Joanna Catherine Scott was born in England and raised in Australia, and that makes this book all the more remarkable. It is a Civil War story, based entirely in North Carolina, and Scott writes in black dialect and white Tar Heel dialect with ease and skill."

—*The Fayetteville Observer*

"In sparse, clean prose, Scott weaves together the tangled threads of three lives. She concentrates less on the history of the Civil War and more on the changes in her characters' lives as disenfranchised people in a world ruled by social class and race. Scott asks readers to think and question not only the world of her novel but our world as well."   —*Romantic Times* (4 stars)

"On the dedication page of *The Road From Chapel Hill* are the words 'For Tom.' With those two words, Joanna Catherine Scott gave life to a slave whose story is lost to history."

—*The (Southern Pines, NC) Pilot*

"A unique perspective [on] those in the South who did not support the Confederacy . . . All the details are historically accurate."

—*The (Durham, NC) Herald-Sun*

continued . . .

For John Lee Conaway,
another child of the South

I think the white man as good as the Negro—
if he will only behave himself.

—ABRAHAM GALLOWAY

CHAPTER ONE

THE train was rickety and jam-packed with what seemed a thousand Negroes. Men and women of all ages, children of all sizes, laughing, shouting, boisterous with liberation, craned their necks to peer around each other at the passing world. With each lurch forward, the luggage racks shook fearfully, threatening to rain down trunks and boxes, buckets, pans and kettles onto unsuspecting heads. Bundles of clothes and bedding filled the spaces in between the seats like stuffing in a mattress and leaked out into the aisle, babies sleeping in the hollows and small children, fly-eyed and runny-nosed, perched triumphantly on top.

A clot of Rebel soldiers stood at one end of the carriage,

half a dozen Yankees further down. The Negroes ignored the Rebels, but the Yankees they treated with jocularity, shouting back and forth across them, laughing when their blank faces showed they could not understand a word. I had never seen so many joyful blacks together in one place. The slaves back at the gold mine had been a miserable, suffering lot, intent on running off at any opportunity. These people reveled in each other like a great big family reunion, the few white civilians on the train bearing their noisy company with impassive resignation, only the flicker of a nostril or the turning of a shoulder hinting at emotions more extreme.

Their joy enchanted me, but at the same time it disquieted. All my life, Negro gatherings had been banned for fear of plots and insurrections. They are free now, I told myself, they can gather if they wish.

In the rush aboard I had not managed to secure a seat, and so clung resolutely to a seat back, half suffocated by the mass of bodies, my small bundle of possessions dangling from my other hand. From the conversations going on around me, I gathered that the Negroes were headed for the city in hopes of finding work that did not involve the dawn-to-dark hard labor of the farm. One spoke of signing for the Union army, another of taking ship north to a brand-new life. I slipped my hand into my pocket, fingering my last few tiny bits of gold. With the price so high it was enough—I hoped it was enough—to support me until I also could find paying work.

The train progressed at a lamentable pace, rattling and creaking and heaving itself along the track like an old mule raised from sleep and inclined at any minute to fall back into it. I became breathless from the closeness, nauseated by the stench of bodies. I had eaten but a bowl of thin potato soup the night before and that morning had taken nothing. I let go of the seat back and began to push my way toward a window where I could lean out into the air, but trapped between the backs of two enormous Negroes, I felt faintness overcome me and the next thing I knew I was being passed hand to hand along the aisle and deposited in a broken-bottomed seat beside a window where the rush of air revived me. A woman with a basket on her knees sat on my other side and she was kind, calling out to the jostling legs and backs, "Get on out of the way, this poor thing is like to passed into eternity."

Here I found myself knee to knee with another white woman, very pale and thin, who gazed about her as though in bewilderment and did not return my nod of greeting. Next to her was a Negro woman with a washboard jammed between her knees and a baby in her arms, the child fussing and coughing and rolling up its eyes, the mother soothing it and humming, although the child was so feverish and sick that the minute I set my nurse's eye on it I knew that it was done for.

Time rattled on, the train alternating between a crawling pace and a complete wheezing stop while it seemed to contemplate the wisdom of progressing. The sky darkened, the streaming air grew chill, and a rainstorm clattered overhead. The pale woman set up a wail for somebody to close the window. It was broken, however, and no amount of tugging by an obliging pair of strong black arms could get it closed, and all the other windows in the same forlorn condition. I pulled my cloak across my hair and crossed my arms and hunched my

3

body to keep warm, from time to time scratching at myself—greybacks, perhaps, from my companions on the train. Or bedbugs from the rooming house in Goldsboro where I had spent last night bedded with a large fat woman so afraid of being robbed that she packed her bags and bundles into bed around her, forcing me so close to the edge that I spent the night grateful to be barely more than skin and bone.

Now, dazed with sleeplessness, I fell asleep and dreamed about Mama. She stood above me, brushing out my hair with hard, unsympathetic strokes. And then her voice, "Such curl, it is unnatural," and the wrenching downward stroke, bringing tears into my eyes. Confused sounds, images of faces that I seemed to know, and I was standing by her grave. It was open, nothing there but bones.

A dreadful shrieking startled me awake—a passing train—and I sat shaking and disoriented, my cloak fallen to my shoulders and one hand raised as though to fend off an attacker.

"Lord, Lord, now the poor child is having nightmares," said the old Negro woman next to me. Shifting her basket on her knees, she took my hand, and bringing it gently down, nudged against me with a sympathetic shoulder.

"Child, ain't no one goin' hurt you now."

For one disoriented moment I wanted to fling myself facedown onto this kindly woman's lap and weep, but the basket saved me from myself, squatting there as if to say it owned the space and no intruders were allowed. And so I turned my concentration to the window, watching the damply swimming sky grow blue and bluer until all traces of the storm had vanished back behind.

We rocked through countryside where here and there a farmhouse regarded us with melancholy burned-out eyes, as though in mourning for the naked fields, which at that time of year should have been vigorous with newly sprouting crops. Negroes seemed everywhere about, walking, walking, bundles on their heads and children dragging on behind. The pale woman watched them through the window. She looked across at me. "Wandering," she hissed, "just wandering. It cannot come to any good."

I did not respond. I was thinking about Tom. Where was he now? Had he made it all the way to Canada? Perhaps, with the war over, he was heading home with all the rest. Perhaps if I watched closely I would spy him. Perhaps if I had not left Chapel Hill so hastily, I might have . . . No, I had to leave. I had to make this journey. I had to know the truth.

CHAPTER TWO

IT was April eighteen sixty-five, and back in Chapel Hill word was out that General Sherman's men were handing food out to the poor at Durham railway station. The news spread farm to farm as though a telegram had been sent posthaste to every one of them, and pretty soon the road was thick with bone-shanked men and women, their children at their heels dull-eyed from near starvation, hurrying to see if this were true. Negroes, black skeletons almost, and women thrown into the trade of prostitution by the war jostled amongst them, while along the edges clots of Rebel soldiers trudged.

On a farm just south of town, Clyde Bricket lay on a cot

beside the kitchen window, fulminating at the pure bad luck of having had his rotten leg cut off above the knee but three days back. When he first heard about the rations he had figured he would go for them. Ma and Uncle Benjamin could heave him up onto the horse and someone at the other end could stuff the saddlebags. But then Doc Berryman came by and said, "Young man, you try a damn fool thing like that and you will purely bleed to death."

Uncle Benjamin could not go for rations. He was blind, both eyes blasted from his head by a field gun backfiring, and him intending to be nothing but a chaplain, it weren't right. The hired nigra could not go. He had run off before the war was even done. And Ma, who had a pair of seeing eyes and two whole legs, said, "If I go gallivantin' off, who will take care of you?"

Clyde said, "Old Mary will, o' course," but Ma said, "I would rather starve than leave my boy when he is like to go to heaven while I am away."

Clyde said, "Miss Genie were supposed to be my nurse, she promised me. But then she up and left me, I do not understand it. She done shoulda stayed, she shoulda. And she coulda gone for rations."

It was early in the morning. Ma had been out hunting wild turkey eggs in the woods and come back home with two, which she was getting ready to cook up for Clyde. She pulled her clay pipe from the corner of her mouth and spat into a tin.

"Boy, you quit your whining. It were me as told her to be off, we could not feed her, we did not have enough. I said to her, I am his ma and it is me as how will care for him, and that is that."

At which Clyde quit whining and moaned instead, "But what about the rations, who will get the rations?"

And Ma said, "Why that boy Tom, o' course. He has come back. He is down there at the cabin with Old Mary." She stuck her pipe back in, and with both eggs in one hand, cracked them with a quick flick of the wrist into the pan.

"That Tom? He has come back?"

"Large as life. I come behind Old Mary's cabin and saw her crying on his neck, and him saying, I did not think to find you here, I thought you woulda run, and her saying, I coulda run, I woulda, but I figured you'd come looking for me here."

Ma jabbed the frying eggs with a knife so that the yolks spread out and hissed on the hot surface. "And after all these years of bein' good to her, never done her wrong." She rattled the pan back and forth, loosening the eggs so they would not stick. "Anyways, her boy is here, he has come back."

"Then I am done for. I am a dead man."

"Don't be a fool. Tom ain't going to hurt you." She slid the eggs onto a plate, pulled a spoon out of a drawer, and carried plate and spoon across to him. "Here, hoist yourself up and eat this, it will do you good." She went off into the room where she and Uncle Benjamin slept and came back with the good red quilt. "Red is good for lifting up the spirits." And she spread it out across him, then went to the door, where she let out a shrill three-noted call, "Old Maaa . . . ry."

Behind her, Clyde clutched the spoon, eyeing the fried eggs balefully. "But it were me as got Tom catched back before the war when he were living in the woods. He'll blame me for it."

Ma turned back into the room and made a spitting sound. "He's just a nigra. Nigras cain't remember one day from the next, he has clear forgot what happened five year back. And he is starving just the same as us, he is skinny as if he never had a bite in all his *en*tire life."

"But all these nigras free now, they will not do anything at all, I heard it at the hospital."

"This one has come home to his ma, so we have got him. We will send him off on Transportation for the rations. I figure he can haul a good amount."

"Let that nigra ride my horse? I will not do it."

"You better do it if you want them rations."

"What about Old Mary? I'd trust *her* with my horse. She would not dare to steal him."

"Old Mary got the rheumatiz. And anyway, she got to take care of the baby."

"Baby? What-all's this about a baby?"

"Some little yeller thing Tom brung with him. He calls it Baby Gold, I heered them talking 'bout it. Its ma got took by bushwhackers, its pa as well, so he done scooped the poor thing up and brung it with him. It were good o' him, he coulda left it. It were a good thing that he done, which means he has grown up a good man, even if a nigra, and will not blame you even if he do remember five year back." She sniffed. "He brung a cat with him as well, a big ol' black thing, stray I guess. You goin' eat them eggs or not? Then hand them here, I'll feed them to your uncle Benjamin."

She went and shouted at the door again and when Uncle Benjamin appeared, tapping his cane against the doorpost, then against the table leg until he found the stool, she settled him down with the plate and spoon and went back to the door.

"Where that old woman got to? If we don't get that Tom movin' quick there'll be no rations left."

Clyde said, "He will not do it. He will see me here and hate me, he might kill me in the night for what I done, leading the patrollers to his hideaway and getting him all shot up in the legs like that, and sold away as well." Clyde's voice quavered. "I believe he has come back to kill me."

Uncle Benjamin, who had been turning his head from voice to voice, said, "Son, if he's come back to kill you, then he's come back to kill you, we will jump that puddle when we come to it. But right this moment we should give the good Lord thanks we have a strong back come among us. That boy can do more than go off riding after rations, he can plow and plant and work the fields. You better be right nice to him or he will take his ma and that there little child and run off and leave us to our certain doom."

When Clyde's face began to twitch with nervousness, and him saying, "I do not dare to face him, I do not dare to face him," Uncle Benjamin said, "Son, without Tom we will starve," and so Clyde quieted and shrugged and said with a dramatic peevishness, "Well, then, I will prepare myself for death," at which Uncle Benjamin twisted round and knocked his cane against Clyde's cot and chuckled in his throat.

"I'll be the one to speak to him," he said, and skidded back his stool.

MINUTES later, Tom stood in his mother's cabin door regarding Uncle Benjamin. Here was this half-starved blind man commanding him because he was a Negro. Ever since he left the gold mine and took up as a Union spy in New Bern three years back, Tom had not been slave to anyone and had grown accustomed to it. Now, though, for a moment, he felt an echo of the fear that used to take him by the throat and make his brains freeze in his head and his body become slow and awkward so they called him simpleton. Had he been a slave once? The notion had become impossible.

A large black cat with yellow eyes came out of the cabin and wound itself around Tom's legs, looking up at Uncle Benjamin. It curled its lips back and made a loud miaow.

"That's Rebel Cat," Tom said, but Uncle Benjamin went on standing quiet, waiting for an answer.

"Who owns this farm?" Tom said.

Uncle Benjamin turned his head to one side as though he had not heard, or had not understood.

"Who owns this farm?"

"Why Clyde, o' course. Now his pa is dead the farm belongs to him."

"And where is Clyde? Why does *he* not come to ask me?"

Behind its scars, Uncle Benjamin's face took on a reproving look. "I don't see what," he started, and then as though someone had whispered caution in his ear, his tone turned more conciliatory. He had been a preacher once and wore a wide-brimmed preacher's hat, which he now took off and with an unctuous motion set against his breast.

"Clyde is injured. Three days back he had his rotten leg cut off again. He lies suffering upon his cot."

Tom looked beyond him at the fields, unplowed and weed-ridden. He looked at Uncle Benjamin, stone blind. Up at the Bricket cabin was a one-legged boy and an aging woman. Not a soul to work the farm.

"You used to have a hired boy called Amos. Where is he?"

"Run off. Took the shotgun with him." Uncle Benjamin's voice took on a pleading quality. "There's no one here but you can go for rations. We'll let you take the horse."

"Did you say you had a horse?"

Uncle Benjamin brightened. "Name of Transportation. Clyde brought it with him when he came back from the war. Ain't much of a horse, but enough to get you to the station and haul some rations back." He hesitated. "Of course we'll give you and your ma a share."

"I think if there are rations to be had we're entitled to our own."

Tom turned back into the cabin where the low sound of crooning could be heard. He took a worn jacket off a hook and pulled it on. "I'll come speak with Clyde."

"I'd not do that, the boy is . . ." Uncle Benjamin screwed up his face and made a sucking through his teeth.

Tom, halfway across the dooryard with Rebel Cat behind him, turned. "The boy is what?"

"Afraid of you."

"As well he might be. I'll take myself along and see how much afraid." And with Uncle Benjamin tapping in his wake, Tom strode off down the path, across the bridge above the creek and through the long grass toward the Bricket cabin.

A flood of memories went with him—how he had run off to the woods so long ago and lived in a den by Morgan's Creek, how he had hunted animals with rocks, ripped them apart with his bare hands and swallowed them down raw because he was afraid to build a fire, how his toes froze in the winter and went black so that he feared he'd lose them. How one day he had walked out of his den and found Clyde pissing up against a tree, pale pink little organ in his hand and terror on his face, how Clyde went shrieking to betray him. Then the headlong flight before the posse, the shouts of "You, boy, Tom!" and the barking of the gun, pain lifting him and smashing him back down. And then his sale to traders.

Tom breathed heavily. He could not go beyond that. His journey with the traders to the gold mine he had long since trained himself to block out of his mind. If he thought about it now he might do something foolish. The traders took him to Miss Genie, he must think of it like that.

He looked across the dismal fields again and at the Bricket cabin. Though larger than his mother's, it was no finer, with broken shingles on the roof, the chimney crumbling and the porch rail half collapsed.

By the time he stood beside Clyde's cot the emotion in his heart was pity. This pathetic crippled boy cowering underneath the quilt was not worth hating or resenting, or doing much with at all except to offer charity. He dismissed Clyde's ma, who, when she realized he meant it, went to stand out on the porch, straining her neck to peer in through the window.

"You own this farm?"

Clyde bunched the quilt beneath his chin, his skin stark white against its redness. "My pa, he's dead, so it belongs to me."

"I see you have no crop in."

Clyde turned back the quilt to show the bloody bundle of his amputation. Tears stood in his eyes.

"You understand you'll starve without a crop?"

Clyde nodded.

Outside, Uncle Benjamin tapped his way up the three steps to the porch. Rebel Cat, who had taken a position on the porch rail, watched him come. As he reached the top, the big black cat reached out a paw toward him and then drew it back, as if giving him permission to pass on.

Tom heard the door latch click, but Ma's voice spoke sharply and it stopped.

"What do you plan to do to save yourself?" Tom said.

"I thought . . . I hoped . . ." Clyde drew his breath in hard and rushed into coherent speech. "Sir, Mister Tom, I done repented for what I done to you, getting you shot up and catched the way I did. But I have seen the light, I swear it for the truth." A sly look crossed his face. "Sir, I been a soldier for the Union. I been fighting for the nigra to be free."

14

Tom laughed. "I doubt that."

"It is God's truth. I were a Union soldier."

Tom pulled a stool up and sat down with his forearms on his knees and his hands clasped in between them. "The truth, is it? So how did you accomplish that?"

"I were . . . my pa, he were hiding out from them recruiters. He did not want to go to war, he had a farm to run. And Fred Hintner's pa, his boy had gone to war and got hisself shot through the head, and his pa, he were upset, he said, God strike me dead, but I will never fight for that Jeff Davis. And so my pa and Fred Hintner's pa and another feller too, they dug theirselves a cave and lived out in the woods and never went to war. But they got caught. Them recruiters, they knowed fellers hid out in the woods and they went hunting after them. It rained the night before, the ground was soft, and they fell clear through on top of Pa and his two friends, and they jumped up outa that there hole and run, and them recruiters shooting after them, and they shot Pa, and he were clear stone dead and I were upset just like Fred Hintner's pa, and I stood up by Pa's grave and said I will not fight for that Jeff Davis either, and Fred Hintner's pa, he said, I know a feller who can help you get that organized, and then . . ."

Tom laughed. "And then there you were, a Union soldier by mistake."

Clyde looked offended. "It were true I had not really thought to do it, just said it out of spite and sorrow for my pa, but I were a good soldier. I were loyal to the Union. I fought good as anyone and did not run."

"And so what happened then?"

"I got took by the Rebels and sent down to that wicked prison over there in Salisbury, and it were bitter cold, everything frozed over, and nowhere to find shelter except by digging in the ground. Them prisoners, they lived in holes just like my pa and Mister Hintner, except they had no food and no warm clothes and no one cared a lick and they were mean men, mean, on account o' all that suffering, and no one would let me share a hole and that was when my foot froze and turned rotten and I near to died."

Clyde looked up at Tom, a pleading expression on his face. "It is God's truth."

"I believe you. That's a story no one could make up. So how did you get out of prison?"

"Took off all my clothes and laid down on the dead pile. They hauled me outa there to bury me with all the rest, but I slid down off that cart when nobody were looking and I run. It were dead cold winter and I thought that I would purely freeze, but I just kept on running till I fell flat down and got picked up by some nigras and hauled off to a hospital." He lowered his voice and looked mysterious. "It were a *secret* hospital."

"Goodness! A secret hospital now! Why would a hospital be secret?"

"It were a secret *Union* hospital. They were taking care of fellers who got sideways with recruiters, got their heads busted or such and wanted to run off to Tennessee or somewheres, but they couldn't on account they had the busted head or some such evil them recruiters done to them—they were right cruel men, bust your head as soon as look at you, they would—and so these fellers were staying at this secret hospital till they was strong enough to run."

He sucked in a hard breath, checked Tom's face again for disbelief, and then went rushing on.

"This hospital, they had it in the cellar of a house outside o' town. It were very dark down there. Them people what run it, they was in a sorta club they called the Red Strings. It were a secret club. They done things to help the Union in the South. Like this hospital for helping sick deserters. There was four on 'em what run it, three women and a big black feller name o' Henry. This Henry, he mighta been a nigra, but he were a fine man"—Clyde hesitated, looking nervously at Tom—"he *were* a fine man, I do not say that just to get on your good side, he were a sorta doctor and he did the ampertations, he were the one cut my leg off the first time. The women soused me up in whiskey and he done it with a saw. He done a good job but the stump took to rotting."

"So why did he not cut it off again?"

"I would not let him. I figured it would only rot again, I figured I were done for, I figured a man ought to see his ma afore he dies, so I come home."

"With one good leg and one half rotten, you just jumped up and came home?"

"My nurse come with me. She did not want to come at first, she were for another ampertation, so I said to her, I said, I will have another ampertation if you take me home to Ma, I will have the doctor do it there in Chapel Hill. And she done it. She come on home with me. On account, she said, she could not bear to let me die after all she done to keep me from the grave, that's what she said. And so Henry stole a horse, a sack o' bones he were but he were a good horse and I still have him, he is called Transportation. And Henry got a feller, he were a Red String too, a big strong feller with a rifle, and he went along with us to keep the thieves and bushwhackers away, and my nurse, she walked all the way from Salisbury to Chapel Hill with me on Transportation. She were a good woman, yessir she were, right pretty too. She were s'posed to stay here with me, she were s'posed to be my nurse after my second ampertation, but she ran off while I were in the hospital and when I come home she were gone. I were . . . I were *upset*. I—"

"You can tell me about that another time. For now I have a proposition."

"A proper what?"

"A proposition. A plan of action."

"You mean a deal? Where you learn to talk so fancy anyways? You don't talk like a nigra anymore."

Tom said, "About this farm of yours."

CHAPTER THREE

A small commotion in the group of Rebels at the far end of the carriage caught my eye. A man wearing a stiff white collar and a brilliant red cravat had come in from the carriage that adjoined and was nudging his way through them, they turning their heads to watch him as he went. He nodded at them, smiling, but the Rebels made their faces blank, eyes moving on him up and down, taking in the size of him, the musculature straining at his neatly tailored coat.

At first I took him for a white man, but then understood he was mulatto, very light of skin. He passed the Rebels and made his way along the aisle one black passenger by one, speaking to each of them as if he knew them, as if he cared where they were going and what would become of them. He shook their hands or put an arm around a shoulder, paid attention to what their women had to say and praised them for their children—I could tell that from the way the women smiled—leaving in his wake an almost visible benevolence that seemed to glow.

Absorbed in my own concerns and worries, I watched him in a manner abstracted, hardly watching really, just letting him be in my vision, not consciously absorbing him. But when he stopped and looked directly at me and smiled into my eyes, I felt a warm sensation, as though I had been greeted by a friend. An inner excitement seemed to light him up, his energy intense and concentrated, as though he must achieve today what was his to achieve because tomorrow was uncertain. He was the sort of man who made you want to trust him, to confide in him, to let him organize your life.

I half smiled back at him, not looking directly, so that it was the row of buttons on his waistcoat that I saw, the breath that rose and fell behind them. I had his face inside my head, though, the delicate pale skin, the sculpted cheekbones, the sensual full mouth. He was clean-shaven and his hair was long and black, not curling tightly like a Negro's, but falling in soft waves on his neck in the manner of a Southern gentleman. When finally I conceded and looked directly at him, he raised a hand and pushed a lock of hair back off his forehead. His coat lifted with the movement, then fell back, revealing and hiding a metal-blue revolver at his hip. The expression in his eyes was almost like collusion, as though we two shared a secret to which no one else was party.

He set his hand against the back of the man in front of him as though to edge his way across so he could speak to me, but just then a Rebel soldier shouldered him aside and wedged himself into the seat across from me between the pale woman and the one with the sick child, tilting his body toward me, one hand atop the other on a knobby cane, his presence insisting on my full attention.

My eyes were locked with the mulatto's, and the soldier, following my gaze, made an impatient clearing of the throat. "Insolence of him," he said, waving a dismissive hand. "Eugenia Mae," he said, and I swung surprised toward him. From the corner of my eye I saw the mulatto move on down the train.

The soldier's eyes turned questioning and disappointed. "You do not remember me? It's Christopher. Christopher Clark-Compton. Surely I am not so changed?"

And it was he, yes of course, it was his voice. I remembered those blond curls, the soft white hands and pure white linen, the way my heart sighed after him. I counted up the years—six, almost seven—since I had been a young lady of Wilmington society, with hoops to my skirts and frilled lace-bodiced gowns, a pocketful of cards with *Eugenia Mae Spotswood* engraved in silver letters, and the carelessness of youth inside my heart. In those days Christopher had been at university in Chapel Hill, boasting that one day he would be a famous lawyer. His father owned a sizable plantation and a house in Wilmington on Market Street, and made investments in other people's businesses so that everybody touched their hats to him and asked for his advice.

Christopher's face was thinner now, and older, his frivolity of manner gone, along with the pure white linen and the soft white hands. He smiled uncertainly and when I smiled back, more surely. Pushing his face toward me, he said, "I am pleased to see you. It has been too long." As though he had forgotten all about Papa's plunge into bankruptcy, our abandonment by good society, our ignominious flight.

"You are just back from the war?" I said.

He moved his head in an inclusive motion. "We have come back from Virginia. We have been paroled." And without waiting for me to respond, "I have an injury. A Yankee smacked his rifle up against my head. It has made me unsteady in a fight. I am in health, but I lose my balance easily."

"And so the cane?"

He shrugged. "I do not like to use it."

"Vanity?" I meant it lightly.

"I'm too proud to admit a Yankee has disabled me."

"I'm sorry, I did not mean to offend."

He pulled his mouth down, glancing at his feet. "These boots, I got them off a Yankee, a dead man."

"The war is over now, all that is past."

"And a good thing too, or we would all be lost. If I ever hear another person say the word *secesh* I swear I will just knock him down."

I looked into his face and it came to me that this young man who seemed so old was changed not just in body but in spirit too. Whereas once he had been open-faced and laughing, saying anything he thought with self-assurance, now a shadow lurked behind his eyes, a sort of furtiveness—no, it was a vacancy, a lack, and with that lack a hint of violence, yes, a propensity for easy violence that was new. I recognized that look, the war had taught it to him.

"What is it?" he said.

"I was thinking of the time your family took me to the beach for a vacation. And you and I sneaked out of the rooming house at dawn and went walking on the sand. We saw a fog bow hanging in the sky above the ocean. The sun was rising up behind it, causing it to shine and shimmer in the light. Do you remember that?"

"I do, most clearly. You were wearing a green gown the color of the sea and your hat was tied by its ribbons underneath your chin. It had flown off and was bobbing at your back, your hair all tossed about." His eyes turned tender. "I thought you the most beautiful creature I had ever seen."

I felt my voice grow stiff. "The war has robbed me of what beauty I once had."

He reached across and touched my hand, his body rocking with the rocking of the train. "We've all been robbed of what we had." A silence, and then, "Your papa? Forgive me, but you seem to be alone."

"Papa is dead."

He watched me, waiting.

"I find it hard to speak of."

"He died a hero, I am sure of that."

Tears sprang to my eyes. I could not tell him. I could never tell a soul. That shameful dying. That despair. The horrid details. How his body, letting go its fluids, stained the cabin floor and soiled the crimson velvet slipper fallen from his foot. The way his body swung so gently while his pale blue eyes bulged from his head as if he had seen something dreadful in the other world.

"Dear cousin, you have suffered." Christopher's eyes traveled over me, seeming to take in my ragged condition for the first time. "You must accept shelter with my family."

I felt a burning coming up my neck. "But I . . . I had not expected . . . I had not planned . . ."

"Tush, cousin. You will stay with us, I will not take refusal."

I opened my mouth to speak again but my thought was lost in yet another shrieking of the train's whistle, the added shrieking of its brakes, and the babble of voices as it slowed and shuddered and came to an uncertain halt, everybody up and gathering their wits and packages and children and shoving for the door as if a prize were to be given for the first one out onto the platform.

As it turned out, there was no platform, just a straight drop to the ground. And no station buildings either, just burned-out hulks, the work, I discovered later, of General Bragg's army as it fled before the Union troops advancing from the sea. Beyond the station yard, across the river, were rows of tents and makeshift shelters among which distant figures moved—a refugee camp, I surmised.

I looked about for the mulatto, and there he was. He seemed to feel my gaze, and turning, nodded, at the same time raising his hand in a gesture that sent through me a thrill of something close to recognition. Tom had raised his hand in just that way when I set him free along the road to Salisbury. It was a gesture dear to me and because of it the notion once more came into my head that this man and I were friends.

As though he read my thought, he smiled at me, and then at Christopher across my shoulder—Christopher once more muttering "Insolence of him"—and set off at a determined pace. I stumbled watching him, and recovering my balance, concentrated on picking my way across the tracks, my arm through Christopher's, not sure who supported whom. Once, glancing up, I thought I saw the mulatto up ahead, but then he vanished in the crowd.

Most of the returning Rebels went off quickly, calling farewells to each other, except one who paused to introduce himself a little breathlessly as "Roland Younger, ma'am, Christopher's third cousin on his father's side, your old friend Sylvie Younger's little brother."

I said, "Of course, how nice," although I could not place him. In seven years a little brother can become a man. I did remember Sylvie, an elegant young lady with a haughty nose who had owned a feathered hat I once had envied. She had been the first of all my friends to cut me from her invitation list.

For a moment I wished I had not made this journey. I had meant to find employment, maybe in a hospital, and rent a room somewhere. Beyond that my plans were vague. A place to live, some useful work, a modest income of some sort—it was enough to think about before I turned my mind to the unsettling matter that had brought me back here to the place I had been born. I had not foreseen being thrust in amongst these people who had once turned their backs on me and now seemed to have forgotten how they hurt me.

We were out of the railroad yard by now, into the commotion of the streets, which were windblown with trash and swarmed with destitute-looking Negroes, whites as well. Wilmington had always been more a black town than a white— domestic slaves and slaves who worked for masters in their trades and businesses, slaves who hired out their own time, free blacks and mulattoes. But although the atmosphere some-times was suspicious and electric, the place had always been industrious and bustling, everybody occupied with what he had to do that day. Now everything was changed. I had seen poverty before, and misery, and ragged, vague-eyed hopeless-ness, but never in my life had I seen so much of it together in one place.

"I don't remember all these niggers lollygagging on the streets," Christopher said. "Something should be done about it."

"They are free men now," I said. "I suppose they may lolly-gag if they choose."

He looked sharply down at me, but just then a mule cart swaying underneath a load of broken furniture cut across our path, a skinny country woman perched on top.

"A little care, woman, take a little care," Christopher called up to her, but she looked back down at him, and gath-ering her wad together, spat an accurate tarry jet that landed at his feet. He cursed and jumped aside, jostling me, apologiz-ing for his language, almost losing his balance, and by the time he had regained it, the woman and her cart had lurched off down the street.

He was still grumbling as we turned the corner into Market Street, where, outside a building on which hung a sign, *Re-cruitment Office,* a line of Negroes stood shifting one foot to the other, the queue stretching well past the broken wooden sidewalk out onto the sandy street.

"See," I said, "*these* men are not lollygagging. They're volunteering for the Union army."

Christopher let go my arm and walked directly at them, making sweeping motions with his cane as though to clear them from his path. They did not budge, but went on shifting foot to foot exactly as they had before, watching him with mild expectancy. He backed away, red-faced, and seizing me by the arm, began to hustle me around them. But I was riled up now, and twisting from his grip, looked up into the passive faces. "I'd be most grateful if you'd let us through."

As if I had just said "Open, Sesame," they stood aside and let us pass, and I called "Thank you" back across my shoulder. Out of earshot, I said, "Even Negroes will respond to common courtesy."

But Christopher's truculent mood had passed. He limped along beside me whistling through his teeth as if not a thing had happened. It made me feel quite breathless, this sudden shifting into anger then back to affability.

"Come along, come along," he cried, tugging at my arm. "I cannot wait to see my parents. It will be a great surprise." He began to run, but stumbled on a broken section of the sidewalk and this time almost pulled me down.

"Behave yourself," I said, laughing, because already I had forgiven him. "You do not want to present yourself to your family flat on your face. We'll be there soon enough."

As we went, I looked about. When last I walked this street all the homes had gleamed with paint, their gardens neat and confident with flowers. Now they had faded, their shutters and front gates askew, slats missing from the fences, paintwork peeling off in patches that made them look diseased. The gardens, with their redbuds and azaleas and wisteria-crazed trellises, were lovely still, their spring colors just as varied and tumultuous, their scents as subtle and seductive, but now the trellises were tipped and tilted, weeds tangled in amongst them, or debris blown in from the street. Gazebos slouched beneath their loads as if they had lost heart, and here and there beneath them a vagabond sprawled out asleep.

"Here we are," Christopher said.

He pushed aside a low wrought-iron gate and we went together down the walkway of a house I well remembered, a tall-pillared mansion with a broad verandah on the lower level and a curved balcony above. We had barely stepped onto the verandah when the door smacked open and a woman flew out and flung herself on Christopher, almost knocking him down.

"My son! My son has come back home!"

Another woman followed making little mewing sounds, and the two of them half strangled Christopher with welcome. He gave himself up to their embraces, kissing first one then the other, crying, "Mother! Aunt Lavinia! How good to see you both again!"

They dragged him inside, calling, "Colonel! Colonel! Look what we have here!" and Colonel Clark-Compton came running with the collar of his shirt askew.

Throughout all the kissing and weeping and exclaiming I stood out on the verandah, uncertain what to do. I had half a mind to slip off quietly and go in search of modest lodgings as

I had planned, and had even turned and started down the steps when Colonel Clark-Compton's voice behind me called, "What have we here? What have we here?" and when I turned he had me in his arms as though I were a long-lost daughter, kissing my cheeks and pushing me away from him to examine me more closely.

"I do believe young Christopher is right, it is Eugenia Mae." His voice broke, and with as much excitement as the women but more gently, he ushered me inside. "Look, we have Eugenia Mae come back to us as well. We are becoming quite a family." He looked behind me. "Your papa?"

"Hush, Father," Christopher said. "She finds it hard to speak of." His voice dropped to a respectful murmur. "Another of our Southern heroes."

"Ah," the Colonel said, gathering me back into his arms, "there are so many we find it hard to speak of."

He was weeping, and I soon gathered that of their three children only Christopher remained, his elder brother killed in battle, his little sister dead of yellow fever. Their welcome to me was so genuine and so affecting I had no choice but to be received into the family, astonished by it, discombobulated, all my own plans tossed into the air. And yet I felt relief as well, reluctant, a sort of giving in while at the same time glad to have a place to breathe.

CHAPTER FOUR

JUST after noon, Tom had headed off on Transportation, a sway-backed old rip with one eye missing and no enthusiasm for the journey. Rations were not the first thing on his mind, although he was as hungry as the rest. What occupied him was the deal he had just made with Clyde. It had been easier than he expected. The wretched boy seemed almost glad to make it. When he had hauled the rations back, he would ride across to Raleigh where someone from the Freedmen's Bureau would help him draw up papers making him and Clyde joint owners of the farm.

In exchange for that, Tom would work the fields and hunt and make sure everyone was fed. And if Clyde died, of rot perhaps, the farm would go to him. It was a hard bargain he had made, and he hoped Clyde's ma and uncle Benjamin would not take against it, but he did not intend to act as slave to anyone again.

His fellow travelers jostled round him in their tattered clothes and naked feet and broken-down straw hats. He was the only one amongst them on a horse. None of the others had so much as a mule, although a number pulled small carts and wagons and one man had a goat with flour sack saddlebags.

As they came closer to what he supposed was Durham station, he pulled out of the crowd, which now milled around a group of dingy buildings, one of which seemed to be a general store. It was from here, apparently, that rations were to be distributed, although the door was shut and locked and pounding on it brought no response. One man said the train was late, another that it had already been and gone. An argument broke out, a fist was swung, the combatants dragged apart by men with cooler heads and sent off like naughty children to sulk in their own corners. People who had arrived earlier sat or squatted on the ground, their heads swinging from the newcomers to the railway line beyond, as if they had already had this argument and come to no decision.

A man and woman sat on the bank beside the road, the woman suckling a child. Tom dismounted, looped Transportation's reins around his arm, and sat beside them.

"Hey," he said.

These two were starving, they told him, because their master had turned them off his farm to fend for themselves. All they wanted, they said, was a chance to work. Tom looked at the baby at the woman's breast, a pretty thing, deep brownish black with a fine fuzz of hair standing straight up. He thought of Baby Gold, her pale skin, how thin she was. He thought about the plowing and the sowing and the working of the farm. He said, "I have a proposition." But his voice was lost in the sudden shrieking of a train and the hallooing of the crowd, which in one body rushed up onto the narrow platform, feet thundering and echoing against the planks, the entire structure shaking.

The man leaped up and rushed with them. Tom, with *proposition* still warm in his mouth, followed at his heels. He caught up at the station steps where the shoving, shouting crowd prevented either from advancing. The woman, watching from the bank, saw him grab her husband's elbow and shout something in his ear. Then both men turned toward her. The child lay sprawled across her lap, asleep, and as the two came up she fumbled with her bodice, covering herself.

"What? What's wrong? No rations after all?"

"They can wait," the man said. He sat down on the bank beside her, leaned back on his hands and stuck his legs out straight. "So what's this proposition?" he said, looking up at Tom.

The woman, urgent, said, "But what about the rations?"

Tom looked down at the child. Pale blue milk bubbled at one corner of its mouth. "I have a child," he said, "not mine. A tiny thing. She does not thrive." He let his eyes glance briefly off the rough cloth covering the swollen breasts.

The woman's face brightened. "That chil'," she said, and clutching her own child in one arm, scrambled to her feet. "You give that chil' to me, she'll thrive. I may be low and starvin', but I got milk to feed God's multitude."

CHAPTER FIVE

THE Clark-Comptons did not live alone. Their house was occupied by Yankee officers who had taken it over for lodging, the family relegated to the slave wing of the house which these days held no other occupants, their servants having all run off. During the day, when the Yankees were off doing whatever Yankees did, they crept cautiously about the house as if they were intruders. Today, however, in the excitement of our homecoming, they ran about as if they owned the place.

After hugging me and kissing me and exclaiming, Missus Clark-Compton's first act was to look me up and down assessingly and declare I needed bathing and some decent clothes. In a flash, she had me out the back door and across the yard into the kitchen, and in another flash sitting in a tub before the fire, where she rubbed my back herself, declaring that the servants would be most surprised to see she could do well enough without them. Aunt Lavinia danced around us, receiving my clothes with a wrinkling of the nose, holding them at arm's length as she went off with instructions from her sister-in-law to "Burn the lot of them. It's the only way to get rid of the little villains."

As Aunt Lavinia vanished from the room I sprang up from the tub, suds and water sluicing off me. "No, no, wait! Oh, dear! Oh, Aunt Lavinia! Missus Clark-Compton! No!"

"Good heavens, child! Sit down. You're quite indecent."

"Don't let her burn my clothes."

"Tush, tush, sit down. It's all right, dear. You're safe now."

"You do not understand. In my pocket. The pocket of my gown. I have some gold."

She was across the room and out the door before I finished and I heard her shouting "Lavinia! Lavinia!" in the yard like any common fishwife while I stood bolt upright, naked as a brand-new piglet, one foot half raised, and would no doubt have gone running after her except I heard Aunt Lavinia call back, "Why Kate, comport yourself." I sank back in the tub.

Missus Clark-Compton reappeared, panting and triumphant. "A narrow escape, but here we have it—gold!" And she laughed down at my few small nuggets glistening on her palm as though a fortune sat there. "Where did you get these?"

And while I told her about working in the gold mine out by Salisbury, she dropped them one by one into a mason jar,

34

helped me from the tub, and rubbed me vigorously with a threadbare but capacious towel that had been warming by the fire. Then she went off to see what could be found in which to clothe me and came back with something in a lacy pale cream floral, along with undergarments and a pair of shoes.

"The gown is dated, I'm afraid, but things have been impossible these last few years and all the ladies of the town are dated. We'll have a grand time, when we can afford it, catching up with fashion."

She held the gown up and I burst out laughing. "If you'll let me have a pair of scissors and a thread and needle I'll adjust it to a simpler style, one more suited to a nurse."

Missus Clark-Compton lifted her face and set on me a pair of blue astonished eyes. "A *nurse*? What *can* you mean? Surely you do not intend to *work*. My dear, we may be in straits, but to *work*? To hold *employment*? I will hear none of it. A young lady of society should never *think* of such a thing."

"Society?" I countered. "Surely there is not much of society remaining."

"We must keep our heads up, dear, we must hold on to our pride. After all, your father was my second cousin. Or was it third? No matter, there is a connection. We are family. We must help each other."

I swallowed the urge to say, "So why did you not help my father when he needed help? Why did you let him break his heart alone?" because with all her losses, Missus Clark-Compton seemed intent on mustering all the family she could.

With that thought I kissed her on the cheek. "Thank you,

Missus Clark-Compton, but I cannot allow you to support me."

"We are family, you must call me Cousin Kate."

"Cousin Kate, I must pay my own way in the world. The gold is yours to pay for my expenses. And when I have found work I intend to pay you rent, with something extra for the food I will consume. It is important to me to be independent."

She swept out of the room and I thought I had offended her, but no, back she came with Aunt Lavinia following. The fire was dying and I shivered in my towel while they considered the matter back and forth, or at least Cousin Kate considered it while Aunt Lavinia acted as her sounding board.

These two women could not have been more different. Cousin Kate was tall and vigorous, with a forceful thrusting head and strong opinions. Aunt Lavinia was of middle height and vaporous. She seemed to have a mauvish haze about her, as though caught up in a web of sorrow that would not let her go. She had lost both son and husband in the war before she came to live with her brother and his wife for comfort.

Both women were thin as fence wire, but while Cousin Kate's thinness had a tensile quality, Aunt Lavinia's seemed fragile. Cousin Kate was blue-eyed, her hair wound in a neat brown plait about her head and staunchly pinned in place. Aunt Lavinia's hair was reddish, greying at the temples, curled in ringlets at her neck like a young girl's, the body of it swept up onto her head in a complicated topknot of straying locks and slipping pins, which now and then fell—*ping!*—onto the floor. Her eyes were mauve and seemed to fade into the sorrow that surrounded her.

Since I stayed resolute and Aunt Lavinia had no strong opinions, Cousin Kate at last conceded that the family was indeed hard up these days, and since God had turned me into an orphan, perhaps he intended I should fend for myself—a little, not too much. A rent would be agreed on when the time was right, but as for food, while the objectionable Yankees billeted themselves upon the family, let them provide it.

Then she fell to worrying about where I could be accommodated, the slave quarters being none too spacious, and now with Christopher quite taken up.

"We have the little garden house," Aunt Lavinia ventured. She turned to me. "You may remember it, Eugenia Mae. It used to be quite pretty but has fallen into disrepair. Perhaps Christopher . . ."

Cousin Kate considered. "With vagrants wandering the alley, I do not think . . ."

"The back fence is solid," Aunt Lavinia said, "the hedge inside it dense. And the gate's lock is formidable."

"Perhaps Christopher could live there and Eugenia Mae with us. It would be more proper."

My towel slipped and I snatched it back around me. "I'm sure I'll find it perfect. It will be just the thing."

"And you will be *independent*," Aunt Lavinia said.

Cousin Kate hesitated, looking from her to me and back again. "All right, Lavinia, you have won."

Aunt Lavinia shot me a triumphant look. "The Yankees

have a hospital. I'm sure they must need nurses. Perhaps our officers might help you find employment." She glanced at Cousin Kate. "Perhaps if you do not approach them forcefully, if you get them on your side . . . ," she finished faintly.

"*Our* officers! Lavinia, how *could* you! They are not *ours*. They are intruders, interlopers, squatters in our home. And as for *help* or *get them on your side*, we are nobodies to them, a conquered people with no rights. Why, Eugenia Mae, my husband may not even carry a weapon to defend himself. When first they came here, I entertained the officers and general staff, I received them in my home, I had the servants dish up the best meals I could muster out of the provisions we had left, I let them drink the last of the Colonel's fine whiskey, I made conversation with their presumptuous whiskered faces, listened to their opinions on our way of life, held my tongue while they made remarks about how backward we are here, how quaint, with such queer attitudes. I bore it all.

"And what did I get for all my courtesy? Why, they walked about our home as if they owned it, examined the portraits of our ancestors, declaring they would make nice souvenirs to carry back with them, pulled down books from Christopher's law library, valuable books with leather-embossed covers which his grandfather passed down to him, and opined that they would make a fine display in this room or the other of their own. And they admired the house itself—oh, they admired it, and declared it much too large for so few people and a perfect place to billet officers. Within twenty-four hours we had become a rooming house, no, hardly that, since they pay us nothing for the privilege."

She stopped, heaving with outrage, and Aunt Lavinia said in a small voice, "The food, Kate, the provisions, we were starving." She turned to me. "We are quite well-off now. We have no money, but we have a storeroom full of smoked and pickled meat, and flour, and lard, and sugar, coffee, candles, tea. And they do not ask how much we use of it, or even if we hand a little out the back door to our friends. In that they are most generous, we are fortunate to have them. And sometimes the captain, the one who keeps his beard trimmed very short—he does it for the weather—sometimes in the evening he likes to have a conversation in the garden."

She stopped abruptly, glancing across her shoulder as if some spy might be listening outside the door. "He's very kind. And he's a surgeon at the hospital. Perhaps if I should ask him . . . Kate?"

But Cousin Kate was still digesting the first of this long speech. "Well yes, if consolation can be had, it's that we do not have to stand in line for rations. Not that we would," she went on hastily. "To wait in line in the public street with all the riffraff and a shopping basket on my arm for some condescending Yankee quartermaster to dole a ration out—it is unthinkable. No one of quality will do it, those who have no servants left to send would rather starve."

"Starve?" I said. "When there are rations to be had? Is that not traveling down the road too far with Southern pride?"

Cousin Kate's voice took on a plaintive note. "Here I was, the kindest of kind mistresses, and yet the second Union troops came marching up the street all our slaves but one jumped up and fled. The one who stayed, a houseboy I was training up to be a butler, turned in an instant from a perfect servant who understood his place to a cheeky fellow demanding wages for his services—can you believe it, *wages*? I told him if it's wages you want you can find them elsewhere, you'll not make a monkey out of me. So off he went, where I do not know, and now you see us servantless. They will come back, though, when the poor deluded things begin to starve. I expect any day to see them creeping one after the other with their tails between their legs."

As though that subject had been dealt with and decided, she straightened herself up and turned to Aunt Lavinia. "I think you fraternize too much, it is not seemly."

Aunt Lavinia was saved by Colonel Clark-Compton's voice wondering outside the door when supper would be served and did we want the bathwater thrown out? She immediately went into a flutter, exclaiming she had quite forgotten, she must get busy before the officers came home. As for me, I was glad for the interruption since I had grown quite chilled.

OVER supper, which we took in the kitchen, Colonel Clark-Compton said, "As you see, Eugenia Mae, we do not eat together with our boarders and must eat unnaturally early on account of it. The Yankees have a corporal who does their cooking, as if they suspect we'll poison them. I would like to get my hands on some of their whiskey, but their generosity does not go that far. Come, child, eat up, eat up, you are too thin." He eyed me anxiously. "You are unwell?"

"No, quite well, thank you, but unused to food of such richness and proportion."

"Little by little, then, little by little. We'll fatten you up in no time."

He turned to Christopher as if to urge him too, but Christopher was having no problem at all. Indeed, he spoke not one word for the entire meal, just ate steadily through whatever was heaped upon his plate by an attentive aunt or mother, occasionally catching my eye to grin through bulging cheeks like a squirrel who has come upon another squirrel's hoard of nuts and is bent on getting them all down before he loses them.

The Colonel regarded his son's enthusiastic progress with affectionate complacency, then fell to eating with a matching gusto and there was silence for a while. He was an imposing man, very tall and of military bearing, with a gentle swell behind his shirtfront. He did not look as though he had been starving, not a bit, and although any mention of the losses in the family reddened up his nose and made his pale eyes shine with damp emotion, he was well under control, full of plans and ruminations and categorical announcements.

"They cannot stay forever," he declared, and after a while I gathered he had had a run-in with some of the Negro troops brought in to guard the town.

"To be guarded by Negroes, yes, it is too much," Cousin Kate said sympathetically. "They could have sent a white regiment, it would have been the decent thing to do. But as if to rub our noses in it that we have lost our darkeys, they must send blacks to guard us."

"And they are so *very* black," Aunt Lavinia said, "not at all like our sweet Southerners."

Cousin Kate sent her a look and Aunt Lavinia subsided.

41

The Colonel wiped his moustache with his napkin, looking blandly over it from one woman to the other. "Once we rejoin the Union and do not have to go cap in hand about the place we'll see to it they are got rid of."

"You think we will rejoin the Union soon?" I asked.

"Oh yes, shortly, shortly. I have done my part, I have been to Washington and petitioned for a pardon from the president. Many others were there, Southerners, with their begging caps in hand. It was a humiliation, but the entire war turned out a humiliation, and at least Mister Johnson is a Southerner. It would have been too much to beg from Mister Lincoln. Still, even Mister Johnson likes to see us dangle. He has our pardons ready—a great stack more than a foot high was sitting on a table in the center of the room—but he intends to make us squirm before he hands them over."

He forked a mouthful of ham between his moustache and beard, chewed on it with a thoughtful air, the moustache appearing to enjoy it just as much as he, and swallowed noisily, washing it down with a gulp of water.

"I do not think Mister Johnson the best man in the world for president—his chin is weak, although he scowls and pulls his mouth down to disguise it—but with him in office I am confident we can get this business settled to our satisfaction."

"Then you are satisfied to have the slaves go free?"

"My dear, they may be free, we have had that forced upon us and must take it, but after all, the race depends on us, they can do little on their own. It makes for an awkward situation, but that will soon be sorted out."

"Surely you don't think they'll be returned to slavery?"

"No, although it would be easier for everyone that way. But adjustments can be made, accommodations."

He raised a hand, palm down and fingers spread, tilting it judiciously from side to side. "A few men with good sense in government, and the Negro will be in the place that God ordained."

A pair of images came into my mind. The first was my dear Tom kneeling on our cabin floor in Gold Hill. I had come home unexpectedly to find him shaking gold dust from his hair onto a cloth. I knew what he was saving for—his freedom. It was late afternoon, sunlight slanting through the window, and it seemed as though a golden emanation issued from his head. The second image overlaid the first, as though they happened simultaneously—the collusive, luminous mulatto smiling at me on the train.

Christopher belched suddenly and set his hand against his mouth. He pushed his plate away.

CHAPTER SIX

BACK on Bricket's farm, Clyde sat in the slat chair on the porch and thought about the proposition he had just agreed to. The decision had been easy. Something had broken in him with the second amputation of his leg. His manly fire was gone. He had worried on it, and rejected it, and wanted to confide, but there was nobody he dared confide in, not Ma, not Uncle Benjamin, who with his blasted face was still a man, or else why would Ma come stepping from their bedroom every morning glowing like a girl in love?

He thought about the people he had trusted in his life, the ones who had not let him down. Ma, of course, although she could be cranky. Uncle Benjamin, who had always called him son. The Irish soldier who shouted "Holy Mother! Holy Mother!" and had his throat torn out by a ricocheting bullet. The nigra Caesar at the Salisbury prison who went off on the dead cart. Miss Genie who had nursed him back to life and walked all the way from Salisbury to Chapel Hill with him on Transportation. Henry who had cut his leg off the first time in the half dark of the cellar hospital.

When he got to Henry, Clyde came to a stop. Henry had been big and black, as big and black as Tom, but he had been a good man and reliable, not the sort to let a feller down. Maybe Tom would be like him, someone to rely on. More than anything in the whole world Clyde needed someone to rely on. Someone who would take onto his back the great responsibility of keeping everybody fed. Someone with two legs. He thought admiringly of Tom's two legs, the way, when he was sitting on the stool beside the cot, they had seemed so thick and solid, a serviceable pair of legs, legs to run a farm with. Legs he could rely on to bring rations home and not run off with his horse.

He scanned the road with anxious eyes. Even on an old decrepit horse like Transportation, Tom should be back by now. Behind him in the kitchen, Ma clashed a pan down on the hearth as if to say, "I told you so, you cannot trust a nigra." Clyde's ghost leg throbbed. He thought that he might cry.

But then a great surge of relief, because here came Tom, with Transportation wheezing underneath the saddlebags and two pairs of skinny black legs coming on behind. Clyde hoisted himself up, the slat chair screeching on the wooden floor. Yessir, he told himself, he knew a good man when he seen one.

"That nigra back yet?" Ma called from the kitchen.

"Three on 'em," Clyde called triumphantly. "That Tom, he brung us back some help."

THEIR names were Grace and Enfield and they had no last name, refusing to be called after their master. Tom installed Grace and her baby Glory in his mother's cabin while he and Enfield spent the night on Bricket's porch. Next morning early, the two men set out walking the bedraggled fields, waving their hands and talking in excited, almost disbelieving voices about wheat and corn and runner beans and, Look, right here can be the pumpkin patch, and here we'll grow tobacco for Ma's pipe, and there . . .

They walked around the barn, then went to stand inside, craning back their heads to eye torn patches of blue sky that looked back down at them with cheery disregard, and talked about the price of nails and ran their fingers down the rusted edges of the plow and pulled back Transportation's twitching upper lip to show long piss-colored teeth and figured he was even older than he seemed, putting him to plowing would just kill him. Then they went off to the corncrib, ducking their heads to go inside, and rattled at the crib and told each other it wouldn't take much fixing, and toed some rat-chewed cobs lying on the floor and talked about how Rebel Cat would see to that.

As they walked together back to Bricket's cabin, Clyde came stumbling to the front porch on his crutch and called out, "What-all you two up to?" in an accusing voice.

Tom and Enfield took their hats off and stood looking up at him. Clyde took hold of the rail with his free hand.

"You Tom, what-all you and this Enfield feller up to?"

"Planning," Tom said mildly. "Planning crops and such."

"You got no right to plan with him. He ain't the owner of this place. You gotta plan with me."

Enfield set his hat back on. "I'll go see about some stove wood. Mornin', Clyde."

Clyde watched him go. He looked at Tom. His chin was trembling. "You ain't the only boss."

"You're right." Tom's voice was soothing. "Come on down here and I'll tell you about the cabin I've been planning."

So Clyde hitched his way down the steps and sat on a log with his bandaged stump sticking out while Tom drew an outline in the dirt for him to make remarks on, and then Uncle Benjamin came and crouched down with them and made remarks on Clyde's remarks, demanding to have his finger led around imaginary walls.

"It'll be bigger than your cabin," Tom told them, "because my father likely will come home someday, and maybe some of my mother's other children too. It'll have a large main room and two rooms with doors for sleeping, and a stairway in the corner of the main room and two small attic rooms above. And at the back we'll build a pair of lean-tos, one to store things, sacks of vegetables and such, and one for just in case we gather in some extra people, and we'll build a shelter in between them for cooking in the summer. We'll build an outhouse too, up near the woods to keep the smell a long way off, and with a good deep hole so it'll last, and put together so it can be lifted up and set over another hole."

"What's wrong with a shovel in the woods?" Clyde said, and Uncle Benjamin said, "Son, don't be difficult."

"The most important thing," Tom said, "is that our cabin will be set directly next to yours, like the two arms of a hinge, with a roofed walkway in between the porches so we can visit with each other in bad weather. That way we'll not be arguing about who's boss. We'll be one family."

Ma leaned across the porch rail, pipe in mouth, watching the men crouched in the dust. When Tom came to the part about one family, she took her pipe out of her mouth and said, "Danged if I ever thought the day would come when I would have a nigra for my family."

Clyde looked up at her. "Ma, this here nigra done set about to save our lives."

"Benjamin, what-all you think o' this? You want a bunch o' nigras for a family?"

Uncle Benjamin shifted his weight from one haunch to the other and turned his face to the sound of Enfield chopping wood. He turned toward Ma. "Go on inside, Ma, this here is for the menfolk to take care of."

She spat across the rail into a patch of dusty nettles. "Amazin' how a bellyful of food can change a man."

Uncle Benjamin sighed and hoisted himself upright. " 'Scusee," he said, and tapping his way up the cabin steps, he put his arm around Ma's shoulders and drew her inside.

Tom turned to Clyde. "You put your mark to our agreement."

"Yessir, don't you be gettin' skittery. We made a deal. Although it don't seem fair a nigra gets to write the words."

"If you like," Tom said gently, "I'll teach you how to read and write. I have a Bible that the Yankees gave me, and a storybook as well."

"One time before Pa died, I asked if I could go to that there school for boys they used to have the other side of town and he said, You don't need no learnin', you is jest a farmer."

"I think a farmer needs to read and write. Otherwise any slick man with a contract could cheat him out of everything he owns."

"I figure you ain't cheatin'. You ain't that sorta nigra."

"Do you figure I'm the sort of nigra you could treat as family?"

Clyde cocked his head, worry creasing up his forehead.

"It seems to me," Tom said, "that if we're going to get along together on this farm, best we do it like a family. Then we all stand up for each other and no one gets the short end of the stick. After all, if I get up and leave and take the others with me . . ."

"You ain't about to do that, are you? You ain't about to leave?"

"I guess that depends on Ma." Tom nodded at Clyde's stump. "I'm handy. I could make a wooden leg for you to strap on easier than spit. You could practice for a while and then you wouldn't need that crutch."

"Think I could plow a field if I had a leg like that?"

"I once saw a man with a wooden leg build a bridge clear across a river."

49

"Is that a fact?" Clyde ruminated. "A wooden leg—that is right nice of you."

"Why don't you go tell that to your ma?"

Clyde pushed himself to his feet and hitched his crutch beneath his arm. "Mister Tom, sir, I surely will do that."

"If we're going to be family, you'd best call me Tom."

CHAPTER SEVEN

NO sooner arrived in Wilmington than I fell deathly ill. I had not been ill the entire time I was away. The upcountry climate must have agreed with me, but back in the low country I succumbed. Perhaps I took a chill as I stood shivering in my towel while Cousin Kate and Aunt Lavinia discussed what should be done with me. Or perhaps some affliction passed to me from my companions on the train—the child across from me was sick to die.

Whatever the cause, I slept that first night with Aunt Lavinia in a narrow slave cot—for which Cousin Kate apologized until I thought she might fall over with apology—and woke next morning with a headache so severe I thought I was about to vomit, and shivering with an ague that caused my teeth to knock together. Sweat poured off me, and my blood boiled and pounded in my head, then fell away until I lay shivering again, clutching at the quilt for warmth.

Cousin Kate sent Aunt Lavinia off to beg assistance of her friend the Yankee surgeon, who came in his socks and pronounced me ill of "one of these deuced swamp fevers of the South." He produced a phial of something, I do not know what, and instructed Cousin Kate to dose me every hour and keep a damp cloth on my head.

By noon my symptoms had not lessened and I had others too—a neck so stiff I could not turn my head, a heavy drowsiness that held me like a prisoner and prevented me from speech. When Aunt Lavinia or Cousin Kate bent over me I saw a strange distorted face and heard whisperings and bellowings, but I could not make out who these people were, or whether they were dreams or devils come to carry me away.

By day's end, when the surgeon came back from the hospital, I was so stunned with drowsiness I knew I was approaching death. The surgeon—Doctor Wilkins was his name—held my wrist and set his hand against my head and cursed in his moustache. Aunt Lavinia, who had been fluttering about him like a moth about a lamp, set her hand against her bosom and began to weep.

"Quite a pantomime she put on," Cousin Kate told me later, and there was admiration in her voice. "Before we knew it, Doctor Wilkins had sent for a carriage and off you went to the Yankee naval hospital, which saved your life. You would have been in heaven now if Lavinia had not had that fellow dancing to her tune."

I woke to figures moving in a darkened room. My headache had dulled to a low buzzing, but I could not think where I might be and sank back into sleep. I woke again to darkness, then to light. This went on for I do not know how long, and then all I remember is a sort of mystification of the mind in which I did not know what I was, a person or a spirit or a timber in the roof. I had a sense of falling into somewhere deep. I remember high black walls around me with dim light at the top, and noises spinning down and bursting somewhere close, as though I had tumbled down a mine shaft where blasting was in progress. The detonations boomed and I felt nausea rise, and then a sharp metallic clatter and a dreadful singing on which I seemed to rise and fall and rise again, and then the headache and the fall back into sleep.

They told me afterwards I fought with death like this eleven days. On the sixth day they gave me up, and again on the seventh. On the eighth they kept me warm and forced a little water into me and waited, and on the ninth, Doctor Wilkins declared I would not last till dusk and had me moved off into a passageway where I would not discourage the other patients with my struggle to the grave.

Aunt Lavinia and Cousin Kate were sent for, and bade me a piteous farewell. Christopher came too, and declared he loved me, an orderly reported to me later, which set Aunt Lavinia off into a paroxysm of weeping. He came close, and with one hand on the bed head, the other on his cane, bent as though to kiss me, but Cousin Kate prevented him and hustled them both off. Colonel Clark-Compton did not come. He had gone to Washington again to try to wring his pardon out of Mister Johnson.

On the tenth day, so the orderly reported, Doctor Wilkins became impatient. He had sick men to care for who had some chance of recovery, and I was taking up a cot. First thing next morning I was to be taken home to die.

But next morning, when they came to get me, and saw me lying blank-faced with my eyes wide open, they left me there and sent out for a priest, who came in his cassock with a cross around his neck and a prayer book in his hand and made himself ready to commit my soul to God. No sooner had he touched my forehead in a blessing than he snatched his hand away and declared his business was to bury the dead, not the living, and everyone came crowding and declared he had performed a miracle. What I remember, and I think what brought me back to consciousness, was the odor of his hands. They smelled like roses.

A few days later I was sent back home. I say home, because something had happened to my sensibilities while I was in the hospital. The evening I fell ill, I had gone to bed a stranger the Clark-Compton family had elected to call cousin. When I returned, it was to home. I do not apologize for that, I did not act to make that change, and did not dwell upon it at the time, but since then I have come to understand that sometimes our intentions count for little in the face of circumstance.

I went home living, although barely. Christopher had repaired the garden house and was anxious I admire it properly before I was installed inside, which I did try to do, leaning on his arm and crying a little and saying, "Oh thank you, oh thank you," hardly knowing what I said. He patting my hand and demanding further admiration—of the symmetry of shingles on the roof, the clever way he had repaired the window, the pretty pale yellow paint he had applied with his own hand. It was not until Aunt Kate said, "Christopher, the poor girl is exhausted," that he gave me up to her and Aunt Lavinia to be tucked into a soft bed in a pleasant sunny room with a view of trees and a trellis budding out with roses, and beyond that the hedge hiding the back alley. Christopher had rigged up a bell that sounded in the house and tied the wire to my bedpost. I was to ring it for anything, just anything, he told me, and went off to his new office, where he was embarking on the practice of law and already had several clients, planters who were arguing with the Freedmen's Bureau about contracts to hire Negroes and the wages they would be obliged to pay.

If I had not had Cousin Kate and Aunt Lavinia to assist me through my convalescence I never would have made it, a fact which in later days came to play sorely on my conscience. At first I was confused and sometimes did not recognize them, calling them by names of people I had known in other parts. Other times I would see them speaking but could not hear a word, or heard words disjoint, which confused me even more. I had lost coherent speech and it was weeks before I could fully command the words to fit a situation. I slept a great deal and dreamed even when awake, talking to people who came and went about the room, not at all surprised at their appearance out of air or their vanishing back into it.

It was not until six weeks had passed that I felt strong

enough to allow Christopher to help me out into the garden, where I lay limply on a chaise in a mixture of befuddlement and joy to be alive. He sat beside me talking excitedly of his business and the good things he had heard about himself from friends of clients, of his plan, when he was rich enough, to take a wife and breed a family of his own. He did not tell me who this wife might be, and when I roused myself to make inquiry, he laid a finger alongside his nose and smiled a secret smile. From this I gathered that perhaps he had not asked the lady yet and so I did not press him.

In those days it seemed to me I had never been away from Wilmington, that the last years of my life had been part of my delirium. Papa's fall into bankruptcy and our ignominious flight to Gold Hill, Papa's failure as a miner there, his suicide, all seemed like stories somebody had told me long ago and I had half forgotten. My flight to Salisbury, the long war years of working in the secret Union hospital, the walk back to Chapel Hill with Clyde, all were part of that same book of fairy tales. Even Tom, to whom I had been so attached, became a distant figure, one hand raised in a gesture of farewell, vanishing into the woods.

There had been a war, though, there had been a war. Christopher spoke of it from time to time, and I came to understand it, too, from the circumstances of my family and from the conversations of the guests they brought to visit me, tense-faced people who sat about talking of this one or that who had been picked off by Yankee bullets, every one of them, it seemed, obsessed with reliving every moment of those years and complaining of their dreadful consequences—the way they had become *reduced* and now struggled to put food into their families' mouths, the way they could not get along without their slaves, the way the Negroes, under the pernicious influence of freedom, had become demanding and ungrateful, which proved they were not fit for anything but slavery.

Especially they complained about the Negro troops sent down to guard us—the impudence of them, the arrogance, the unadulterated nerve. It was an affront, they said, a calculated insult. And the way they mingled with the freedmen and got them all stirred up, this being the same complaint I had heard growing up about the black sailors coming from the Northern ports who flaunted their freedom before ignorant coloreds. In those days the Negro sailors had to carry passports, sometimes they found themselves locked up, but they were free men and for the most part did exactly what they pleased. Now, though, everyone was free, the local Negroes and those flooding into Wilmington in search of better lives. And the whites were frightened, whispering of vengeance planned, tormented by old fears of being slaughtered in their beds.

Christopher appeared one day with Sylvie Younger on his arm, declaring she had come to pay a visit. I remembered Sylvie's haughty nose and asked if she still had her feathered hat, at which she patted my hand as though I were a child and smiled maternally. While we talked, I thought about her as she had been before, rather sly, with a slim waist and a bosom I used to envy almost as much as her hat, and a way of tapping young men on the wrist with her closed fan that sent them into raptures of desire. Now she had changed, or perhaps the way I saw her in the world had changed. Her nose was just as haughty and she still brandished a fan, but whereas I once had seen her as grand, stylish, in some way invincible, I now saw her as pathetic, needy, reaching out for friends. And she was growing older now, of course, approaching thirty. Was it Sylvie Christopher was targeting to be his wife? I watched the two of them together but neither one gave anything away.

Sylvie came regularly after that, and I was grateful for her visits. They seemed to anchor me. Sometimes she brought with her others of the upper-class young ladies, who fell at once to filling me with all the latest gossip—marriages and love affairs, suspected swains, expected proposals. I kept my ears laid back, but not a hint did I get of romance between Christopher and Sylvie. At last I asked her, cunningly I thought, if she did not think my cousin admirable, the way he had set his heart upon prosperity, and his mind and will to labor on achieving it. She considered, twisting the little finger of one glove. "I have always thought him admirable, even when he was a little boy. Do you not think him so?" Which turned my question on its head and set me to protesting admiration while the circle of young ladies exchanged furtive, knowing glances. I resolved never to employ cunning on Sylvie again, she would beat me at my own game every time.

Gradually my world solidified, and as I ruminated on those unlikely, dreadful years of gold mining and war, I grieved for my papa again. With that grief came back the memory of that awful night at Gold Hill when I heard him weeping in his loft. Creeping up the stairs to comfort him, I found myself seized and caressed in the way a father does not caress a daughter, and his voice—"Tilda, oh my Tilda"—whispering against my hair. And after that the nebulous night fancies crystallizing into hard suspicion.

On afternoons when Doctor Wilkins came back early from the hospital, he would come to visit me. He would draw up a chair beside my chaise out in the garden, and inquire how I had done that day. He had a gentle manner that drew confidence and seemed interested in my life and what it had been like. When he discovered I had been a nurse he was delighted, and so one day I told him about our basement hospital in Salisbury, how we had helped dissenters from the Southern Cause.

"We called ourselves the Red Strings," I told him. "By that time I had become an abolitionist."

He nodded with approval, and so I spoke about the woman who had owned the house, and how she was from Boston.

He replied he was from Boston too, it was a stronghold for abolitionists, he had known several. He asked about my life before the war and I told about our farm, how well-off we had been. "Nineteen slaves we had," I said, and watched him blink. "But then Mama died and Papa failed at business and everything went wrong. We had to sell the house, the farm, the carriages, our furniture, Mama's eggshell dinnerware, the silver passed down from her grandmama . . . the lot."

He looked sideways at me, an inquiring look. "The slaves, you sold them too?"

"It was the old times then. Papa had no choice."

He did not speak. I felt that he was judging me.

"I was a child," I said defensively. "I had no say in the matter."

"So when did you become an abolitionist?"

"Before the war, although I did not call myself so at the time. You see, I had this slave, his name was Tom . . . but no, I must go back. After Papa sold the farm he took employment in a gold mine out by Salisbury. Did you know we had gold mines here, out in the center of the state?"

"I did. My father held investments in something called the Gold Hill Mining Company."

"Gold Hill? How strange. Gold Hill is where Papa took employment. He called himself a supervisor, but he was really just a miner." And I told about Papa's disappointment in himself, and my resentment. "I was not a loving daughter to him. I blamed him for his failure. I will regret that to the day I die."

"But you were young, child, and the young are often hard. They do not understand. They think the world belongs to them and ought to dance to their command. That everything their parents do is to advance their comfort. Which might be true, of course, but then when parents fail . . ."

He stopped, looking at his shoe, which he moved to make a half circle in the dirt. "Since you have confessed to me, I will confess to you. My father made some good investments, but he made some bad investments too, and the bad outweighed the good. All the money set aside for my education had to go to pay his debts. For years I was resentful, and all because I had to work my way through university." He laughed a small tight laugh. "Callow youth. So selfish."

"But you were reconciled? Please tell me you were reconciled."

"We were, but years were wasted, years. And then he died."

A horrible thought took hold of me. "He did not hang himself, do not say that."

He turned his gaze full on me. "You are a strange girl indeed. Why would you think that?"

"Because . . ." And then it all came tumbling out. How Papa in his struggle to appease his daughter had turned his pockets out to buy a crippled slave, how he gave him to her as a gift, and how, as time went by, the slave's legs healed and he worked hard and never caused a moment's trouble. How, when war broke out, Papa set his mind to eluding the recruiters by buying passage to a copper mine in South Australia. And how she, Eugenia, set herself against the notion.

"That slave, the one called Tom? When Papa said he'd sell him for the passage money, that he would haul me with him to a far-off land of savages and strangers, I went into a panic. And besides, I could not bear to see Tom sold. You see, I had no friends at the gold mine and Tom had been so good to me." I hesitated, stepping carefully. "He had become . . . a sort of friend. I had grown . . . fond."

Doctor Wilkins shifted in his chair.

"Don't look at me like that. It is a common thing, or was, here in the South, for a mistress to grow fond. There was no harm in it, no sin. After all, the Bible says 'Thou shalt love thy neighbor as thyself.' How can we love our neighbor as ourselves if we then turn around and sell him? I could not do it, I simply could not do it. I wrote a freedom paper out for Tom. I robbed Papa."

"It's all right, child. I understand. God's love turned you into an abolitionist."

Gratitude rose in my throat. Tears rose in my eyes. Oh, what a good man Doctor Wilkins was.

"But I did worse. I stole the cigarette tin where Papa kept the gold nuggets he was saving for a rainy day. And now the rainy day was here, and what did I do? I ran off with his umbrella. I ran away to Salisbury and set Tom loose along the way. It was in Salisbury that I took up working for the Red Strings, it was they who told me that by freeing Tom I had become an abolitionist. Which they considered was a good thing, as I did myself, and yet by freeing him I helped destroy my father."

"He hanged himself?"

"How did you know that?"

"You told me when you asked about *my* father."

There was silence for a while, and then, although I had not been thinking it, "Doctor Wilkins, I have heard that suicide is sin. Do you think God would have refused Papa entrance into heaven?"

"Oh, child."

"You do think not?"

"I think that God sees deep into our hearts. I think he does not judge us for despair, or else the entire South would be denied entrance into heaven."

"Some say that is true."

"It is not true, as it was not for your papa. Don't cry, child, all that is past. You have made up for your sins by your good work in the Red String hospital, and your father was a good man, of that I have no doubt. After all, did he not breed you? Come, come, cheer up."

But I did not cheer up. I sighed. I set my hand against my forehead. I gave a little moan.

"What is it? There is more? More wickedness?" He said it lightly, trying by jocularity to lift me from depression, but I did not respond. The sun had dipped behind the trees and the sky was boldly orange. Shadows and bright patches shifted in the garden.

"It is about my mother. She . . . I mean . . ."

"You said she died when you were but a child."

"No, that was my mama."

"I do not understand." And he looked at me so kindly that I found the sentence forming on my lips that I had not yet fully spoken in my heart.

"I suspect Mama was not my mother. I suspect my father bred me of a slave. That is why I came back here to Wilmington. I came to find if it is true."

To this day I remember how his face closed. He edged his chair almost imperceptibly away and I knew I'd made a great mistake. We had spoken of a position for me in the hospital when I was recovered, but now I saw the possibility fade off behind the studied kindness of his smile. At least, I told myself, you did not tell him all there is to tell of Tom. At least you did not tell him that you loved a slave, a Negro, that you miss him, that you think about him every day.

DOCTOR Wilkins was in the habit of meeting Aunt Lavinia in the garden after supper. I would see them through the window of the garden house, she with her arm through his, their heads together, murmuring words I could not catch. That evening when I saw them there, What if he should betray my confidence? I asked myself. And what if Aunt Lavinia told Cousin Kate? And Cousin Kate told Christopher? And the Colonel— what if he should hear?

Frozen with foreboding, I watched until the darkness swallowed them. I did not sleep that night, and by morning was half demented from exhaustion so that I spent all day in a fluster waiting for a word, a hint, the lifting of an eyebrow, a pursed lip. Doctor Wilkins never came to sit by me and ask how I was doing after that. It was a lesson to me, and an answer to a puzzlement I had about his friendship with Aunt Lavinia. How, I had asked myself, can two people be in love when one condescends to an entire race of people, while the other's mission is to raise those people up? Now I understood that he and Aunt Lavinia shared the same beliefs. It made me look into my heart and wrestle with my own.

To find a Negress, an ex-slave, and declare myself to be her daughter—was that why I had come back to Wilmington? And what would I do then? Go live with her in some backstreet hovel? Give up my lovely little garden house, the affection of my family—because by now I had come irrevocably to see the Clark-Comptons as my family. Give up everything I had? I could not think I had been so . . . so what? Perhaps even then I had been sickening. Perhaps, I told myself, I should be grateful for my illness. It had left me weak, but somehow it had purified me, restored me to my proper place in life.

And yet there were the dreams—or were they visions?—of the luminous mulatto smiling at me on the train as though we shared a secret. He would lean toward me, opening his mouth as if to speak, the bright sun lighting up his face. And then the shove, the elbowing aside, and his collusive wink before he was replaced by Christopher leaning toward me, also smiling, as though by some sleight of hand one man had been transformed into the other. And I found that I resented it.

CHAPTER EIGHT

TOM'S cabin was complete, with a rainproof shingle roof and shutters on the windows and a good wide rocking porch. It would have been done sooner, but there had been the Brickets' cabin roof to fix as well, and the rails on their front porch, and the barn and chicken coop and corncrib and the fences. He and Enfield made some benches too, with Clyde getting in the way, and a table big enough for all of them to sit at underneath a tree.

When everything was done, Enfield helped Tom's mother move her few possessions out of her old cabin, then slung his blanket on his shoulder and moved in there with Grace and Baby Gold and Glory. Tom's mother climbed up on her new porch, and shading her eyes with one hand against the setting sun, looked along the track that led out to the road.

"I fancy I would like a rocking chair," she said, "so's I can set here in the evenings and watch out for your father to come home. He'll come at sunset, I saw it in a dream."

After that, when supper had been cleared away, Grace would bring Baby Gold and Glory, both stiff-bellied with her milk, and set them facedown on Tom's mother's knee. With her eyes fixed on the far end of the track, she patted the jutting little backsides till the wind came burping out and they fell off to sleep. Then she let her hand rest gently while she rocked, her eyes still watching, watching. It made Tom want to weep for her, an old woman bathed in the glory of the sunset, hope written on her face, and the tender movement of the chair, its soft click-click against the boards. It made him want to sing.

When the chickens had been chased into their coop and Transportation locked up in the barn, he would sit beside her in the afterlight and tell her his adventures since he was sold away, and she would tell about his father and the children she had lost before he had been born, and the others too, the ones he half remembered, sold away to strangers when he was just a little child.

"They let me keep my youngest since they figured you was just a simpleton. I used to thank the Lord for that. Dear Lord, I used to say, thank you for making my poor Tom a simple-ton." She turned to look at him. "And now you ain't. It is a miracle."

She was fascinated by his new last name. "Maryson," she murmured, "Mary's son," and after a while refused to answer to her slave name of Old Mary, insisting she was now Missus Maryson.

"Did my father have a last name?"

She made a deep sound of disgust. "His name is Morgan, like the big white marse. He is called Nathaniel Morgan. And"—she turned and set a reprimanding hand against Tom's mouth—"don't you speak of him as if he's dead and gone. He's coming back, I feel him coming, getting closer every day, I feel him in my bones."

But all she ever saw down at the far end of the track was a shadow in the woods that sometimes seemed to be a shadow and sometimes seemed to be a horseman, loose and easy in the saddle, his horse shifting beneath him. She did not mention him.

Tom saw him too, and set himself to go on down and challenge him. But then he thought best not, because he did not want his mother frightened. And anyway, he told himself, the fellow was just nervous about Negro plots and plans and insurrections the way the whites had always been. When he saw them living peaceably he would be satisfied and go away. Clyde, on the other hand, had no such qualms and one evening crept around and came up from behind. But when he sprang, no one was there. Three times he tried to catch the watcher in the woods. Three times the watcher vanished, as though he and his horse had purely stepped inside a tree. Clyde shook himself off like a puppy who has fallen in a pond and resolved to keep an eye on him and if that feller came one inch onto the road he just might find his hat shot off his head.

Each night when the dark came down Tom would swing

forward in his chair and go inside and light a candle and figure on a piece of paper. When first he came back home he had dug a hole out in the woods. In it, in one of his mother's herb tea jars, he had buried the gold nuggets he had scavenged at the mine and kept about him ever since. A handful of Confederate specie he set aside to be changed into Union money. That and the money he had saved out of his pay while he had been a soldier should see them through until they could bring in a crop. No matter what hardships they faced along the way, he would not draw upon his gold. Once he had planned to buy his mother with it. Now, when he looked across the small estate he shared with Clyde, he seemed to see figures moving in a vast expanse of fields and buildings, a herd of handsome cows lowing to be milked, a windmill making its thunk-thunk, children laughing in the yard. He figured if he went to church and prayed, the Lord would, in his own time, tell him how to spend it.

But church he found discomforting, with the Negroes in the upper gallery the same old way, and the preacher preaching to the white folks, telling them they were bosses of the whole creation still. Others felt it too, so the freedmen had a meeting with the elders, who agreed to let them use the church on Sunday afternoons. But the first time they set about to do it, a white man came along to listen just like before the war. It was Samuel Morgan, which made Tom angry and embarrassed because he once had been his slave.

Of all the freedmen in the congregation, Tom was the only one who had traveled on his own account more than thirty miles from home, the only one who had been in the Union army, and consequently the only one accustomed to acting like a free man. And so while the others quailed and murmured, he rose up to his full authoritative height and went to stand in front of Mister Morgan.

"Sorry, Mister Morgan," he said in a firm voice, "this meeting is for black folks only."

At which Mister Morgan said, "Well Tom, I see you are a troublemaker still," and went on sitting with his leg crossed on his knee and one foot jigging in the air the way a man does when he's thinking about violence.

What the freedmen needed, they told each other outside in the yard, was a place where they could meet and a preacher of their own.

Tom thought about this hard, and one night when they had come in from the fields and he was coaxing Clyde through chapter six of Genesis, Clyde astonished and excited by the vision of an ark of gopher wood unfurling verse by verse above his finger, a notion started up inside Tom's head.

"Rooms shalt thou make," Clyde read, "a window shalt thou make . . . and the door of the ark shall be set in the side . . ."

"Clyde," Tom said, "that's what we need to do."

"What-all?" Clyde said, blinking.

"We need to build."

"But the rains is over. It ain't about to flood."

"Not an ark. A place where we can start a church."

"Why's that? You got a fine church in the village."

"We need to build another church, a church for the freedmen."

"You mean a nigra church?"

"Yes. A place where we can hold our meetings."

Clyde screwed up his face, tilting his head to one side. "Ain't no need for buildin'. Uncle Benjamin, he got a house on Preacher Lane."

"A house? What sort of house?"

"Jest a house, a plain ol' clapboard house, not so big, but there it stands—if'n it ain't ruined or tore down or some squatter took it over. Bet he'd be glad to turn that place into a church. Why, he could be the preacher. He can preach the thunder of the Lord."

Tom laughed. "I think the freedmen have had a bellyful of the thunder of the Lord."

Clyde sniffed. "Well, there is *that*. So who's the preacher gonna be?" And before Tom could answer, "You figurin' to be the man? Well, my. This readin' and writin' business is a grand thing, ain't it just?"

Tom's stomach tightened. "A preacher? Me?"

"Then who? Come on now, Tom, you ain't shy, is you?"

UNCLE Benjamin's house had fallen into disrepair during the war, but no squatter had taken it over, just weeds and possums and a long brown snake that stood up on its tail and hissed at Tom and Enfield when they went to check it out.

When they heard what was proposed, freedmen from all over came to haul and hammer, and then to sit on logs and boxes and the floor while Tom, shy at first but with increasing confidence, delivered his first sermon, a mix of Bible texts and an account of his own life since he had been sold away from Chapel Hill. He had not meant to tell of it, but standing there before the freedmen he felt something unblock in his heart, and he told about his journey with the slavers, about the pain he suffered in his legs from being shot.

"Sometimes in the winter even now," he said, and rolled his pants legs up to show the scars.

The congregation craned to see, calling "Lord, Lord, brother!" and half crying, caught up in his tale.

He told of how he had been sold into the gold mine. "I thought I had been sent down into hell because back then I was nothing but a simpleton frightened of the dark, but the good Lord had a plan for me, just like he has a plan for you."

He paused to look around and saw Enfield nodding at the back. "Brothers and sisters, the good Lord powered up my voice to howl and wail so loud they never sent me down that mine again, but sold me to a lady who was kind and pitied me and set me free."

"Lord! Lord! She set him free!"

"She told me, 'Run, run north to Canada,' and that was where I headed, but the Lord, he took me by the hand and led me east. I met two turpentiners there, black men like myself, and worked with them, and then the Union army came to New Bern and we all jumped up and went to join them. They called us contrabands, since we were spoils of war, and they taught us how to read and write and talk as well as any white man, and taught me how to read a map and read the stars, and put a musket in my hand and trained me how to be a scout and help them fight for freedom."

"Freedom! Yes, Lord! Freedom!"

"So here I am. I started out a slave so scared of everything in the whole world that I could barely speak, and now I own a farm and a cabin of my own and am not afraid to tell a white man he's not welcome in my church. The Lord took a poor slave with his head turned down and made of him a man as good as any other. Yessir, he worked a miracle on me. And he wants to work a miracle on you as well."

He paused to let the *Hallelujah, brother*s, and the *Amen*s and the *Lord, Lord, Lordy, Lord*s settle down, looking anxiously around the congregation. He wanted something for these people, but how to say it? He would rather be a listener sitting on a box and have someone else tell him. He looked at the man who had called out, "Freedom! Yes, Lord! Freedom!" At his bare feet and his ragged clothes and old straw hat.

"Brother," he said, "who still tells you morning until night what to do and what you cannot do? Is it your own self or another? And you there, Enfield, didn't you come to live with me because your master pushed you off his farm for wanting wages for your work? Who of you has not been jostled in the street and jeered at, accused of insolence if he says hey or how-do to a white man? And how many beatings have you seen, how many murders, since freedom broke around your heads? Why, the other day, I heard a fellow say that he was better off when we were under slavery. Is this what that good man Mister Lincoln meant by freedom for our suffering race? Brothers, sisters, when I was living on the turpentine plantation, before I ran off to the Union, a wise man said to me,

'Tom, freedom's not a gift. You got to hunt it down and catch it. You got to snatch it in your hand.' "

Now he could barely hear himself, the shouts and weeping, clapping, stomping and the *Yes, Lord*s were so loud. He stopped, perplexed once more by where to go from here, and looked down at his Bible for a text.

"Read it, brother! Read it!" someone said, and as though a spigot had been turned inside his head, Tom knew what it was he wanted for his people. "Raise your hand if you can read and write," he said into the sudden hush.

Everybody looked around, but no one raised a hand.

"Brothers, sisters," Tom said, "we need everyone to learn to read and write and cipher and know about the world, all the children and the adults too. That's the way to bring our people out of ignorance and let the light in. That's the way we will learn to make our own way in the world."

Next day he rode across to Raleigh and begged twelve copies of the *Primary Speller* from the Freedmen's Bureau. The woman there told him she hoped before too long a freedmen's school would be set up in Chapel Hill. She did not know when, but assured him, with one hand on his coat sleeve and damply shining eyes, that if he waited they would get a schoolma'am from the North, an expert teacher.

Tom thought about that for a while. "Thank you, ma'am, I figure that would be right popular."

He went down the front step and headed along the street to where Transportation twitched his flanks beneath a shade tree, guarded by a little boy who sat beside him in the gutter and stood up with his hand out when he saw Tom come.

As he rode back home, the packet of readers and a copy of the Ralcigh *Standard* tied behind his saddle, the image of the woman's hand on his coat sleeve clung inside Tom's head, and it was not until half the journey was behind him and he stopped to water Transportation at a creek that his resentment faded.

"Yessir, old boy," he said as Transportation creaked back up the bank and stood before him with a daft expression on his face and his legs trembling like an old man who has got himself a little tipsy. "Yessir, I'd say we can teach ourselves just as well as any Yankee schoolma'am."

BACK home, Clyde's ma was in a temper, stomping about with a sour look on her face. When she saw Tom coming up the track, she flopped down on her front step and savaged at her pipe, blowing smoke about and glaring at Tom's mother, who was rocking on her porch. When Tom said, "Hey, Ma," she reared away as if he smelled of something bad.

He sighed. Ma had become a problem. "That Old Mary done got above her raisin'," she would say. "One day she will take a fall." As if Tom's mother had been set on earth for nothing but to do her bidding.

Sometimes Ma would come across to their front porch and peer in through the window, where Tom's mother might be mending clothes or putting up preserves.

"Missus Maryson, indeed," she'd hiss, and Tom's mother would look up and nod at her and smile as if she were a visitor. "Come on in and set," she'd say, "I'll make some tea."

But Ma would just stand there talking to herself and grumbling in her throat, and when Uncle Benjamin came tap-tap along the wooden walk between the cabins, saying, "Come now, Ma," she would rear away.

"I do not understand it," she would say, "I do not understand it." But she would go along with him, and perhaps accept a jar of jam or pickles, until outrage overcame her once again.

Tom talked to Clyde about it, and Clyde said, "Ain't none of our concern. Them two old women got to figure out a way to get along. Ma, she has a tough head, she did not speak to Pa for nigh on fifteen year afore he died."

"But we can't wait fifteen years."

"Ma just ain't accustomed yet to Old Mary turning into Missus Maryson." Clyde sniffed, wiping his nose across the back of his hand. "Still and all, I reckon she'll get it figured if we leave her be."

CHAPTER NINE

I had recovered from my illness, but was still too weak to seek employment. I am strong of constitution, though, and found myself growing restless and impatient with my prescribed regime of total rest. And so I walked about the garden, finding it more and more restrictive as the days went by, and at last ventured out onto the street.

Aunt Lavinia's Doctor Wilkins was no longer a problem since he had been transferred, leaving poor Aunt Lavinia in a state of whispering dismay. "It appears," she told me when I inquired after him, "it appears he has a *wife*." Her dismay, I also suspected, was tempered with a thrill—that *she* should be the center of a scandal! She seemed to wrap this notion up and carry it about with her, a small bundle of triumph hidden in her breast. "A *wife!*" she would say, and her eyes would glow with something not quite proper.

The first day I left the garden I walked gently along Market Street to the corner of Second Street and back, enjoying it the way one does when life begins again after an illness. The day was warm, the sky blue, the birds singing in the live oaks that made a wall of green along the center of the road. Spanish moss dripped off them, and further down was the bustle of the early morning market. It all seemed so familiar, and at the same time strange because of the sad condition of the houses, the filthy alleys where refugees both black and white were just now waking out of sleep, and in the absence of chamber pot or privy, crouching or standing face-on against walls. Others were shaking together their few possessions in readiness to go once more to beg or stand in line for rations. Market Street was wide and open to the breeze, which smelled of river water and the sweet dankness of the swamps, but as I passed each alley the stench of wretchedness and human excrement lurched out of it like a madman desperate for company.

The new energy that comes with convalescence brings with it euphoria. I have seen it often in my patients and I was no exception. Not even the filth and the pitiable condition of the people creeping on the streets could damp my spirits. It seemed to me that I was back in childhood, in one of those lovely long days when all was well and nothing yet gone wrong. Lighthearted is not the right way to describe my mood. It was as though I had turned into my young self, a pretty girl with tumbling curls, and, I do admit it now, that childish petulance of manner that comes of being doted on. And yet I think it was that morning I resolved, when I was up to it, to work amongst the poor, to find some occupation that would allow me to relieve their suffering and at the same time put a little money in my pocket so I would not be obliged for everything to the Clark-Comptons.

Each day I walked a little further, despite Aunt Lavinia's horror that a young lady should walk about the streets un-chaperoned and, what's more, with no hoops to my skirt. I told her that the war had not just freed the slaves, but it had freed me from my hoops as well, and I had no intention of be-coming enslaved to them again. She fluttered for a while. "Oh dear," she said, and, "What will people think?"

I said, "I care not what they think if they have nothing more to occupy their minds than hoops. I must walk and get my strength back up so I can find employment. Fresh air and exercise, I have always found, work wonders for a convalescent."

She backed off then because I was a nurse and spoke out of experience, but sometimes when I pushed open the gate and set off down the street I would see her in the garden from the corner of my eye and know she watched me anxiously. Sometimes I would slip away without telling her goodbye, but even so I felt anxiety follow me along until I turned a corner out of sight. I did not resent it. Aunt Lavinia's heart was kind and her concern for me was tender.

Cousin Kate's concerns were more substantial. "The streets are dangerous," she said, "and foul. Who knows what illness you will trail back home? Smallpox, maybe—I have heard of several cases—or some malignant fever."

"Cousin Kate," I said, "I cannot spend my life sitting in the sun or strolling graciously about the garden. I am accustomed to activity."

"Then we'll have a ladies' afternoon. We'll organize a cribbage tournament."

I would have laughed if she had not made this suggestion with a look of perfect hopelessness.

"You'll be accosted," she said, reverting to a stronger argument, "you will be robbed, who knows what? Murdered. And it is not proper, Lavinia is right on that. A young lady of your class should not be wandering alone. The alleys teem with low life."

The teeming alleys were a sore point with Cousin Kate because the back wall of our garden abutted an alley, which, although it was public property, she regarded as her own and was much offended that a Negro family came to sleep there with their backs against her bricks. Each morning she would arm herself with a broom and march to the back gate. There she would feel about inside the hedge that backed onto the wall, bring out a big black key, unlock the gate, and with a swift determined motion, swing it back. "Shoo! Shoo!" she would hiss, as though the poor creatures were stray dogs, and sweep them off about their business.

These people were not violent, or at least we had no evidence they were, but Cousin Kate was convinced they would become so. They had a little boy of maybe three years old, a sad little thing constantly coughing and running at the nose. Once or twice an old man joined them, but mainly it was just the little boy and his parents. I presumed they were his parents.

Sometimes after supper in the evening I sneaked out with a pan of leftovers, and glancing furtively across my shoulder, unlocked the gate and set it down before them. While they ate, I walked up and down the alley, not daring to leave them with the pan for fear they might make off with it and bring Cousin Kate's wrath down on my head. When they were done and their fingers licked, I sneaked the pan back to the kitchen, where I washed it and set it on the shelf, relieved to have got away with my small charity.

But one night I was discovered. As I slipped back through the gate with pan in hand, Cousin Kate was waiting. "Eugenia Mae," she said, "while you live under my roof, you will obey my rules. I know these sorts of people. Give them handouts and we never will get rid of them. It's like feeding a stray dog. One starts to do it out of pity and ends up with the creature living in the house."

After that she watched me and made sure any leftovers were locked securely in the pantry.

One evening, hearing a commotion, I took the key from where it hung inside the hedge and let myself into the alley to find the man holding the little boy up by his feet while the woman pounded on his back, the child vomiting and gasping.

"What's going on? What's wrong with him?"

The woman pointed to some matter on the ground and then across the alley to where yellow flowers were growing on our neighbor's fence.

"He's been eating those flowers?"

"No miss, these miss." And she indicated with her foot a small pile of rhizomes attached to stringy roots.

"But this is yellow jessamine. Did you not know it is poisonous?"

She looked at me accusingly. "He were *hongry*, ma'am."

"But you should have watched him. You should not have . . . here, bring him into the garden. I'm a nurse. Let me give him an emetic."

I pushed the gate open, but as I turned my back they fled off down the alley.

CHAPTER TEN

I had intended, when I was ready for it, to apply for employment to General Ames, who was the Union officer in charge
of Wilmington. He and his men were headquartered at City
Hall. I arrived there early on a Monday and was civilly greeted
by a clerk, who invited me to take a chair in an anteroom.
There I waited, while townsfolk who had arrived before me
were called in one by one to present their petitions to the
general.

All this was very public, nothing confidential, the sound of
angry, begging, or obsequious voices clearly heard by everybody waiting. It seemed that every Rebel in town was busy
trying to get a pardon, or to get back a plantation which the

Freedmen's Bureau had declared abandoned, or to ingratiate themselves with General Ames for their own ends. I believe that many thought emancipation had been a big mistake, a sort of joke on them to make them toe the line. Others took it as a necessary evil, sour medicine they had to swallow. All thought "something should be done to get things back to normal," no one was quite clear what, but they did mean getting back to normal in a very Southern sense.

I was growing restless, and being in need of a privy, got up to inquire where one might be found. In the hallway, I came upon a man who seemed not to belong there. He wore no uniform and lacked the stiff bearing of a military man. There was no one else to ask, and he looked kindly, so I told him my plight and he was good enough to direct me to a privy in the yard. Coming out, I was embarrassed to find him waiting for me.

"Come along," he said, "I've been expecting you all week."

"You have?" I said, but he was already heading for the steps, and so, bemused, I trotted after him to an office with a sign fixed to the door: *Superintendent of Education, Freedmen's Bureau.* This he entered, and turning to me, thrust out his hand.

"Ashley," he said, "Samuel Ashley. I'm very happy you have finally arrived. I had begun to fear . . . no matter. Sit down, my dear, sit down." And he pulled a chair up to his desk and took his seat behind it.

"Before we go any further, you must be aware that the native people here regard me with suspicion and attempt to undermine my work. If you work for me, they will despise you too. Feeding the freedmen, that the whites can understand. But teaching them to read? There we come slap up against their fiercest prejudice. My teachers are excluded from society. Sometimes they are threatened. They are spied on through their windows, followed in the streets and called abusive names. I have tried to make this situation clear in our correspondence, but now that you are here, I must put it to you plainly that if you prefer a more congenial life, you would be best to go back home and find genteel employment."

The word *employment* stimulated me. "I assure you, sir, that I am not genteel at all. I used to be, but these days I am accustomed to all sorts of things."

"Well, then, I am glad to hear it. We have eight schools set up so far, fifteen hundred freedmen total. It is slow, every sort of obstacle is purposely set in our way, but we are making strides." He shook out a handkerchief and wiped his extensive forehead, then removed a pair of round wire spectacles and wiped them too. He rearranged them on his nose.

"You look unwell," I said. "You have been ill?"

He pulled a rueful face. "In this place of agues and swamp-bred fevers? Never!"

"Could you use a nurse?"

"A nurse? I do not understand."

"Sir, I'm sorry, but you would not let me get a word in edgewise. You have mistaken me for someone else. I am Miss Eugenia Spotswood. I am a nurse."

"You are a Southerner."

"And I would like to help."

He looked at me a long time, doubtfully. "Well, then," he said at last, "if you have nothing against Negroes."

AND so I became an itinerant nurse on a small wage. My task was to go house to house wherever I was needed and do what could be done for the sick and suffering, of whom there were a great many in the town and across the river too. Most of those across the river had come up from the south with Sherman's army. A sorry lot they were, half naked, some completely, grown men lost to modesty talking to themselves. Some were on hands and knees like dogs, dragging limbs astink with gangrene, or hitching themselves along on hands and buttocks, leaning on branches torn from trees. Others had been shocked out of their minds by liberation and the grueling trek that followed it. Having lived within the confines of one plantation all their lives, they had been scared into stupidity by the world's enormous cruelty and size. These unfortunates did what they could, huddling together, eating what they could beg or scavenge, sickening, and in some cases with relief, lying down to die. And to make matters worse, smallpox was in town, bent on turning epidemic. The hospital had but a hundred beds, and so the sick were left at home until someone obligingly gave up and freed a bed. I did my best for all of them, I tried.

When Cousin Kate discovered the nature of my employment, she threw her hands up in the air. "You will fall ill again, you will be struck down." But I assured her I had already been so ill God would not have it in his heart to strike me twice.

And he did not. I stayed healthy as a horse, no doubt due to all the walking I must do to see my patients, and saw more suffering and death than I had seen at the gold mine and the Red String hospital combined. Every house was swelled with refugees, as many as ten people sleeping in one room. Rheumatic fever, bilious colic, diseases of the eyes, earache, toothache, feverish colds, pneumonia, running sores, food poisoning, starvation—such things could only be expected with the town so crowded and so filthy, every overhang and corner and abandoned ruin squatted in.

Each morning I would walk down to City Hall, where my new employer could be found furiously writing at his desk. He was supported by the American Missionary Association and it was to them he wrote. I never knew a man write letters at such a pace, constantly reporting and requesting, begging sometimes, for provisions, clothes, books and other school supplies. At first I would present myself to him and receive my orders for the coming day, but as time went by I needed less and less direction, and then none at all.

The Freedmen's Bureau teachers, although Yankees, were nice girls full of good intentions. They would have me come to class and dose their students with whatever potion I might have on hand. These I got from Mister Ashley, who never gave up on petitioning the Missionary Society to send everything they could, from spelling books to fuel to bed-sacks. Anticipating winter, when the weather would turn sour and chilly, he begged for sheet-iron stoves and lengths of pipe.

Part of my responsibility as I went house to house was to encourage school attendance, to persuade people used to being whipped for opening a book that education was the secret to advancing in the world. I also taught a class two evenings a week to mothers, giving them advice on how to care for babies and small children, and in the process persuading them that they must make their children come to school no matter how much they protested, and if they fell sick, to send them back to school the minute they were on their feet again.

"These people," Mister Ashley told me, "are living in such wretchedness and squalor that they seek darkness rather than light, and so they must be literally hunted up and their children dragged forth."

I did my best to drag them forth, and did have some success. However, it was the orphans that concerned me most. Little children, some barely out of babyhood, ran about the streets, growing wild and furtive, learning to pick pockets and steal from stores.

"Something must be done," I told Mister Ashley. "Somehow they must be gathered in. We must find somewhere for them to live."

"Yes, yes," he said, "we must." And he wrote a letter to the Missionary Society begging for money to set up an orphanage.

These street children were as swift as rabbits. They trusted no one and would as soon continue starving as walk into the arms of strangers. When they sickened so they could not run away, I had them taken to the annex of the smallpox hospital which had been created from an old warehouse. When they recovered, Mister Ashley insisted they be kept there.

"If we cannot have an orphanage," he said, "we can at least keep them safe and feed them." And so their faces would be seen peering from the windows of the warehouse like trapped animals.

"Education, we must give them education," Mister Ashley said.

Which turned out to be a problem, since these orphans were so wild they could not be trusted on the streets for fear they would revert to their former condition. And so each morning they would be tied together one behind the other with a piece of rope—there were seven of school age by this time—and not released until the schoolhouse door had closed behind them. At first they refused to sit still at a desk, but jumped about and threw things, paying no attention. Eventually the teachers' kindness tamed them, and they learned to sit and listen and at last to find pleasure in their schoolbooks. It was months, though, before they could be trusted to be led along the streets unroped.

The citizens used this to blame us. "Look at that, a coffle," they would say. "These do-good Yankees have already taken up old Southern ways."

Christopher reported this to me, his face creased up with worry. By this time he and I were solid friends, although not entirely easy with each other. Christopher's affection was gallant, protective, proscriptive in the manner of a father or a husband or much older brother. My work disturbed him. He found it both demeaning and commendable, and did not know how to speak of it. And so he did not, speaking rather of his clients, how they multiplied, of his father's frustrations finding freedmen who would work the farm without demanding wages until a crop could be brought in and sold—where else to get the money?

One day, though, he came urgently to accost me on the street. His law office overlooked the wharf and he had been standing at the window when I appeared below him led by a small child who had been sent to bring me to her sick mama.

"Aha!" he said behind us with such force that the child panicked and took flight.

I spun around. "Christopher!"

"Eugenia Mae," he said.

"Is something wrong?"

"No, no. Yes. I mean . . . there's something I must tell you."

The child was waiting just around the corner. I could see one eye and the green ribbons twisted in her hair. I said, "I must go. I have an urgent case."

"They are saying—do you know what they are saying about you and your Yankee friends? They say you are *consorting* with the Negroes."

I looked into his eyes and saw there genuine concern that I, a member of his family, someone he loved, should fall under public criticism. "Of course," I said. "They say so many things. We have learned to take it lightly."

"Lightly? I had hoped to marry in a year or two, but if my business fails . . ."

"I understood your business has been doing well."

"It's barely on its feet," he said impatiently. "Eugenia Mae, can you not see that talk like this could ruin me?"

"What would you have me do?"

He looked perplexed, turning his head from side to side as though looking for something he had dropped. "I do not know." And then, as if he had found whatever he was looking for, "Must you do this work, Eugenia? Must you?" But I made no answer and after a long look at me he sighed mightily and did not demand one.

That night I dreamed again of the mulatto. I could not put him from my mind.

CHAPTER ELEVEN

ONE night, when all Tom's tasks were done and supper over and his mother settled on the porch, he went to sit beside her. "What do you want most from freedom?"

She did not hesitate. "I want your father back and the two of us get marry legal with a bunch of flowers in my hand and a flower in his buttonhole."

"I want that too. I want that very much."

"And I want you to get marry too. Some nice girl to make you happy."

"But I *am* happy. I'm happier than I've been in my whole life."

She swept her arm out. "But what-all's this *for,* this farm you bust your heart on every day?"

"What do you mean? It's for us, of course, for all of us to live on and support ourselves."

"And what when we all dead?"

"Oh, I see. You're talking about grandchildren."

"A nice girl, Tom, some nice girl from hereabouts. Ain't you never been in love?"

He made a humming sound, thinking of that morning at the gold mine when he woke to find Miss Genie standing over him with urgency upon her face. "Quick, Tom, you must run. Papa is going to sell you. He is going to Australia, to some godforsaken copper mine. He plans to take me with him. He plans to sell you for the passage money. You must get out of here at once." And then, tears welling in her eyes, "Tom, I love you. There, I've said it now. I want you to be free." What had happened to Miss Genie since he did not know. Had her father found another way of buying passage to Australia? Had he given up the notion? Had the two of them been swept off in the war?

After a while he went inside, where he prized a spent candle stump out of a bottle neck and replaced it with another candle, which he lit with a burning twig pulled from the fire. He blew the twig out, stood a moment looking at the ember, then settled down to read the Raleigh *Standard.* The front page told about an "enterprising gentleman" who had imported twenty white laborers into North Carolina as an experiment to see if white men could grow cotton, rice, sugar, and tobacco "in as great perfection" as black men. Tom thought about this for a while and figured Clyde, with his new wooden leg, could do it just as well as he could, and then he turned the page. A name he knew stood out at the bottom of a paid announcement—Abraham Galloway, his wartime friend, the Union spymaster from New Bern:

FREEDMEN OF NORTH CAROLINA, AROUSE!!

MEN AND BRETHREN:

> *Lo ! The waking up of nations,*
> *From Slavery's fatal sleep,*
> *The voice of the Universe,*
> *Deep, calling unto deep.*

These are the times foretold by the Prophets, "when a Nation shall be born in a day," the good time coming. Four millions of chattels, branded mercantile, commodity, shake off the brands, drop the chains, and rise up in the dignity of men.

The time has arrived when we can strike one blow to secure those rights of Freedmen that have been so long withheld from us.

To learn how to honorably and usefully fill our new position, and to discharge our debt of gratitude and our new obligations, is the principle aim of the Emancipated Colored People. To this end a Mass Meeting of the Colored Citizens of New Bern was held on August 28th, and resolutions were unanimously passed in favor of holding a Convention in the city of Raleigh, on the 29th of September, and invitation was extended to all Freedmen of North Carolina.

From all sections let delegates be sent to represent you. Let the entire colored population of North Carolina assemble in their respective townships, and speak their views on this all important subject. Let the leading men of each separate district issue a call for a meeting, that delegates may be chosen to express your sentiments at Raleigh on the 29th of September, and let each county send as many delegates as it has representatives in the Legislature.

Rally, old men; we want the counsel of your long experience. Rally, young men; we want your loyal presence, and need the ardor of youth to stimulate the timid. And may the Spirit of our God come with the people to hallow all our sittings, and wisely direct all our actions.

> *Abraham H. Galloway,*
> *John Randolph, Jr.,*
> *George W. Price,*
> *Committee*
> *Sept. 8, 1865*

"Galloway," Tom said aloud, "Abraham Galloway." He sat back in his chair, his mind flown back to New Bern and the man who trained him as a Union scout. A bold, handsome fellow he had been, with a quick mind and an air of easy confidence. "Listen up," he used to say when Tom was nervous starting on a mission, "do everything I tell you and you'll come out all right." Once the two of them had climbed a tree to get a better look at the territory they were going into. From up there they could see for miles. Galloway had swept his arm in a wide arc.

"See this, see all this? It's America and it belongs to us."

To this day Tom had not forgotten the sensation that gripped him, the longing for a sweep of land to call his own. He stared out the window at the dark and thought about the shadowy watcher in the woods. He looked back at the newspaper spread on the table and read the words of the advertisement aloud. He glanced up at the date. Saturday, September nine. Barely three weeks to the convention. Plans buzzed in his head. Tomorrow he would read this out at church.

Which he did to silence. Then an old man called out, "What's this express sentiments, what-all's that mean?"

"It means, what do you want to do now that you are free that you're still not allowed to?"

"Amen, brother!" the old man shouted. "Say it loud!"

Tom pulled a pencil and paper from his pocket. "See this paper, see this pencil? I'm going to write down what you want and we'll elect some delegates to carry it across to Raleigh and read it out to the convention."

"Amen, brother!" the old man shouted. "Write it down!"

Tom looked at him. "So, Tanner Hanley, what is it you want? We need the counsel of your years."

The old man sniffed. "Want nothin' but a wage so I can buy myself a piece o' land."

A man stood up at the back of the room, turning his hat between his hands. "Sir, my wife and me and our three young uns, we been turned off the farm where we was born and raised and lived on all our lives, no other way to earn a dollar, and now we livin' in the woods, my young uns starvin' and my wife a-cryin' all the time. I want someone make the old marse take us back and treat us right. I ain't got nought against him, I never done him wrong when we was under slavery, and do not intend to wrong him now. I figures if we treats each other right we'll get along just fine, but that man just don't want to get along. I want someone to make him."

This speech broke the hesitation and for the next hour the freedmen spoke their grievances and concerns out loud, calling on Almighty God to be their witness. The thrill of it affected everyone and the meeting was noisy and tearful. At the end, Tom called order for the final prayer.

"Dear Lord," he prayed, "with your guidance, we have decided here today that we want the law to treat us equal, that is our sentiment. And, Lord, that means we need to have some colored folk in government to keep an eye on things. Please help us choose the right delegates to carry our message to the convention on September twenty-nine. Amen."

A mason jar was passed around to gather up a contribution for the man living with his family in the woods, and the following Wednesday night at ten o'clock agreed on for election of the delegates. Then everyone went tumbling outside into the sunshine of the yard, glowing with accomplishment, and set off home, tipping their hats to the gaggle of students from the university who stood hard-eyed and unresponsive in the lane, turning their heads to look at each one as they passed.

WEDNESDAY came. It was the first time a meeting at the Preacher House had been held at night and Tom, looking at the tiny turnout, regretted sending the congregation off to think about their vote. On Sunday, a late-night meeting had seemed to him a fine touch, a sort of trumpet blast to signify that now they could meet anytime they pleased. But since then old fears had set in with the freedmen, memories of patrollers, and more recent threats as well, that if they got in too deep with this troublemaker Tom—Maryson, was that his name these days?—they just might find themselves plumb out of work.

Tom looked around him, counting. Fourteen men, and they so nervous they insisted the meeting should be held in secret in the attic room. Tom cursed under his breath, but followed them outside and locked the door and climbed behind them up the outside staircase. Everybody squatted on the floor and someone lit a candle. Light flickered on tight-drawn faces.

"Let's begin," Tom said.

But an air of listening had come over the meeting, not to his words, to a low whispering like wind in leaves that rapidly resolved itself into the whispering of voices. A rock came hurtling through a window. Another, and a third, in quick succession. The candle guttered and went out.

"The students, it's the students!"

The freedmen jumped up in a body and stood poised.

Scrambling sounds, dark figures climbing through the windows, and then everything was shouting, the crack of fist on jaw and stick on skull, the harsh whoop of a man punched in the gut, the crunch of feet on broken glass. Someone inside shouting, *"Rally for freedom!"* Someone outside shouting, *"Fire it!"* A pistol shot, a cursing in the dark, a cry, *"Police! Police!"* Then silence and Tom's voice, "Get out! Everyone get out of here! Meet me at my house!" And the freedmen tumbling through the far-side windows.

Within half an hour the meeting had resumed in Tom's kitchen, one man with a bleeding eye, one with a split lip, one holding to his ribs and swearing underneath his breath, several bloody-faced. Tom's mother, clucking her tongue, cleaned them up and bandaged them, and when it all was done not one had the courage to become a delegate. Tom, they said, must go alone.

When the village policeman came riding up next day, Tom was feeling truculent. He came onto the porch and watched him slide down off his horse and limp across.

"Constable Pike," Tom said.

The policeman nodded and pulled a folded paper from the pocket of his shirt. "This here is a statement from one of the students about your activities last night."

"We held a meeting. We're entitled."

Constable Pike pressed the paper flat against his leg. "It says here in this statement your men were planning insurrectionary proceedings."

"We were electing delegates to a convention."

"It says here that after these proceedings . . ."

"We came back here when the students attacked our meetinghouse."

"Well now, did you? All I know is there was a big row with the blacks in town last night, all the students in on it, and others too. People got beat up. Went on till one o'clock." The policeman stretched his leg out painfully. "Someone whacked a stick on my bad leg."

"If the citizens of Chapel Hill decide to have a brawl, that is their own affair. My men are not responsible."

"It says here . . ." And he began to read one word at a time, thick-tongued and laborious.

"*We got to bed about one o'clock. I felt a little afraid the Negroes might attempt something, but we had a double-barreled gun in our room so we went to sleep trusting in God. About two o'clock some Negroes, for it could have been no white man, came up in the campus and broke into the Halls of the two literary societies, tore up curtains, cut up the rug kept for saving the carpet, cut the seats, and locked us in our room.*

"*George and myself were sleeping very soundly, and did not hear the noise which the rocks made, tho' we heard the glass fall. We struck a light and woke up Battle and Barlow, who room near us, and we went out on the steps but could see no one. We also searched the adjoining room but to no purpose. I suppose they fled immediately on the perpetration of the act. We examined our room and found two very large rocks. Both windows were shattered considerably and our bed was covered with wads of grass. Our bed is immediately under one window which is generally kept raised at night.*

Last night providentially we lowered it. If it had been up we might have been seriously injured. We sat up the remainder of the night keeping watch by turns.

"This morning at the Chapel Mister Woodford addressed us and gave us some very excellent advice. The students have just had a meeting to see about patrolling the campus. I feel very thankful to My Heavenly Father for his care over us. I think the danger is all over."

"Who wrote that? What's the student's name?" Tom held his hand out for the paper, but the policeman folded it and slipped it inside his jacket. "No concern o' yourn."

"My men did not do this. And who's this boy to say it could have been no white man?"

"Come set." The policeman pulled a twist of chewing tobacco from his pocket and held it out inquiringly. Tom shook his head, but he did sit down beside him on the step.

"So what's your version of the story?" Constable Pike asked, and shoved the tobacco into his jaw. While Tom talked, he chewed slowly and intently, and when the story was all done, made a hawking sound and shot a greenish dark brown jet onto the dust. "Them students up to the university, they are a sorry lot."

For a while they sat in silence, just the wet sound of the policeman's chewing. At last he said, "I heered you done come back. Sam Morgan told me, the one you done belonged to. He says watch out for that nigger Tom, he is a fomenter of trouble."

"Sam Morgan who had me hunted through the woods and shot down like an animal? Who sold me off to traders? Left my mother with not a soul of family to care for her in her old age?"

"Easy, there. It were the way things went."

Another silence, just the chewing, punctuated by spitting.

"Sam Morgan says as how you used to be a simpleton, not good for nothing, but have turned into a sly one."

Tom said nothing, observing in his mind the young boy he once had been, terrified by life into stupidity. "I'm a free man now," he said at last. "I've been free since three years back when I went to New Bern and took up with the Union army."

The policeman whistled. "You done that, did you? Well, I ain't never had nought against the Union, never did think nothin' of the war. Done us no good here in the village. Closed down the university so everybody lost their way to earn a living. Now folks so poor they cain't barely pay one lame policeman. And all them students dead, thirty-five in all. It were a waste. No sir, it were a bad idea to go to war."

"It was the war that freed the slaves."

"It were that man Lincoln, much good it did him, got him shot clear through the head."

Once more they sat in silence. Tom looked up at the sky. Almost noon. His head was growing heavy from lack of sleep.

Clyde came thumping on his wooden leg, a bucket in each hand. "Hey, there," he said and set one bucket down midway between his cabin steps and Tom's. "That there's for your ma," he said and hoisted his leg onto the first step of the Bricket cabin. Then he took hold of the rail and hauled himself and the second bucket up onto the porch and went inside.

"Good man, not one drop spilled," Tom said to his vanished presence.

Constable Pike, who had stopped chewing on his wad

while this went on, twisted his head from side to side, stretching out the tendons. "I heered about this from a feller in the village."

"Heard about what?" Tom said, although he knew.

"About this here . . . living arrangement . . . like you-all was family."

Tom stretched out a leg and pushed his hat back easily. A vein was pulsing in his temple. "It works out pretty well."

"It ain't proper."

"How so ain't proper? We're all freedom colored now. And I thought the good Lord wanted us to help our brother in distress."

"I heered you stole his land right out from under him."

So that was it. *Stay easy, don't confront him.* "Clyde and I, we came to an agreement good for both of us."

The policeman sniffed. "So what you people up to here?" He looked about suspiciously, and at that moment Grace came along the path with Baby Gold slung on one hip and Glory on the other, the pale child and the dark. She nodded, looking shy, and went on up the steps to Tom's cabin. "Missus Maryson? You there, Missus Maryson?"

"I heered about this from a feller too," the policeman said.

"A feller on a reddish spotted horse?"

The policeman turned his face around and looked Tom up and down. "How you know that?"

"Evenings he's been sitting down there"—Tom indicated with his chin—"just inside the woods."

"Jest sitting?"

"Watching. Frightening my mother."

103

The policeman flushed along his neck and up his cheek beside the ear. He was about to speak, but Tom rose, cutting him off. "Constable, I sure do thank you kindly for the company, but I can't sit here all day. There's work to do. Clyde with that leg and all, he's . . ." He swung around, suddenly angry. "You call that fellow off."

Constable Pike's face took on an aggrieved expression. "He ain't my feller. And you got no right . . ."

"You call him off."

Tom stood over him, one hand outstretched to help him up. For a moment Constable Pike regarded it suspiciously, then, gathering his breath together, he let it out in a great sigh and set his hand in Tom's. "I'll see to it," he said.

His voice took on a whining edge. "I ain't got nothin' against freedom for the nigras. It's them students up to the university give me the gripes. Next time you hold a meetin', you-all let me know. I got a bone to pick with them."

He limped over to his horse and hoisted himself up. "You-all have a fine convention." And he pulled his horse around and rode away.

CHAPTER TWELVE

WE had been invited to the Waddells' house for supper. Cousin Kate and Aunt Lavinia were dressing in their faded frills and furbelows with all the fluster and excitement of a pair of debutantes getting ready for the first ball of their lives.

"Always so much of a relief, an invitation," Aunt Lavinia said. "Tonight we will be civilized." She took a hand mirror, the only one she had managed to smuggle from the house, and had me hold it while she admired her reflection piece by piece.

Cousin Kate said, "Do help me with this bow, Eugenia. There, that's better. I intend to pay the Waddells back as soon as I am able, and every single friend who has invited us. Lavinia, your hairpin."

When the hairpin had been retrieved and fixed back into place, and another dangler also, Cousin Kate examined me. "Eugenia, will you please wear a hoop, just one, for decency?"

I laughed. "I find it not indecent, but conducive to a good day's work."

"But we're going out for entertainment." She snatched the lid from a large potbellied basket in the corner, and plunging her arms into it to the shoulder, rummaged in its contents, pulling halfway out a corset, a lawn petticoat, an impressive pair of pink flounced drawers, a sad-looking silk stocking.

"Aha!" she said at last. "I have it!" And pulled completely out a three-hooped petticoat, wrestling with each hoop as it caught in the basket's mouth until—snap-snap-snap—it appeared in its unwieldy glory. "Just the thing," she said. "Do wear it, dear, wear it for me."

I could not resist that argument and so conceded, and she taped me in. "Much better, so much better. What do you think, Lavinia?"

Aunt Lavinia, of course, agreed, and the two women declared us ready for the evening.

THE Waddells lived a short walk off and we set out, all five of us, like a triumphant procession, Christopher tapping smartly with his cane and supporting Aunt Lavinia at the elbow, the Colonel doing likewise for Cousin Kate. I came behind trying to corral my skirt, which seemed enormous, although it was quite modest in relation to the vast expanse of well-hooped scallops going on in front. After years of going hoopless, I had forgotten how a hoop will swing and swing as though some frightened animal inside my skirt was struggling to get out.

Mister Waddell was a handsome man in his own way, reddish of complexion and powerfully built, with a straight aristocratic nose and a balding head that seemed to speak not of age but of accumulated wisdom, and a moustache and beard that flowed together in an elegant and greying dignity. He had been a Union man at first, as many were, and did not want the war, but when all was said and done and Southern pride was on the line, he went Confederate. He was a speech maker, no doubt came orating from his mother's womb, and was already talking as he strode out of the house to meet us on the path. A good deal of handshaking went on, and flattery passed back and forth, and I thought perhaps that I might like him.

"Come in, come in, come in," he said, beckoning with both hands, and it was not for several moments that he realized his enthusiasm blocked us from obeying. He laughed then, a big man's laugh, and stepping back, planted his right foot in the soft soil of the garden. It was then I knew I would not like him, not because of what he said, which was brief and underneath his breath, but because of the look which flashed across his face, there and not there, his bluff smile taking over in an instant. I can hardly put a word to what I saw, anger certainly, but something more, a sort of personal humiliation, as if he had been made to look a fool and would store the memory up and get revenge. On whom? The gardener? No, I'm making all this up. And yet there was something, there was something.

Inside, we barely had time to greet his wife, a self-effacing pretty woman, before he planted himself before the mantel shelf, tucked two fingers of each hand into the slits of his waistcoat pockets and looked about with a complacent air.

"I made a speech at City Hall last night," he said importantly. "A group of the more levelheaded Negroes invited me to give them some advice on how they should proceed now they are free."

Behind him, a mirror edged with stiff gilt-painted leaves gave his head and shoulders back into the room like the rear view of a family ancestor. It made my hackles rise. This man may once have been against the breakup of the Union, but he was no friend to the Negro.

"What possessed them to do that?" I said, and felt the Colonel turn to look at me.

Mister Waddell's eyes rested on me for a moment and moved on. "I set them straight," he said, "on some untoward expectations they had got into their woolly heads. Friends, I said, I wish you never to lose sight of something. A large majority of the people of North Carolina are whites, and whether you get the vote or not, they will always control the state. You cannot resist without inviting destruction upon yourselves."

"Colonel, but—," I said.

"Eugenia!" the Colonel hissed.

Mister Waddell removed his fingers from his waistcoat pockets, inserted one inside the collar of his shirt and stretched his neck, at the same time turning his head one side to the other. It struck me that he looked remarkably like a cockerel about to test his early morning voice. Perhaps my thought showed on my face. In midstretch he paused, his finger still inside his collar and his head turned to the right so that the fibers of his neck stood out like rope.

"I told them frankly that I look upon universal, unrestricted, free suffrage as a curse instead of a blessing, that only those who can read and write should be allowed to vote."

"Sir," I said, "when the Negroes learn to read and write, you will have no objection to their voting?"

"That said," he continued, "and the matter dismissed"— and he dismissed my question with his eyes—"I spoke to them about ambition. Do not strike too high, I said. Ambition, within decent bounds, is very commendable, but remember, by that sin fell the angels. You ought, I said, to strive to show the world that you deserve the freedom and privileges now bestowed upon you. But let me tell you that in order to succeed, you will have to prove yourselves an exception to every instance of emancipation which has ever happened in the history of your race."

"But sir," I said, "you seem to have told them what to do in order to succeed, and in the same breath told them they cannot do it."

Mister Waddell turned his head to me again, a slow, deliberate motion. He said nothing, just looked at me politely, as though he thought I might have said something but now realized he had been mistaken.

I persisted. "Sir, is this not a conundrum?"

He put the knuckle of a thumb into his mouth and closed his teeth on it, his eyes closed too, and his head bowed, as though he prayed for patience. That granted, in a voice censorious and fatherly, "Miss Spotswood, you are very young, a girl of no experience in life."

I saw my poor papa again, the way his hair had gone from full and heavy on his head to thin and wisplike, his face worn like a sandbank eroded by a stream. I saw myself as well, tattered, barefoot, a bonnet on my head Cousin Kate would not offend a vagrant with, and the heat and daily grinding of the gold mine. I smelled the makeshift stink of death in the hut which served as hospital.

"Sir, in my short life I have had more experience than any girl would wish."

"Then it's time for you to marry and address yourself to concerns proper to a woman."

He turned toward his wife, inquiring when the meal was to be ready, and talked a great deal at the table, addressing most of his remarks to the Colonel, who agreed with all he said, and a few to Christopher, who said that he agreed. I think he was afraid of Mister Waddell. He was a man of consequence in town and Christopher in need of business.

Mister Waddell did not speak to me again, although several times I caught him watching me, and once, with half an eye on me, he spoke enthusiastically about the notion of declaring freedmen orphans so they could be rounded up and forced to work. I did not rise to his bait, though, and was happy when the meal was over and we left.

THE Colonel would not let me walk behind as I had coming, but insisted that he take my elbow. Since he had Cousin Kate by the elbow with his other hand, and the sidewalks were not designed for a procession of that width, I was in danger of falling off into the gutter.

He said nothing as we came down Third Street, but as we turned the corner onto Market Street he drew his breath in hard, then blew it out again.

"What is it?" Cousin Kate said. "Was the meal too heavy?"

"My dear," he said, and I understood he spoke to me, "my dear, a small word of advice if you are not averse."

"Not at all. I'm always open to advice."

"Mister Waddell is a man of influence. It might be best to humor him."

"To agree with everything he says, you mean?"

He pressed my elbow in a sympathetic way. "He has his views, as have we all."

"I have mine too."

"Yes, yes, child, of course, of course."

We continued on, he deep in thought, his pace dragging so that we barely strolled. At last he drew his breath in hard again, then blew it out, at the same time shaking his jowls like a horse just come in from an early morning gallop. "My dear, I will confide in you. I am, as all plantation owners are these days, brought down. The war was hard on us. We lost our sons."

His voice fogged up and caught. He cleared his throat. "On top of which we have lost our labor force, as well you know. The blacks refuse to work except for pay and we have nothing left to pay them with. Which means, my dear, that we must find other ways to make a living until things settle down."

"Other ways? Like what?" Cousin Kate spoke sharply.

"I have been considering a shipping agency."

"Shipping? You would go into *business*?"

"I have been made an offer by a pair of Christopher's clients. CC Importers, they call themselves. They have a warehouse on the riverfront with offices above."

"You mean Cannerty and Coombes, those two?"

"Yes. Is it not a strange coincidence that all our names begin with C? It will be an easy matter to add one more above the door. CCC Importers, it has a ring to it. Of course, not yet," he went on hastily. "I would have to prove myself."

"Those men are boors."

"They are making money."

"I do not trust either one of them. You will get yourself in trouble."

"They have Christopher to counsel them on legal matters." The Colonel laughed uneasily. "Surely you trust Christopher?"

Cousin Kate sniffed. "Their wives are not appropriate."

"You would not be required to socialize."

Cousin Kate said nothing. She increased her pace so that the Colonel and I were forced to increase ours. In a moment we were at the house.

"My dear," the Colonel said, "I cannot see another way."

A few days later, the Colonel came to breakfast with a copy of that day's *Journal* in his hand. When he had settled in his chair, he snapped it open.

"Have you seen this piece of fandangle?" he asked, addressing Christopher. Christopher held his hand out and the Colonel reached across and slapped the paper into it. Christopher spread it on the tablecloth beside him.

"Freedmen of North Carolina, arouse!" he read. "The time has arrived when we can strike one blow to secure those rights of Freedmen that have been so long withheld from us. . . ."

The Colonel listened in silence, and when he had done, "A convention to express their sentiments? In Raleigh? No good can come of this, no good at all. And this 'all important subject,' what can that refer to?"

Christopher consulted the paper. "I suppose 'those rights of Freedmen that have been so long withheld from us.' "

The Colonel made a sound inside his nose. "So much for Mister Waddell's wise advice. Who are these fellows anyway? Who is this—what's his name?—the first signer? He must be the ringleader."

Christopher consulted the paper again. "Galloway. Abraham Galloway."

"Of the Brunswick County Galloways?"

"Abraham." Christopher looked thoughtful. "I do not know an Abraham. But of course he's colored, it's simply a coincidence."

Cousin Kate put a bland expression on her face. "No doubt he's of the family."

The Colonel looked at her. "For shame, my dear, and you a lady."

Cousin Kate's face flushed and her bosom swelled, but the

Colonel ignored her, turning once more to Christopher. "Have you heard anything about this so-called convention?"

But Christopher had not and the two of them passed the paper back and forth, the Colonel saying, "Secure their rights? I'd like to give them rights, the rights to get their lazy carcasses back into my fields," and Christopher, nervously, "What do you think it means, 'The time has arrived when we can strike one blow'? Do you think they're planning violence?" and the Colonel, "So they intend to speak their views, do they? What can they have to say that we've not heard a thousand times already from the Yankees and are tired of?"

He reached out with his fork, speared an enormous sweet potato from the serving dish, and held it before him, eyeing it like an enemy. "*That* is what I would like to do to these meddling Yankees and their cohorts. Find out who this fellow is."

As he said it, I realized who the fellow was—my luminous mulatto from the train. I do not know why this came to me. It was purely intuition.

I was returning home from work along the waterfront, enjoying the sensation of a cool breeze on my face and listening to the chatter of the watermen and the chatter of the terns. Water slapped against the docks and a pair of small boys, swimming naked and illegal in the river, were hauled out by a policeman who boxed their ears and sent them running with their clothes wadded in their hands. Aside from their vanishing pale bottoms, the wharves were almost empty. I looked about in puzzlement. Vagrants who all day had wandered in the streets should by now be straggling to the waterfront to bed down for the night. Where could everybody be? Surely the entire vagrant population had not been taken by the smallpox.

A little white girl planted herself in my path, one hand held out. I had seen this child before and had tried to help her. Once I had succeeded in taking the outstretched hand, intending to lead her to Mister Ashley in hopes that he would find a place for her with some kindhearted family. But the child was skittish and I could not hold her.

Since then, it seemed, I saw her everywhere, as though she understood that here was someone who could be touched for a few coins. She would appear before me as she had today, one hand held out and her hair in a tangle down across her eyes. Usually she was quick on her feet and furtive in her movements. Today she seemed heavy and sluggish, listing to one side like a ship about to founder.

"Child," I said, "I can give you more than coins. I can find a place for you to live where you will have food each day, if only you will come with me."

The child dropped her hand and stepped back, glancing about as though she suspected an ambush. In that turn of the head, I saw the rash of pustules on her cheek.

"Come, little one, you're sick, let me help you. I'm a nurse."

The child stood rooted, eyes turning side to side, her skinny body tensed for flight.

"Where's your mother? What has happened to her?"

The child reached up and took hold of one ear and pulled at it, her mouth opening, straining, as though some great grief was in her head and she was fighting to control it. She staggered and

115

seemed about to fall. I reached toward her, but she twisted from my grasp and bolted.

I clicked my tongue, exasperated with myself. "Gently, take her gently," I whispered, but I knew that if I did not take her soon the child would die.

The sky dimmed suddenly, as it does at that time of the year, and I turned away and headed toward home. My course took me past the Methodist church on Front Street, a shabby building which had lost the windcock off its spire. A crowd of Negroes and poor whites stood outside the church, men and women both, and children darting in and out. Approaching closer, I realized the place was so jam-packed that all who wanted could not get inside. This explains the empty wharves, I told myself.

A wave of laughter and then silence. I asked a woman what was going on and learned that some famous orator from New Bern was inside making a speech. Curious, I nudged and squeezed and elbowed my way up the steps and through the entryway into the body of the church. And there he was, my mulatto from the train, in full bass voice.

"Unity is what we need, and must have, if we are to stand with our heads held up as citizens of this country, which belongs more to us than to the white man. From first settlement, it was we who worked the fields and grew the crops and broke our backs out in the sun, and died beneath the lash to make this country rich. Since we made it, it belongs to us, and no matter what the law might say, we are its citizens. And as citizens, we will have our rights, the right to stand as witness in a court of law, the right to educate our children, the right to vote, to have a say in what goes on. Brethren of New Hanover County, we must come together, forgetting petty differences, because together is the only way. The black man must have equal rights before the law with whites. To achieve that, we must be steadfast, it is the most important thing. If we stand steadfastly together, we will complete our freedom."

Abraham Galloway, I whispered to myself, so this is what you are about.

As on the train, I could not take my eyes off him. He had a charm that made you want to look at him and never look away. His manner was easy and forcible, both at once, his voice carrying clearly, and his serious intent made more serious by the joking way he had. He did not drone or preach, but laid his argument out simply and then told a story which made his listeners laugh and fixed his point securely in their minds.

"My brethren," he said, "white people tell us we are lazy, worthless, and inferior, that whipping is the only way to make us work. They say we have descended from the apes, that we have not the ability to discipline ourselves or the intelligence to have a say in our own government. Brethren, you think that you are free, that General Sherman freed you, or the Union army, or Mister Lincoln, rest his soul, but you are slaves still, and will be until the black man has the ballot. Only then will you be truly free. And let me tell you this. The white man needs us. North Carolina might beat her knuckles off rapping at the doors of Congress, but she will never get back into the Union without Negro suffrage."

This drew a great stamping of feet, and when it faded, "I'm somewhat down on Andrew Johnson, who might like the darkeys very well, but he likes the South more and would go with old South attitudes. But I don't want to marry any white man's daughter. All I ask is our full rights under the law. The white man says he doesn't want to be placed equal with the Negro. Why, if you could see him slipping around at night, trying to get into Negro women's houses, you would be astonished."

A shrill voice over to the right called out, "Ain't that the truth!"

Her words were taken up and passed woman to woman around the congregation, each one turning to another, laughing, whether from hate or outrage or amusement I could not discern.

Silence fell again and all eyes turned to Abraham, who had been standing with one forearm on the podium, his eyes traveling with the traveling words, alert, assessing, sympathetic. "I do not wish to be considered the white man's enemy. No sir, I think the white man as good as the Negro—if he will only behave himself. I am half white myself, and it is no credit to me because I am a bastard. My father was a white man, and one of the chivalry of North Carolina at that. But I love the Negro more than I do the white man, and want to see him elevated to his proper position. We want to be an educated people, an intelligent people. We want to read and write and acquire those accomplishments which will enable us to discharge the duties of life as citizens. And we want to be allowed the privilege of voting."

The hall broke into applause. Abraham stepped back from

the podium, unsmiling, nodding slightly as his gaze went around the room. Raising his hands, he waited quietly for order.

"I know that the white people, or some of them, will object to this. But if they refuse to allow us the privilege of free suffrage, I am willing to compromise the matter with them. I am willing that the test of education should be made to rule in the matter, for both white and black."

He drew his breath and looked around, a wicked twinkle in his eye, and leaned across the podium, lowering his voice so that everyone leaned in to hear. "Grant the right of suffrage to every white or black man in North Carolina who can read and write, and one half the white people of North Carolina will be debarred from voting."

Again he stopped for a barrage of cheering, and I admired, and would at later times admire even more, the way he had with a crowd, the way he could control it and persuade it to his point of view, and at the same time make his listeners love and trust him.

"Many of our men fought bravely for the Union. Many of us died. If the Negro can handle the cartridge box, he can handle the ballot box. If he is capable of one, he is capable of the other."

Once more the stamping and cheering so that the entire building seemed about to fly off into heaven.

"Now, I overheard two white men talking a day or two ago in New Bern. One of them said to the other, 'I don't favor this Negro voting, for if they are allowed to vote they have the majority here in New Bern and the first thing they will do will be to elect that scoundrel Galloway to mayor.' " And when the laughter had again subsided, "We have many warm friends among the whites. Others, who say they are our friends, are perfectly willing to give us Bibles and spelling books, but want to deny us the rights to which we are entitled. To gain them, brethren, we must take a long pull, a strong pull, and a pull together."

Cries of "Hurray for Galloway!" and it was clear that he was known here and was popular. One fellow called out, "Galloway for mayor!" and he looked down, smiling, and called back to him, "Sir, I would not start so low as mayor!" and the meeting broke up on a new wave of laughter.

ABRAHAM'S speech was on the thirteenth of September. Eight days later, another mass meeting was held at City Hall, and another five days later at the colored graveyard. On the twenty-eighth, the *Herald* newspaper became impatient.

> *Just what the Negro population of this state are aiming at it*, it fulminated, *is difficult to conceive. Their minds have been filled with wild notions of their right to the ballot and their purpose to secure that right. Public meetings have been frequent among them. Conventions and delegates and voting have been prominent topics of talk among them. And thus they have gone on, forgetting that they are poor people, that the laboring season is fast passing away, that they must henceforth shift for themselves, and that they have nothing laid aside for the winter— forgetting that they now have families which their indi-*

120

*vidual efforts must support, that they have no master to
go back to in the hour of need—in fine, utterly neglectful
of that great fact that henceforth they have only their
individual labor to rely upon for support.*

*What this convention is for does not appear. But we
hear that they are actually applying to the state constitutional convention for admission to its deliberations, fail-
ing which they propose to do some awful things in the
way of protestation.*

*Now how seriously wicked appears the conduct of
those fanatical agitators who have inspired all this useless
political tomfoolery among the ignorant blacks, the result
of all which will merely be disappointment. What punish-
ment can be too severe for such criminals?*

I was sitting in the garden when I read this. I let the paper
fall onto my lap, the last sentence crawling in my mind like
something evil. Around me flowers tumbled in abundance. A
bird called in the tree above my head, and somewhere in the
distance the muffled tapping of a woodpecker. A small green
lizard skittered on the path.

Chapter Thirteen

T HE convention was to start on Friday. Tom arrived the evening of the day before. Not knowing where to spend the night, he took himself to the Freedmen's Bureau, where he had got the readers. The same young woman who had given them to him listened to his problem, her head tilted to one side like an inquiring bird, then pulled a pair of blankets from a shelf and led him into an adjoining room, where she offered him the floor. This, Tom discovered, he was to share with half a dozen other delegates, one man from as far away as Statesville, whose location he remembered from his study of the map when he had been a Union scout.

A man from Caswell County had a bloodied head, which

the Bureau woman—Miss Troover was her name—had washed and bound up in a bandage. He had got it, he told the others in the dark before they went to sleep, from the man who used to be his owner and for whom he now worked under contract.

"He said as how this yere convention were for nothin' but a-plottin' and a-schemin' and I had no business gettin' into trouble of that sort when I had little ones to feed. Ain't that I am a-goin' for, I told him, I am a-goin' to espress the senteements o' those what sent me. That was when he whacked me first, with his bare fist. Enough of fancy double-talk from you, he said, and when I said it's clear as stillwater to *me*, he took a stool and near to broke my head."

"My ol' marse," a deep voice said out of the dark, "he threatened me with thumbscrews if I come, so I snuck off in the night."

"You goin' back?" a third voice asked.

"I is."

Several men spoke at once.

"What's that?" the deep voice asked.

"You oughta stay in Raleigh. Keep away from that ol' marse."

"Nah. I goin' back. He try to put them thumbscrews on me I will kill him."

"They'll hang you for it."

"I'se a free man now. I'll run."

"They'll track you down."

"I ain't afraid o' them no more."

"Maybe not, but if you kill that man it will be bad for all

of us. The white man, he'll say look at that, niggers are just animals the way we always said."

"Well, then, I won't kill 'im after all. I'll jes' run."

"Oughta stay in Raleigh like I say."

"Will you shut up with Raleigh?"

A scuffle started.

"You-all quit that. You is grown men."

The scuffle stopped and there was silence for a while. Then the man from Caswell County said, "He gotta go back home."

"How's that?"

"We *all* gotta go back home. We gotta go back to those what sent us and tell what happened at this yere convention. That's why they sent us to espress their senteements."

Tom said, "And what *are* the sentiments of those who sent you?"

"Just want to be men like any other. They done sent me here to say it."

TWO conventions were going on in Raleigh that weekend, one black, one white. President Johnson had turned a man by the name of William Holden into a provisional governor. His task was to gather up such Union loyalists as he could find and set up a government to make some voting rules. Mister Holden was a fiery man and very energetic, with a high domed forehead and a determined mouth. People loved him, hated him, trusted him entirely, or doubted him with vicious spite. He did not care. He went about his business like a bull at a gate, and yet with the subtlety of bulls he could on occasion creep, appearing behind an opponent, head down, horns swinging, while the poor fellow was still pulling on his pants.

Mister Holden's convention was being shouted back and forth beneath the high arch of the Capitol on the main square of town. A few blocks away was the African Methodist church, a plain wooden building, small and painted white, crammed with what Tom calculated might be three hundred men on the main floor, with cushioned seats and carpet. Maybe a hundred more, men and women both, hummed and fidgeted on bare wood benches upstairs in the gallery. Reporters were there too, local men and white men come down from the North, he could tell them from the notebooks in their hands and the alert way they turned their heads about.

A sensation of amazement took him as he pushed his way through the onlookers crowding in the street and did not abate as he pushed his way inside. All these black faces gathered in one place, all these black opinions, the jocularity and laughter with underneath a seriousness of purpose the like of which he never had witnessed in his life. Much backslapping went on, and calling across the room or upstairs to the gallery, one man chanting "Glory, glory, glory" in a deep black voice. A sort of jubilation, a sort of thrill, possessed the room. It made Tom want to jump and shout.

At last, as though a trumpet had been sounded, everyone fell silent and three men came in from the vestry. Three chairs were ready on the platform, and a pulpit with a sloping top. Two of the men sat down. The third Tom recognized as Abraham Galloway, neat and handsome in a dark blue suit with matching waistcoat and a red cravat. He held a judge's gavel in his hand and knocked it hard against the pulpit, smiling out across the congregation.

Tom smiled back as though his face would burst and barely heard the words of introduction, just sat there smiling, smiling, the man from Caswell County's voice singing in his head. *Men like any other*. When Abraham's eyes came to rest on him, Tom raised his hand in greeting, and Abraham lifted his hand back.

"Hey there, Tom Maryson. It's a fine thing to see you here today." And everybody craned their necks to look at him, which made him proud and bashful all at once.

He looked up at the statue of Mister Lincoln back behind the pulpit. It was set on a bracket fixed onto the wall, head and shoulders large as life, the wall swathed in black mourning. Above it, on a canvas edged in black, were words Tom could not read from where he sat, he supposed they might be something that good man had said. He thought about what he might say if he had been the president who freed the slaves, something wise and beautiful that people would remember. *Men like any other*.

To be president, what would that be like? He could not imagine it, and fell to watching Abraham, admiring his confidence and the way, each time he rose to speak, he seemed to glow. Tom looked at Mister Lincoln and back at Abraham, who shared his name. He thought about his Union army days in New Bern, how, when Abraham was teaching him to be a scout, they would sit together on a riverbank or by a creek and trail their hot feet in the water. How, little by little, Abraham had told him of his exploits after he fled slavery in Wilmington. How he had linked up with a gang of abolitionists in Canada and helped slaves cross the border from Ohio. And met John Brown and conferred with him about his plan for Harpers Ferry. And spied out the Carolina coast for General Butler ahead of the invading Union. And met with Frederick Douglass and given his opinion on the vote for Negroes, and with Mister Lincoln too, while the president sat completely still, one elbow on the table, and listened to him with a look of concentration on his face. How, in New Bern, thousands upon thousands of Negro runaways had gathered round him, looking to him as a leader. There was no boasting in him as he told these stories, no Look at me, look at what I've done. He was a man of serious intent. Tom smiled to himself. He thought it might be good to have two presidents, one white, the other black. He thought he would like Abraham to be his president. If he could vote, he would cast his vote for him.

On the second day, in the afternoon, the man from Caswell County was asked to stand up in his turn and express the sentiments of those who sent him. He rose slowly, pulling himself up on the back of the pew in front, the bandage on his head still oozing blood. He stood a moment, bowed and wavering, and a man rose on each side and took him by the elbows.

"I been sent to say we want to be men like any other."

A sobbing broke out in the gallery, a woman's voice, and then a running murmur, a man's voice calling, "Say it, brother, say it!" And then a chant, a deep low song, *Like any other, men like any other,* passing back and forth across the room. It went on for a long time, a prayer, an invocation, a resolve, and then Tom heard his own name called. He rose and stood a moment, thinking he might cry. Then out of the mass of faces, he saw Abraham's and spoke to him.

"My people sent me here to say they want the law to treat them equal. And they want coloreds in the government to keep an eye on things."

Had he asked too much? Abraham's face had gone completely still, his gaze once more moving back and forth across the congregation. Then an odd thing happened. As Abraham's head turned side to side, the congregation's heads turned with it, like pins following a magnet. They began to crane and peer to see who he was fixing with his eye, and then to turn toward each other. As eye caught eye, heads began to nod, a murmur started.

Abraham raised his hands and silence fell. "And we will get that. We will have our own men in the government. We will keep on until we do. The only way to silence us will be to shove the ballot down our throats."

After that, Tom flung his whole mind into the proceedings, cheering with the others when a speaker took up for the right to vote. Although on the last day he was disappointed because the committee charged with writing a petition to be carried to Mister Holden's convention did not put suffrage in it. The need for decent wages, decent hours of work, protection against cruel employers, collection of just pay, these went into it. Education too, an end to biased laws, care of orphans, reunion of families split apart by slavery.

These were all good things to ask for, but what about the vote? And the wording of the paper was so humble, so groveling, begging rather than demanding. *As our longer degrada-*

*tion cannot add to your comfort, make us more obedient as
servants, or more useful as citizens, will you not aid us by
wise and just legislation to elevate ourselves?* The wording
sickened him, but Abraham seemed satisfied. Tom could not
understand it.

On the last day, when everything was finished, Tom pushed
his way through the crowd and went to read the sign above
Mister Lincoln's head:

*With malice toward none, with charity for all, with firm-
ness in the right, as God gives us to see the right, let us
strive to finish the work we are in, to bind up the nation's
wounds, to care for him who has borne the battle, and
for his widow and orphan; to do all which may achieve
and cherish a just and everlasting peace among ourselves
and with all nations.*

Tom stood a long time, emotions breaking over him he
never would successfully describe. Relief, perhaps, and triumph, belief and disbelief, and fear and pride. Ambition too,
and pity for this man who had achieved so much and in the
end paid for it with his life.

A whisper back behind him. "Tom?" And he turned into
the embrace of Abraham, who apologized for not greeting
him more fully before this, he had been overwhelmed by business. The two men went along the aisle together, down the
shaking wooden steps, and out into the crush of onlookers,
which by now had more than doubled. As they broke out of
the crowd, Abraham led Tom off to a quiet bench beneath a

tree, where he listened with attention to his account of what had passed since they last saw each other in New Bern, and in his turn gave an account of what had passed with him.

He laughed. "As for me, I seem to spend my whole time making speeches."

"Do you make speeches about voting?"

"All the time. Why?"

"Why didn't we put the vote in the petition?"

"We did. We came to them as citizens. Only citizens can vote."

"But we didn't ask for it straight out."

"Increments, Tom, increments."

Tom had never heard the word before, but understood instinctively.

"So you think one day we'll get the vote?"

"I do. I do indeed. I do not think that God has brought us through the Red Sea just to let us wander in the wilderness, but if we come at them flat-on we'll panic them." He nudged Tom's arm. "You remember that night in New Bern when we bluffed the Union recruiter into promising us equal pay with the white soldiers?"

Tom nodded. "We didn't get it, though."

"No, but what we did get was the start of understanding that if we act together we can get things done. Tom, you must have heard the bluster about how the white man has to lift us up, to civilize us. But we can't trust them to lift us up. We have to lift ourselves. And for that we have to change the laws."

"It's going to take a miracle."

"And I have come to understand how miracles are made.

Not one man raising up a saintly hand and calling on a generous God, but an entire race standing side by side demanding, not of God, but of their fellow men. As you said yourself, we need our own men in the legislature. We have to organize the black man and make him understand that when the vote does come, and come it will, he has to put every Negro capable of such an undertaking into office."

"You?"

"I'm going to the Senate."

"They'll kill you first."

"I intend to do it though every white man in the South stand in my way."

They sat awhile, each occupied with his own thoughts. Then Tom said, "Mc, I intend to be a farmer."

Abraham stretched out his legs and crossed them at the ankles. He leaned back comfortably on the bench and hooked his elbows on the wooden slatted back. "I'm all for it."

"I've got some gold buried in the woods."

"Where did you get that?"

"At the gold mine, when I worked there."

"And you've kept it all this time?"

"Yessir. Thought I'd lost it for a while, but then I found it."

"What do you intend to do with it?"

"There's this new freedmen's bank. There's interest to be had and I was wondering . . ."

"The Freedman's Savings and Trust? Don't do it. It could too easily go under. Invest in something solid, something real."

"Railroad bonds?"

"You'll be defrauded. Go for land."

"I was wondering that too."

"Buy every acre you can lay your hands on. But do not draw attention to yourself. Remember, increments, Tom, increments." He laughed a rueful laugh. "I'd do it too if I had more than six cents to my name."

AS Tom rode home on Transportation, he let his thoughts wander as they might. The countryside crept by, step by creaking step. He was a lucky man, he thought. When he had been sold into the gold mine and they sent him down the shaft, he had howled like a kicked dog. He was not embarrassed by the memory since the fellow who had howled was someone else, a stranger he had left behind. He pitied him and yet he had been lucky. He would buy land with his gold. And one day Abraham would be a senator, Tom did not doubt it. He would like for him to be the president.

"A good man, Abraham," he said aloud, and Transportation turned his ears back, slackening his pace still more, like an old man ripe for conversation. Tom flicked the reins. He thought about Miss Genie and then he set her on one side and let her travel with him.

CHAPTER FOURTEEN

Now it was fall. Elections had been held and Mister Holden had been beaten out for governor by Mister Worth, a good enough man, a Quaker, but unable to control a legislature dominated by old Southern attitudes. With Mister Holden and his cohorts sparring on the other side, the months dragged on and on until it looked as though our constitution would never get rewritten in a way to get us back into the Union. Meanwhile, most of the military had been pulled out of Wilmington, the offending Negro brigade as well, and the city government turned over to much the same people who had always run it.

The minute the Yankee squatters, as Cousin Kate called

them, left the house, she began once more to entertain. Her meals were simple, but these days no one minded. The increasing frequency of invitations was an indication that a sort of normalcy was starting to take hold. Everything was talked about over these meals, from the presumptuous Negroes who thought that if they worked the fields they were entitled to a share of the crop, to the new store that had just been opened up on Front Street by Mister George Z. French, a big handsome fellow in a broad-faced way, and very hairy. He had been a sutler for the Union army and had an almost magic way of securing goods the ladies had not seen in years. Few among them could afford to give him custom, but oh the thrill just to stand outside his window admiring his display, or to sweep by haughtily, pretending not to look but looking anyway. They called him "that *caah*petbagger Gizzard French," and seemed to get as much thrill from not buying as buying from him.

Despite our entertaining, we still had no maid, although plenty were available. We had a yardman Christopher had hired, and a man who served as handyman and groom. Neither lived on the property, this was insisted on by Cousin Kate. "Enough that I should have these impudents around by day, I will not have them here at night scheming how to steal me blind while I am sleeping on my bed."

No one lived in the back alley. The vagrant family had not been seen since the yellow jessamine adventure, and Cousin Kate policed the alley, advancing on it every morning with her broom, sweeping off anyone who thought to take their place.

Cousin Kate had sway over the hiring inside the house, and

although the Colonel nagged and wheedled her to get herself a cook, a maid, she would not budge. "How dare these creatures come to my back door demanding to be paid? And we ourselves so short of money Lavinia and I must patch and mend and turn the gowns we had before the war. A new pair of hose these days is nothing but a luxury. And as for undergarments! Rather than hand good money to some lazy trollop, I would rather get down on my hands and knees and scrub the floors myself."

And she had become quite good at it. Each morning a great flurry of activity would take place inside the house. Up would go the windows and a vengeful shaking out of quilts and pillows start. When that was done and the air below the windows a tumult of small feathers, she and Aunt Lavinia, their skirts pinned up beneath capacious floral aprons and their hair tied up in dusters, would advance from room to room in search of dirt like a pair of soldiers tracking down an enemy. The yardman was allowed to pump water for the tank up in the attic, since that was done outside, but let him tote a pail into the house, or haul a shovelful of ashes out? It was forbidden.

"I will not let that Negro step across my sill," Cousin Kate declared. "I will not let him see what he and his benighted race have brought us to. I will not tolerate that *face* of his, the way he never smiles. Why cannot he smile? Why can none of them these days? A normal Negro always smiles. I do not know what has gone wrong with them. Our sweet niggers have been turned into strange creatures by this . . . this *emancipation*. They walk around as though they have great solemn things to think about and have completely lost their manners. They do not even have the courtesy to step aside when Lavinia and I walk down the street. We are obliged to step around them. Freedom is not good for them, it will all end in disaster."

She stopped to draw a breath. "As for this yardman of Christopher's, he is a gloater, and he keeps his hat stuck firmly on his head to mock me."

The Colonel said, "He's just feeling his oats. They all are. They'll settle down. Meanwhile, wife, you need a maid. Perhaps Eugenia Mae, since she's out among these people every day . . ." He looked imploringly at me. "I'm ashamed to have it said about the town that my wife—*my* wife!—has turned herself into a servant. I'm ashamed to have my friends come here and eat our food and go off clacking their tongues that we're too poor, or too mean, to pay for a little household help."

"Too poor? I am too *proud*."

"A white maid then?"

"I'll not have white trash in my house, holding out their hands for pay and stealing money from my purse behind my back."

"Chinese then? I hear they have become available."

"And I hear they are completely faithless. For the offer of a nickel more they'll jump up unannounced and leave guests waiting at the table."

And so the argument went every morning, with Christopher interjecting soothing lawyerly remarks and the whole thing ending with the Colonel marching red-eared off along the street, leaving Cousin Kate clattering about the house in a callithump of mops and brooms and polishing cloths, Aunt

Lavinia flustering along behind like a caboose to her engine, with scrubbing brush and kneepads, a pail awkward in one elbow.

At noon they bathed and rested and became ladies, and as the sun began to set, transformed themselves into a cook and scullery maid. When they came into the dining room, red-faced and staggering beneath a loaded tray, the Colonel would mutter in his beard, and ignoring them both, make a loud clatter with his knife and fork, addressing his remarks to Christopher as if the two of them were all alone. "It's underdone again," he'd say. "It's burned." "Good God, what *is* this brew?" And once, to Cousin Kate's clamp-mouthed indignation, "If I saw this on the street I'd purely step around it."

If guests were present, he would make excuses. The cook had proved unsatisfactory and had been sent off that very afternoon. The maid had gone to see about her mother, who was sick. And everybody nodded and was sympathetic, telling stories of their own unsatisfactory help.

ONE day, having finished my home visits, I came back to the Freedmen's Bureau office at City Hall and was busy making notes on patients' cards. I was alone, the hour near sunset, the building emptied of its workers and no preparations going on for entertainment or a meeting. The only other office in the building with its doors still open was the library down the hall, which had taken to staying open late into the evening so members could come by after supper. Everything was silent.

A sound behind me made me start with that little fearful gasp one makes when one is not expecting anything and something happens. Turning, I found a Negro woman standing in the doorway. She was obviously poor, but neatly dressed and shiny in her cleanliness.

"Hello," I said, and set my hand against my heart. "You startled me."

She looked at me, slitting up her eyes. "You're the one give us the food."

"I'm sorry, I see so many people every day."

"When we was living in the alley."

"Ah, yes, I remember. How's your little boy?"

"He daid. He et them roots, miss, and he daid."

I rose, feeling the skin beneath my right eye twitch. "I'm sorry about that, so very sorry."

She said nothing.

"I *did* tell you not to let him eat them," I went on. "Yellow jessamine is very poisonous."

The woman's eyelids lowered, just a momentary flicker, and I wished I had not said it.

"Gladys, am I right?"

"Gladys Horton, miss. My husband's name is Jacob. He got a good job now, a waiter on the Wilmington-to-Weldon line."

"I'm pleased to hear it."

"Miss, I heered your family don't have no cook."

"You did?" But then I remembered the yardman Christopher had hired, and the way news ran house to house amongst the freedmen, seeping through the walls it seemed.

"I'se a good cook, miss, I run the kitchen for a grand lady in Columbia."

"And now you want to work for us?"

"Yes, miss. Me and Jacob, we doin' better now. It were a shock, miss, we bin born and bred in slavery and the suddenness of being free . . . we got confused." She looked down at the floor and sniffed. "And then our tragedy."

I considered her. "You do not hold ill feelings toward Missus Clark-Compton for sweeping you away?"

"No, miss. I just want work. They tell us work, they tell us go to school, they tell us elevate yourselves. I want to elevate myself."

"You have enrolled in school?"

"Yes, miss, at the Baptist meetinghouse on Front Street."

"Then you'll need time off to continue your studies, I suppose?"

"I cain't elevate myself unless, or so they says."

"Who says all this?"

"Why, Mister Galloway, miss, Mister Abraham Galloway. He say the Negro ought to learn to read and write and learn about the world and work an honest job and save and buy a little house, a piece of land. He say the Negro just as good as white, better maybe, since he never treated no one bad as they did ever. Miss, please miss, we savin' all we can to get a little piece of land, but Jacob's pay jest ain't enough. If I don't find paying work we'll never get to elevate ourselves."

She clasped her hands and bent her knees as though she were about to fall on them.

"Come, come, no need for that. If you are to elevate

yourself you must not beg. You must hold your head up and be proud. I cannot promise anything—the decision is not mine—but I will recommend you to Missus Clark-Compton, and if she will not agree to hire you, I will recommend you to another. Cheer up, we'll find you a position. Oh, and it will not hurt if you do not say you once lived in our alley. I doubt Missus Clark-Compton will remember who you are."

Back home, I had exerted all my powers of persuasion and was about to give up on Cousin Kate when the Colonel—who, it turned out, had listened to our conversation from the hallway—came striding in and put an end to the matter.

"I am not in the habit of ordering you, wife," he said to Cousin Kate, "but you embarrass me before our friends, with your hands bright red from scrubbing and blistered from hot pans, your eyes swollen from the chopping up of onions and your skin exuding garlic."

"Exuding?" Cousin Kate said.

"Exuding, yes. It has to stop. You must hire a cook. It's not as though we can't afford one now I have employment. And regardless of that, your cooking is like to poison somebody someday."

Cousin Kate looked deflated. "There have been criticisms?"

"There has been"—he had her now—"there has been *gossip*."

"Well then . . . well then . . ."

And so Gladys went to work in the kitchen, but not one step inside the house would Cousin Kate let her come. The bowls and trays and platters must be deposited on a bench at the back door and she and Aunt Lavinia carried them inside, which could be quite an undertaking when guests were entertained. Still, Gladys was happy with her job, the quality of food was much improved, and although I flayed myself with guilt about her child she did not seem to blame me.

Meanwhile, I threw myself into my work amongst the freedmen. I went freely in and out of their houses, spending as much time as I wanted, unlike the Yankee teachers, who were persecuted and ostracized at every turn. A trail of poor white children followed everywhere they went, pointing, spitting after them, hissing "Nigger lover," "Nigger schoolma'am," "Yankee nigger lover," even "Nigger whore." If any of these snot-nosed children set about to follow me, I had only to turn upon them with my Southern accent, and holding out my arms, begin enticing them to come to school, and they would flee as though the Devil spoke.

Their parents were the same. "We'll get you," and "Go home, Yankee nigger," were the order of the day for Mister Ashley's teachers, but when I came striding with my black bag of medical supplies, they stood aside and let me pass. Perhaps this was because I was not a teacher but a nurse, and to take care of the sick was in the old Southern tradition of extending charity. Whatever the reason, I was still included in society, although in a chary way. The younger set abandoned me, which caused me little pain. They had abandoned me before and I understood their fickleness. The older generation, though, was forbearant enough of my deluded eccentricity to include me in an invitation which encompassed all the family, although to tell the truth I was coming to prefer the company of Negroes. Poor though they may have been, and much as they had suffered, they were cheery, unpretentious people, inclined to break out into song and dance at any time of day. Sometimes I would see Christopher's eyes resting on me with an uninterpretable look and suspect that something had been said, but when I looked at him inquiringly he would turn his eyes away and smile and shake his head. If gossip or criticism went about, it was not reported back to me.

Sylvie Younger was having troubles, though, making her hard way through a social scandal. In the old days she had been an effervescent girl, full of talk about the latest styles, her latest holiday in New Orleans or Charleston, her latest triumph at some ball where she had been declared the most accomplished dancer on the floor. And always one could count on her for round-eyed tales of who was courting whom and why it would surely come to nothing—usually because the swain involved was secretly in love with her. And yet she never did get a proposal, perhaps because prospective swains suspected she would only love them for the hats and gowns, geegaws and frippery they might provide. Then came the war and so many of the young men went away and died that competition for the ones who did return was sometimes venomous. If a rival's reputation could be blackened it was done without a second thought, the victor carrying her spoils triumphant to the altar.

And now poor Sylvie had the problem of her father. One hungry frozen night, so gossip ran, he had deserted to the Yankees, but as he slithered on his belly across the Union line he was taken for a Rebel scout and shot through the left eye. I do not know where this story started but could well imagine how, as it made its way from drawing room to drawing room, it would have spawned another detail until Sylvie's father was transformed into the very model of a traitor. Sylvie, of course, never mentioned this to me, but I knew of it and pitied her. She had been kind when first I reappeared, bringing gifts for my recuperation, a posy she had made herself, a lavender sachet, a pretty little book of Mister Wordsworth's verse. But character will out. When she learned that I was working, actually *working*, and—*oh, horrors!*—with the freedmen, she grew distant and polite. She did not come to visit anymore and did not invite me to her birthday party.

A full-fledged birthday party was a rare occurrence still. The food, the wine and whiskey and champagne, the fine cigars, the band, the gowns (which must be new) with shoes to match and matching fans and *Darling Daddy, please, that tablecloth is a disgrace, the rug is worn*—it was too much. And so the news that Sylvie's mother had agreed to hire the German band was news indeed. I was hurt, I will confess, when no invitation came for me, and yet I understood. Sylvie was, in some sense, fighting for her life. To be my friend, to be known to be my friend, would open up her flank.

Christopher, however, was much put out at the snubbing I had taken at her hands. He had been invited to the party but refused to go. It was a warm evening and we had brought our coffee out to drink on the verandah. Christopher had given up his cane, but he still put a hand out to the wall or let it linger on the doorjamb while he made the circumspect step down. I sat in the cushioned basket chair, my feet on a low stool, sipping slowly. Christopher sat in the suspended swing. He swallowed his coffee in two gulps and set his cup and saucer on the rail of the verandah.

"The impudence of her," he said, pushing back and forth, the bolts squeaking above him. "I will speak with Roland. I will have him reprimand her as a brother. No, I will speak with her myself. I will tell her she is acting like a parvenue."

The quick tendency to violence that the war had wrought in Christopher had been mellowed by the business of the law, with its rules and orderings and stipulations, its need for slow considered thought. Sometimes, though, his shoulders hunched into a sort of cringe and his eyes turned skittish and opaque. His voice took on a high staccato quality and he lost his way in his own sentences, going over the same words, as though by churning and churning at whatever had upset him—some outrage or insult or indifference—it would be ground to dust and scattered into reassuring air. That evening it was Sylvie's turn and by the time he had calmed down I had quite got over my upset with her.

"I think you've punished her enough," I said. "And you will not speak with Roland. If Sylvie does not want me on her invitation list, then that's an end of it. I will not campaign for her affection."

He patted the swing beside him. "Come sit with me."

"I am quite comfortable, thank you."

"Come, cousin, don't be shy."

"I am quite comfortable."

THE next day Christopher came home with news from Sylvie's brother Roland that her birthday party had not been a success. Not one soul, not one, had come except for family. Her fault was that she had tried too hard to recover her good favor with society. Instead of waiting for inconstant gossip to pass on to its next subject, she had fueled it, inviting to her party everyone in town who had abandoned her, setting herself up for failure.

"Roland was severely miffed with me," Christopher said indignantly. "I told him it was Sylvie's fault I did not come, that she can't insult my cousin and expect me to come smiling to her door."

"Poor Sylvie. We should ask her to come visit. Perhaps now she would be agreeable."

We did not have to ask her. She came shamefaced of her own accord and after that came from time to time to sit with Christopher and me on the front porch, or if I was working late, with Christopher. What they spoke about alone I did not ask and Christopher did not volunteer. I never did bring up the matter of the party with her, and she did not apologize. Because of it, we talked together like a pair of neighbors who can see each other's houses but cannot make their way across the swamp, while Christopher watched us both across his coffee with that half-smiling uninterpretable look.

CHAPTER FIFTEEN

TOM had taken Abraham's advice and used a portion of his gold to buy more land, a swath of woods he'd had his eye on for some time. Negotiations had started out to be a problem, what with his black face and the fact that the property belonged to Mister Morgan, who was not pleased to see an old slave of his buying it from under him. But times were hard, Mister Morgan had no ready money, and he could not seem to get his head around the way he must deal with the freedmen to make them work for him. So he did not back away entirely, and yet he would not come to terms.

"Let me talk with that ol' boy," Clyde said, and within a week Tom owned the woods where he had hidden as a runaway, part of a free-running creek, and quite by accident, the family who had been living in the woods. His deal with them was free rent for three years and a portion of the crop if they would clear the land and farm it. And, by the way, they must go to school and learn to read and write.

The parents of the family from the woods were Elsa and Elijah. They were proud and grateful and worked hard. Elijah and his two boys cleared the land and built themselves a cabin and set about to farm. His little daughter ran about barefooted getting under people's feet and doing jobs about the place. But Elijah would not let Elsa work outside the house. He was a free man now, he said, and would have a lady for his wife.

Tom said, "My old mother is as much a lady and she's not ashamed to work outside. Perhaps your wife should talk with Grace."

So Elijah went off into his cabin and after a while Elsa came out in a new print dress and went along the trodden path and on across the humpbacked bridge across the creek and came to Grace and Enfield's cabin.

It had changed considerably since Tom's mother used to live there. Enfield, also an ambitious man, had once been a shoemaker and figured he could make some extra money on the side. So he had built himself a shady lean-to at one end of the cabin, with wooden pegs fixed up and down a row of wooden posts. He built himself a bench, and with a small loan from Tom to lay in leather and supplies, he went to work. He was the only shoemaker available to the citizens of Chapel Hill, the last having been shot down at Gettysburg, and before long he had a modest flow of customers.

Elsa, having knocked on the front door and got no answer, took herself on down to Enfield's workshop. He had his back to her and was bent over his last, tap-tapping on a shoe sole with a fine-headed hammer while with his other hand he picked tiny nails from a row between his lips. He did not notice Elsa and she went up and down examining the boots and shoes slung on the pegs.

At last she took down a lady's shoe with a neat turned heel. She held it away from her and squinted up one eye. Then she tapped Enfield on the shoulder. He swung toward her, spitting nails onto the ground.

Elsa held the shoe out on her palm. "This here needs a pretty thing to set it off."

"I ain't got no pretty things. I just make shoes."

She held a finger in the air and turned away. Before long she came back with a pair of gleaming red-green cockerel feathers. "I pulled them from the breast," she said, "to get the smaller fluffy ones." And taking down the shoe, she set it on the workbench and arranged them on the toe.

"Grace!" Enfield hollered. "Grace! Come on out here and look at this!"

CLYDE learned to drive a plow again, stumping up and down behind a brand-new mule, talking to it as he went. What he talked about out there nobody knew, but Clyde's loquacity did not require a human ear. He talked his way through life and would address his ruminations and opinions to anything at all—a tree, the blank blue sky, a snorting hog, the mule, which stubbornly ignored him. He would talk to Transportation too, the old horse twitching an ear as if to indicate he heard, turning on Clyde his diplomatic one good eye.

"Clyde Bricket," Uncle Benjamin would say, "you have missed your true vocation." Meaning Clyde should have been a preacher or a politician. He was wrong on that, though. Clyde's flow of talk did not have the purpose of a preacher, to bring the lost into God's fold, or of a politician either, to bring them into another sort of fold. And it was not simply for the sake of talking that he talked, but as though he could not believe a thing had happened if it was not spoken out aloud. Or as if what happened was so tenuous, so prone to change, that even what had happened yesterday could not be relied on as the truth unless it had been seized and trapped in words.

In his spare time Clyde took to whittling, nothing useful at the start, just shapes, but one day Baby Gold came staggering on her baby legs and clambered up onto the porch beside him. He had a box of odds and ends and she scrabbled in the box and drew out odd-shaped pieces he had whittled. One piece had a round fat top with a pair of straight long pieces underneath. She seized it. "Pin," she said, and scrambling down the steps, took herself across to where Ma was hanging out the washing. "Pin," she said, and when Ma heaved her up, tried to pin the sheet onto the line. The space between the legs was too wide and it fell. Ma laughed. Despite herself, she delighted in the child. She set her down and praised her, and the child trotted back to stand below the porch.

"Bad pin," she said, holding the thing up. "Bad pin."

Clyde, who had been watching and making a commentary underneath his breath, said, "Good pin coming."

By week's end he had three sets of a dozen clothespins neatly tied with string. "For next time you go to Raleigh," he told Tom.

Baby Gold did not give up the bad pin, but carried it around with her like something precious. When asked about it she would say, "Bad pin." Sometimes she would spank it. "Poor pin," she would say.

One afternoon Grace put her down to nap, the pin clutched in her hand. As the child relaxed, her fingers loosened and the pin fell onto the sheet. Grace looked at it. She picked it up.

When Baby Gold awoke, the pin had been transformed into a doll, with burned-on eyes and mouth, a dress and tiny bonnet. Delighted, she went off to look for Clyde. And so he started whittling dolls and Elsa taught her daughter how to dress them, Baby Gold and Glory making a delighted nuisance of themselves. Everyone was occupied from dawn to dark except for Uncle Benjamin, who was growing peevish out of inactivity.

"What would you like to do?" Tom asked.

"I'd like to preach the word of God the way I did when I could see. I been thinking on the Preacher House."

Tom said, "But it's a church for black folks now. I don't think . . ."

Uncle Benjamin took off his hat and turned his face to Tom. "To me everyone is black."

Tom said, "I know, but," and Uncle Benjamin said, "I used to care about such things, but the Lord has taught me otherwise. It seems to me he had a purpose in robbing me of sight." He stopped, and when Tom didn't answer, "After all, it is my house."

Clyde looked up from his whittling and said, "You cain't do it, Uncle Benjamin. Everybody and his dog knows you was a slave catcher back before the war."

"But I got saved and turned into a preacher."

"You cain't do it, Uncle Benjamin."

Tom said, "I knew a blind man out in New Bern who caned chairs for a living."

Uncle Benjamin was sitting in Ma's slat chair on the porch, his arms set on the chair's arms and his wide-rimmed black preacher's hat in his lap. He raised his hands briefly to his face, then set them one on each side of the hat, the thumbs against the rim, and bowed his head. He murmured something. Tom thought it was a prayer, but Clyde said sharply, "How's that?"

Uncle Benjamin said nothing.

"You got something to say, you say it out aloud," Clyde said. "We ain't having any fermentations here."

Uncle Benjamin did not look up. "I'm not fermenting. I was quoting from the scriptures."

"Well then, say it clear," Clyde said.

" 'Be sure your sins will find you out.' " He spoke into his hat.

Clyde's head jerked back, but then he understood that Uncle Benjamin was speaking of himself. "Don't be like that," he said. "It ain't so bad. And p'raps the Lord robbed you of your sight so you can be a caner."

Uncle Benjamin sighed. His shoulders shook. His entire

body clenched, unclenched, and clenched again. After a while, he raised his head and seemed to look into the distance. "Lord," he said, "Thy will be done."

The day was bright and although he sat in shadow the detailed ruination of his eyes was more than Tom could bear. He rose and went softly down the steps, intending to see about some chore or other. But the incident had disturbed him and he found himself walking up the hill behind the cabins, down into the valley on the other side.

This was the land that he had bought from Mister Morgan. A portion had been cleared, but the woods around the den he used to live in when he was a runaway he had preserved. He went to the den now. It was so overgrown the entry was invisible and he pulled his knife out of his belt and slashed at it. The vines were green, resilient, and it was some time before he struggled through into the dimness.

His den was not as it had been before. To the left, where the rock gave out, someone had dug back in and braced the hole with a barrel, which had rotted and collapsed in on itself. Tom peered between the pieces into what must once have been a hiding space, but now the roof was fallen in, the hole half full of dirt, and light straggling through the overgrowth above. "Well now," he said. Then he sat down with his arms around his knees and thought about Uncle Benjamin wanting to be a preacher. He thought about his eyes and wondered if they still could cry.

FIRST thing each morning, Clyde would hop out to the porch, wooden leg in hand, and rolling up the left leg of his overalls, prop his stump up on the rail and examine it front, back, and bottom with the piece of mirror Ma kept on the shelf to comb her hair. His stump was clean, no telltale bruisey-looking spots or creeping patches, and so he would strap on his leg and go about his business. But no matter how clean his stump was, he knew for sure that next week or next month the signs of rot would start to show.

This conviction bred in him a kind of cheerless humor at the same time as it bred a devil-may-care attitude about the opinions of the other farmers. That they regarded him as strange, or called him nigger-lover, he did not care a snap. That Tom would stick by him, that was all he cared about, since all he wanted was a means to feed his ma and Uncle Benjamin and keep a roof above their heads when he was gone. It did not occur to him that Tom would stick by him for friendship or because he was kindhearted, or because he needed friends himself.

And Tom liked Clyde, even loved him. When first he cut the deal with him about the farm it had been a matter of survival for them both. But he had come to trust him and responded to Clyde's need for love. If he had thought about the matter he would have thought about him as a younger brother. As for Clyde, he stuck by Tom with the fierce devotion of a dog who has been kicked and kicked by cruel owners and then taken in by someone kind.

THE first harvest was a great success, the second too, and Tom fell to thinking about buying still more land. Clyde had turned out to be a savvy negotiator—slick as hog slop, as he put it—and he and Tom continually had their heads together scheming up another deal. Each time Tom fell to eyeing some new tract of land, Clyde would make the first advance. Strawhatted, armed with a disarming grin, he would approach the owner, who in most cases was flat on his haunches with money problems, and negotiate a price.

This could sometimes take all day or all week or more, the pair of them sitting on a stoop or log or leaning up against a fence, hats tilted on their heads, conversing contemplatively about the weather or the price of wheat or the way farm labor had become expensive now the slaves were free. Sometimes the farmer, with a sly-eyed sideways glance, would inquire about "that there nigger" Clyde had living on his farm. And Clyde would clear his throat and spit and say a lot of words, and by the time a dozen or two had gone by, the farmer would become confused and think he'd asked a question that he hadn't, and not get any answer to the one he had, or thought he had.

Then Clyde would talk about the possum he had caught that morning, or the way they needed rain, and before too long he had crept up on an offer, dropping it into the conversation as naturally as an acorn falling from a tree, and the farmer, not a stupid man, would pick it up and toss it back and forth between his hands and pitch it off into a bush, and then it would be time for supper and the whole thing would be put off until next day until eventually an agreement settled from the air.

Pretty soon more than twenty families were living on the property. Almost everybody had a second occupation so there was no sitting sucking on a pipe or chewing straws, waiting for the crops to grow. A couple of the men had started up a sawmill to deal with all the trees cut down. Tom's mother went full tilt into poultry raising and the dawn resounded with young roosters crowing in cracked experimental voices and the triumphant roistering of laying hens.

The demand for fresh eggs and fat-breasted chickens was so great that within a few years she grew quite wealthy off it on her own account. Chapel Hill was still a poor place, though, and the village did not provide sufficient people with the means to buy. And so, when Tom went across to Raleigh, she would pack her eggs in baskets and string live chickens by their feet around the wagon. Enfield would pack his shoes in too, along with Clyde's packs of clothespins, the dressed-up dolls, and when Uncle Benjamin had got the hang of things, cane-bottomed chairs and footstools and side tables.

Then Tom would pull the wagon round and go rattling and squawking off to Raleigh to sell them into stores or at the open market down along the railroad. Sometimes one of the other men came along to help, but most times he went alone. Clyde could have come, but he would not.

"I been to war," he said. "I seen all the world I want to, I ain't about to go to Raleigh."

CHAPTER SIXTEEN

MISTER Ashley loved the people we were working with. Love quivered in his hand as he wrote his letters to the North, pleading and demanding—shoes, we need more shoes, clothes for fourteen-year-old boys, dishes, cups and cooking pans, more bedding, cots to spread it on, a horse and cart for hauling these supplies to Middle Sound, where he had now set up his dreamed-of orphanage.

I would come into his office early in the morning to find him at his desk, his face pale from the heat, beads of sweat glistening on his forehead and beneath the fine hair of his crown. "Good morning, Mister Ashley," I would say, and he would lift his head unseeing.

"They have sent the wrong things," he would say, or, "They have not sent enough," or, "I fear the shipment I expected has been wrecked." Then he would turn his head back down and go on with his writing, whispering his needs aloud as he recorded them.

With his voice behind me like unanswered prayer, I would sit down at the small desk in the corner and go over my cases for the day. After a while he would register my presence. "Oh, Eugenia, good morning. Sorry to ignore you." And he would push his round wire spectacles up onto his head and wipe the sweat out of his eyes with a capacious handkerchief. "We need, we do so need," he would begin.

The matter of a horse and cart weighed heavy on his mind. He had used one loaned him by the army, but when the Union troops had been withdrawn from Wilmington his horse and cart had gone along as well. As far as the townspeople were concerned, he could whistle for one—no one had one available to lend him. And so poor Mister Ashley, a man of fragile lungs and with a predilection to succumb to heatstroke, must in winter wrap three scarves around his neck, and in the summer set a dripping sponge inside his hat, and cough and sweat his way about his duties on his own two blistered feet. For his trips out to the orphanage he must rent a horse and buggy for a price outrageous as the rent demanded for the Mission House where his teachers lived.

Sometimes, of an early morning at the Freedmen's Bureau office, with Mister Ashley whispering his needs onto the page with a fervor worthy of the Christ, I would ask myself if I cared as much as he. No, I did not think I loved my patients, not the lowest cases, not the hopeless, not the ones who stank and died. Then I would castigate myself, and gathering up my bag of medicines, determine to do better, to love as Christ would love.

It was their souls that Mister Ashley loved, I would then tell myself, and not their bodies. His fervor was not that of a saint, but of a missionary. He had been sent down here to educate, but if he failed at that, he had done his duty if their souls were saved. Then I would castigate myself again, because Mister Ashley was a good, hardworking man. But increasingly I saw that to be a missionary was not the same as being a nurse. My duty was to the body. I must be practical, I must comfort and relieve. I was not required to love.

And yet sometimes, bending over some old man too young for death, some woman rank with sores or rattling with fever, I would feel a well of love, but behind it would come anger, with myself because I could not save them, and with Christ for demanding that I love without allowing me to heal.

A blustery day and I was walking head-down into the wind, my bag of medical supplies in one hand, my other hand clutching my cloak across my chest. I was thinking of a conversation I had just had with Miss Kellogg, a teacher at the Lincoln School at Sixth and Orange. I had gone there for my monthly checkup of her students, who filed before me, baring chests and opening mouths and offering their heads for lice inspection. The school boasted no stove and the wind came through the cracks strong enough to blow my papers off the desk.

"These children must go home," I told Miss Kellogg, "or they will freeze to death."

She herself was chap-lipped with the cold, her cheeks bright red against skin as white as marble, and her fingertips a purplish blue. Still, she shook her head. She had come here to teach, and teach she would.

"Come now," I said, "surely you do not want these children's deaths upon your conscience?"

That made her agree, although reluctantly, and she watched the children filing out the door with such anxiety upon her face I was half expecting her to suddenly cry out, "Don't go! Come back! There are lessons to be learned."

The last one gone, she seized a pair of felt erasers and set herself to vigorously rubbing down the blackboard. "This new teacher Mister Ashley is recruiting," she said across her shoulder, "do you not think we ought to have her living in the Mission House with all the rest?"

"Why should she not?"

"Exactly. That is exactly what I said to Mister Ashley. 'Why should she not?' I said. 'Is she not a human being? Does she not have eyes and ears and limbs and sensibilities? And she is well qualified. Her references are outstanding. Mister Ashley,' I said, 'you constantly complain that we are short of teachers, but when a good candidate appears you set about insulting her.' "

"Goodness!" I said. "I can't imagine Mister Ashley insulting anyone at all, much less a teacher. What was his objection?"

Miss Kellogg turned, a chalky white eraser in each hand.

"Oh," I said. "I see."

"How can we come down here," Miss Kellogg said, "how can we have the presumption to come down here and preach equality for all when Mister Ashley forbids us to so much as walk in public with our colored friends or invite them to eat supper? And now Miss Daffin must not live amongst her fellow teachers. She must be shunted off to a black family, which will trumpet to the world that we missionaries are nothing but a sack of hypocrites."

"What does Miss Daffin say of this?"

"She will not come if she is not housed at the Mission House."

Miss Kellogg swung off to the window, unlatched it, and swung back the right-hand pane. She leaned out into the freezing air and made a loud clapping together of the erasers, chalk dust flying in a cloud. Then she pulled the pane back in and latched it, set the erasers on the railing of the chalkboard, and smacked her hands across her skirt, leaving the imprint of white palms.

"You are a Southerner, Eugenia, yet you associate with Negroes all the time. What is your opinion on Miss Daffin's situation? Will you stand by her?"

"It is not for me to stand or not stand," I said carefully. "I am just a nurse, an employee. Decisions like this must be made by Mister Ashley."

"But he is bending to a prejudice he does not share."

"Come," I said, "stop marching up and down and sit quietly here with me. There, that's better." I set my hands in my lap and gathered up my words. "I sympathize with you, but you do not understand the Southern mind. On the surface we are milk and honey, but underneath is violence. You are a pariah here, you have told me that yourself. You have been spat on in the street and cursed. Never once have you been invited to a white person's home, or even smiled at. Even I dare not invite you home. My family would throw you out the door."

"But you associate with Negroes every day and your family does not throw *you* out the door."

"As you say, I am a Southerner. We have lived in intimacy with the Negroes since the first were brought ashore, but it is an intimacy of a different sort from what we share with people we consider to be equals. Our society is made of rips and reefs and dangerous shoals. One must learn to navigate. For someone like me to be friends with a poor white person would be a breach of manners, of good breeding, but to be friends with a Negro would be a violation of the soul."

"Eugenia, how *could* you?"

"It is the way things have always been down here."

"And you expect me to accept it?"

"I think you try to move too fast."

Miss Kellogg screwed up her forehead. "You puzzle me. You say 'I' and 'we,' and yet you are not like the others."

"I am trying not to be. I truly am. I—" I stopped, teetered on the edge of telling her my thoughts about my mother, my continued longing for dear Tom.

"Go on," she said. "You what?"

I turned and took her hand, my mouth forming my confession, but when I raised my eyes to hers and saw her zeal, I knew I could not trust her. She was a crusader. She would want to *stand by me.*

"Oh, nothing," I said, and squeezed her hand, making a little shrug. "You think Mister Ashley is making a mistake, and that may be, but if it should get about that Mister Ashley's staff is fighting him, the wedge will be in. We must stand together, yes, but we must stand by him. His work is crucial. By providing education to the freedmen, he is equipping them to fight for their own rights."

Miss Kellogg was not satisfied. "It is not enough to fight for legal rights. The Negroes must have social rights as well."

"Have you heard Mister Abraham Galloway from New Bern speak on this matter? He does so very forcefully."

"Abraham Galloway? Is he not an interesting fellow? I met him at the Bureau office when he came to visit Mister Ashley one afternoon not long ago. He's moved to Wilmington. You did not know? He's setting up the Equal Rights League here. They already have three offices, with a couple of hundred members each, men and women both, and black and white, or so he told me. I have not heard him make a speech, though. What does he have to say?"

"That he is for equality before the law and does not care about the social."

Miss Kellogg drew her brows together. "It seems to me they go together."

I said no more, but the intensity of her conviction made me sad. Once, when I was working in the Red String hospital, I had fantasized that one day when the war was over we would break out into a brand-new world where everybody could be friends with whom they wished, and marry whom they wished, and I could marry Tom—yes, I did imagine this—and live with him in a house with a white-railed verandah where we would sit out in the evenings and rock.

Now, though, back inside the real world of the South, I knew it had not changed one bit. I hoped it would, and some days fancied that I felt a softening, but then I would see a white man on the street push out his chest and walk—*thunk!*—into a black man coming along the other way, neither of them giving.

My musings were broken into by the appearance of a small white face above the windowsill, a scrubby child, boy or girl I could not tell.

"Nigger schoolma'ams!"

A gob of spit smacked against the window, giggles and a string of curses rising after it. I rose, and swinging back both panes, stuck out my head to find a cluster of half-naked children poised to flee.

"Wait!" I said. "Don't run."

They stopped, eyeing me suspiciously. "Nigger lover," one of them said. "Yay, nigger lover!" said another.

Before they could get themselves together in a chorus, I said loudly, "Stop it! Stop! Now, come here, children. Come on, don't be afraid. Here—"

I dug in my pocket and produced a handful of coins. "Here, come here, hold out your hands."

They did not budge. I held a nickel to the light and turned it back and forth. Their eyes followed.

"Who will be the brave one? Who will take it?"

A little girl stepped forward with her hand stuck out. For a moment I thought she might be the little girl who used to beg from me down at the wharf, but then I saw she was not. I took her hand in mine, she pulling away nervously, and placed the nickel in her palm. "Buy yourself something to eat, child," I said, and closed her fingers over it.

I expected her to run off now she had the coin secure, but she let her hand stay in mine. She was perhaps five years old.

"Little one," I whispered, "come around to the front door."

She looked back at her friends. "Come on," I said, "I'll meet you at the door."

Her hand slipped out of mine and she turned. My heart jumped. "I have her!" I was at the door in a second, but when I pushed it back the little girl was halfway down the street, dragged along by the older children, two of whom had her firmly by the wrists. "Hey there!" I called. "You bring her back!" She twisted back her head, and then was gone.

While this was going on, Miss Kellogg had not stirred from her seat, nor had her face changed its intense look of reflective thought. When I turned back disappointed from the door and came to sit beside her, she went on as if not a thing had interrupted.

"Perhaps," she said, speaking slowly, as if each thought were just now forming in her head, "perhaps Mister Galloway has a low vision because he is a Negro. Perhaps because he has always been unequal socially he cannot imagine what it would be like for the black race to be otherwise. Perhaps . . ."

"Or perhaps," I interrupted, "he is wise. Perhaps he understands the province of the legislature, which can regulate political equality but cannot regulate human attitudes."

"Which makes my argument," Miss Kellogg said. "The

way to change attitudes is by changing hearts, and the way to change hearts is by setting an example and letting the disbeliever see there is no damage done by it, but only good. Also, we lead the Negro out of his assumption of inferiority, men like Mister Galloway perhaps."

"Oh no," I said, "that's not his attitude. He thinks the black race is *superior*. He doesn't want to *condescend*."

"Superior? What nonsense! It's obvious to anyone—" Miss Kellogg gasped and smacked her hand against her mouth. She turned to me with a look like panic in her eyes, as if expecting me to say "You see?" She was a woman of the best intentions.

I left her with her problem unresolved and set off into the town, my mind on Mister Galloway. Did he really think the Negro was superior? Was not that as wicked as for whites to think the same of their own race? Or was he just a pragmatist with a fine sense of how far he could go in his demands?

The next thing I knew I had walked directly into him.

We both stepped back. I said, "Mister Galloway, I believe."

"Call me Abraham," he said, and as though we had known each other all our lives, we fell into conversation about the sickness in the freedmen's houses. It turned out his own mother was suffering from a fever, and in a minute I found myself hustled up onto the porch of a modest clapboard house on Fourth Street just north of the railroad. A brisk young woman, very dark of skin, met us at the door. She held a baby on her hip and introduced herself as Martha, then looked inquiringly at Abraham.

"Nurse Spotswood," he said. "From the Freedmen's Bureau. About my mother."

At which Martha stepped aside and let him lead me in to where an old woman lay half dozing on her bed.

Abraham leaned above me. "Could it be the smallpox?"

I examined her, asked some questions, and assured him it was not, just a severe chill that had settled on his mother's chest and made her feverish. Martha watched, I thought not unsuspiciously, but when I had prescribed hot soup and showed her how to make a compress, she smiled and told me her child's name was also Abraham and could I find it in my heart to keep an eye on Mother Hester since she herself had no talent for such things.

EVERY day for a week I went back, and when Mother Hester was past the crisis, went as often as I could to check on her. Her cough persisted until spring, when the warmer weather cured it and she took to sitting on the front porch in a rocking chair, where she would call out instructions to the visitors who came looking for Abraham, of which there were many. A meeting of some sort, or a consultation, or the giving and receiving of advice was constantly going on, often, I gathered, until late at night.

Mother Hester was a tiny lady who, though only in her forties, gave the impression of great age the way people do who have been through hardship in their lives. She was, however, agile in her way when in good sorts, and generous of spirit. The neighbors loved her, as she loved them, fussing over their lives like a she-cat stirring with a rough tongue at her litter. She suffered from what she called "bad legs," which from the knees down showed a peculiar mottling like lichen on a fallen tree and were often swollen, some days so much that when I rubbed them with a soothing lineament and pressed my fingers hard I left an indentation in the flesh. Sometimes they hurt badly and her feet and toes would tingle and go numb. Then I would mix a bowl of salts so she could soak her feet and rock and call out to visitors and passersby at the same time.

We grew comfortable with each other and one day she took me by the hand and told me that before the war she had lived right here in this house with someone she called Joel, who was an oysterman.

"He be still here," she said with a triumphant rocking of her chair, "but he is *hiding*."

On the last word of this communication she raised her voice and looked about accusingly, as if Joel might be spying on her through a knothole in the wall and her accusation would go through to him and pierce him like a guilty arrow and bring him stumbling to her feet.

"They told me he had drownded, but it was just his way of getting shed of his old marse. Some hid on steamers and went north, like Abraham, but Joel, he said, Hester I will never leave you, you is all the world to me."

She had a gift, she said, that Joel gave her, and sliding a handkerchief from the bosom of her gown, she unfolded it to show a large black pearl with a swelling on one side as though it would give birth.

Sometimes when I came she asked my name. "Eugenia," she would say as if it were the first time she had heard it, "Eugenia, a pretty name," and she would seize my hand and kiss it. Sometimes, after I had rubbed her feet and dried them on a towel, and was drawing on my shawl to go off about my other duties, she would seize my skirt like a child about to lose its mother in a crowd.

"Why won't you stay? Why won't you stay with me, Eugenia?"

Sometimes, when I had been very busy in some other part of town, or had been called across the river to attend some poor wretch birthing one more child who would not live to see its second birthday, she would hear my footstep on the porch and greet me at the door.

"Where you been, child, where you been so long?" And folding me inside her arms, she would rock me back and forth, her face against my shoulder, her hair soft and springy on my neck and a low crooning coming from her throat. Since Aunt Lavinia's surgeon I had not shared my secret heart with anyone, but Mother Hester's open arms and satisfactory vagueness lulled me into confidentiality.

One day sitting with her on the porch, I said, "The woman I first thought of as my mother was named Hester. She died when I was just a little girl."

Mother Hester raised her face and looked at me and I waited to be questioned, hoped for it, the name Tilda on my tongue, but all she said was, "Well, now, ain't that somethin'. Well."

"Tell me about Abraham," I said. "Tell me about his father."

Her body tensed. "That man," she said, "that *man.*"

"Tell me, Mother Hester."

She turned her head away, looking down. "That *man,*" she said again. "That *look* he give me, and me a chile still, jes' a *chile.* I knew that look. All the young bucks from the Big House brung it with them when they come down to the black girls. An' me with no one to protec' me, ol' Aunt Maylene a-snorin' on her bed. I fought him, cryin' to the Lord. It were my first time. He hurt me. An' he stunk o' whiskey."

She made a sound of deep disgust.

"Still an' all, he give me Abraham. I *loved* that babe. I *loved* him. An' tol' him his papa love him too. I did. I tol' him that. I tol' him his papa were rich and white and lived in Smithville and went out on the sea in boats. I tol' him he would come for him one day—I knowed he would, I always knowed he would—and, God forgive me, send him off to school and he'd set evenings in a porch swing like the little children up the Big House and look at books and learn to read the words and one day his papa would set him free, an eder-cated man, so he could go anywheres he liked and maybe be a pilot or the captain of a ship and sail across the sea. I said, Abraham, you will be a great man, you will do great things. You will make your papa proud."

"Why? Why did you tell him all those things?"

"I knows. I knows that none of it were true. But I tol' my-self, better for my baby to be happy. Better that he have some hope." She twisted round to look at me. "I do not think I done him wrong. Those was good lies I tol'. They made him think he were a big man, good as anybody else. His papa may not be proud o' him, but his ol' mother be. My son, he is a *man*."

"He is that. And after his papa had taken him from you, what then?"

"I were a pretty girl."

"Oh. I did not mean . . ."

"I were sol' off. Lookee," she said suddenly, "lookee up there. That be a *purty* sky."

ONE of the functions of the Bureau was to help freedmen find lost members of their families. As well as teaching, Miss Kellogg had the duty of maintaining a ledger where names of the sought and searching were recorded. People came with names written on a piece of paper and left them in a box outside the office. Those who could not yet write would come in person at a certain hour and ask for her to look through the ledger for this name or another. Sometimes touching reunions resulted from its pages, but now Miss Kellogg had demanded reassignment.

"But we need you, we cannot afford to lose you," Mister Ashley said.

"I cannot on my conscience work for you," she said, "when your policy is nonassociation. Not to walk in public with my students, never to share a meal with them. I can no longer bear it."

I had walked in on the argument and began at once to slink away, but she seized me by the arm insisting that I be her witness. And so I stood there awkward and embarrassed, making an apologetic face at Mister Ashley while Miss Kellogg rode her high horse round and round the room.

"And as for poor Miss Daffin," she went on, "I hear she has lost all ambition to become a teacher in the South on account of your insistence she be boarded with a Negro family. You have run her off, sir, you who complain day after day about the paucity of teachers. You should be ashamed."

I flinched for poor Mister Ashley. "Miss Kellogg, listen to me," he said despairingly, "we are hated enough for our work here. We are railed at, we are scorned, obstructed and frustrated in every move we make. I myself have been abused and stoned and threatened, called odious, distasteful, beneath the contempt of decent people. The only way I can persuade the Rebels to let me set up schools on their plantations is because the freedmen will not work for them if they cannot at the same time learn to read and write. Miss Kellogg, I am sympathetic with your feelings, please believe me. I would house Miss Daffin at the Mission House if it were possible, but the hard fact of the matter is that her skin is black. If the powers that be in Wilmington discovered I had housed her with white teachers, they would have me ridden out of town. Our entire mission would come crashing down around our ears. All our hard work would go to waste."

At this point he wrung his hands, he literally wrung his hands. I have never seen a person wring their hands before or since. "Compromise, Miss Kellogg, compromise," he begged.

But Miss Kellogg would not compromise, and so she left and took a teaching job in Charleston. A year later she would die of fever. When I heard of it, I wept. She had been a forthright woman, a constant source of confrontation, but I had loved her for her unwavering demand that all the world be kind.

Her departure left the missing families ledger with no one to maintain it. Mister Ashley begged me to take it on, which I did with an outward smile and inward shivering disinclination. I was assiduous, though, as is my nature, coming early, staying late, sometimes working Sunday afternoons at my small desk in the corner of the Freedmen's Bureau office, recording other people's hopes and sorrows. But although I did find genuine delight in effecting a reunion, I was like a snail, tracking the names furtively across the garden of the ledger's pages, stalk eyes out for trouble in the form of Tilda, or Mathilda, or Mathilde. Panic seized me when I found one, and then, when details turned out not to fit my situation, panicky relief. If I had found someone who fitted, I think I might have fainted dead away.

Meanwhile, circumstances at home with the Clark-Comptons had improved. We had two housemaids now, as well as a laundrymaid and groom and our own cow, which was taken out to graze each morning by the local cowherd and returned each evening to be milked. Christopher's business was prospering. Just last week he had bought his mother a pretty roan mare with a gig for it to pull, and for himself a stallion, purest white, a handsome beast. The Colonel came home late each afternoon with the helplessly gratified smile of a man who is doing well at business but is not sure why. "I do my best," he would tell Cousin Kate when she inquired, "I do my best. It seems my efforts are appreciated." And yet he always had the air of stepping carefully, as if this good fortune that had come to him was thin ice which any moment now might crack.

CHAPTER SEVENTEEN

ABRAHAM was a mason by trade. He left the house at dawn and finished working midafternoon. The rest of the day and Sundays after church he was busy with the Equal Rights League.

"I have not one jot of faith in what is going on in Raleigh with this rewriting of the constitution," he declared. "Those fine gentlemen are setting out to keep us in our place. We may not be slaves, but by the time they have finished with the *Black Codes*"—spitting out the words as though they were a poison—"we will end up with no more rights than we had before the war, you mark my words. They will call us free because they are obliged to, but we will still be slaves."

The writing of the Black Codes was on everybody's lips. In bar and lodge and meetinghouse and parlor the whites sucked smoke out of their pipes and offered wisdom to each other on how the world should be. Strangers on trains and ferryboats and steamers wagged their fingers, telling how the black man should be organized. Letters flooded through the mail slots of the newspapers, their authoritative, frightened voices declaring something should be done to force the freedmen back to work. Farmers took the law into their own hands, hunting down their erstwhile slaves with dogs. The police assisted them by hanging runaways up by their thumbs until they promised to behave themselves and go back to their old masters.

Meanwhile the freedmen organized.

At last, one bleak, cold, windy day, the fine gentlemen in Raleigh set their hats on straight and shook each other's hands and went back to their families. The day the Black Codes were published in the paper, I rose early to discover Abraham's prediction had been right. The vote had been denied, no black man could hold office, nor could he appear as witness in a court of law, and so on and so forth as things had always been, as if a change of course would be to cross swords with the will of God.

I went at once to visit Mother Hester, curious to know how Abraham would take the news. "Can you believe?" he said, appearing in his shirtsleeves on the porch, newspaper in hand. "They've even backed out of their promise to provide funds for Negro education. Indeed, they have provided funds for no one, black or white."

"No funds for whites? Why not?"

"They're afraid that if they fund public schools the freedmen might attend them and turn out to be intelligent."

"But what about the whites? The ones too poor to pay for education?"

"They'll let them go down with the ship." He smacked the newspaper against the wall. "And to insult us further, they will punish us with death for the crime of intending to rape a white woman."

"Intending?" I said. "They would presume to judge *intentions*?"

He laughed, a short sharp bark, and shook his head. "The one concession they have made is to let us marry legally, or force us to, as though it is our fault they've made us live in sin for all these years."

I looked up from where I knelt before his mother, wrapping her ankles in a new poultice I had dreamed up that seemed to do some good. "What will happen, do you think?"

He nodded back behind me and I turned to find a group of neighbors gathered. One by one from door and yard they came until the group became a crowd. A crowd that rustled with the rustling of the newspapers they carried, as if by shaking out the pages and then shaking them again, they could magic out the poison of the Black Codes printed there. They stood silent save for that eerie rustling, looking up at Abraham. He set his paper on the window ledge, hitched his suspenders onto his shoulders, and in his stockinged feet went out to them.

I had not thought about how tall he was before, but seeing his head and red suspenders move above the crowd as he shook a hand here, patted a shoulder there, spoke a word into an ear, and seeing the upturned faces follow him with what could only be described as adulation, it occurred to me that God had set him on the earth to be a leader of his people.

After a while he climbed up on one of the gateposts, a pair of solid red brick structures he had built himself. They supported no fence or gate, but stood alone like two proud watchmen, and no doubt had been intended from the first for making speeches.

He stood silently a moment, his white shirt and red suspenders glowing in the early sun, and when all eyes were on him and the rustling silenced, "You, my people, stand here this morning fettered, bound hand and foot, by a constitution that recognizes you as chattel, that says Negroes have no rights that white men shall respect. But I predict that before this is all over, we will be allowed to vote for or against a constitutional convention. And we must do it. We must send our own people as delegates, we must represent ourselves. And when the constitution is rewritten as it should be, when we are citizens with all the rights of citizens, we must send our people to the legislature to protect those rights and to advance them."

A murmur ran through the crowd, a cheer went up, a silence fell. A woman's voice called out, "How can that be, Abraham?" and she raised a folded newspaper on a stiff arm. One by one the others followed until the crowd was topped by a strange Black Code salute.

Abraham ran his eye across them. "Let me tell you a story. A large man and a small, two pugilists, agreed to fight till one or the other should cry out *Enough!* The first day the large man thrashed the little one. Next day, however, the little one renewed the attack and got thrashed again. But on the third day when the little one came up to the scratch the big man objected to being obliged continually to thrash him and gave up the contest."

He smiled, spreading out his hands. "Something will give. Eventually something will give."

And something did give. The Republican Congress in Washington grew disgusted with the stubbornness with which the South held to old ways. They became disgusted with the president for "loving the South more than he loved the darkey." In the spring of eighteen sixty-seven they elbowed President Johnson aside and took over Reconstruction of the South, granting blacks the right to vote for delegates to a constitutional convention, and demanding their enfranchisement be written into the resulting document. After which, a new state government would be elected. Highly placed old Rebels were still not allowed to vote, much to their disgust, and the bluecoats were sent down to supervise our good behavior.

Those were heady days. The Republican Party was formed in North Carolina, and Abraham, as he liked to say, "had a peg to hang his hat on." He barely slept, his income slipped, and every minute was spent persuading freedmen to join the Party and register to vote. Everyone who came in contact with him or heard him give a speech went away refreshed, inspired, uplifted in their spirits. Even his enemies went off after a good heckling full of the creative genius that manifests itself in thoughts of *Next time I will say*, or, *I will write a letter to the paper saying*, or in fantasies of flooring him in a debate with rhetoric so brilliant he would never rise again. He would go to Raleigh, he told the freedmen, he would be their delegate to the constitutional convention. He would fight for them.

Even Mister Ashley became swept up in politics. "It is an opportunity," he said, blowing his nose into a large white handkerchief, "it is an opportunity for education."

I had come into the Freedmen's Bureau office to organize my visits for the day, had just pulled off my gloves and was blowing on my fingers, working them back and forth so I could write. "What is an opportunity?"

"To be superintendent of education, it would be such an opportunity."

"Are you not already superintendent? Oh, I see. You mean in Raleigh. You are going to run for office?"

"For delegate at first, and if all goes well, then I will run for superintendent." He turned a beaming face on me, his handkerchief clenched in his hand. "To be in charge of education for all North Carolina. Think of it, Eugenia. Free education for the poor, for everybody, black and white. If I could achieve that in my life I would die a happy man." And he puckered up his face and sneezed into his handkerchief.

"Mister Ashley," I said. "You are not to go outside today or you will not live to run for office."

He did live, of course, and took to campaigning as if he had been bred to it, his nose adrip and his spectacles afog. Before long he had earned the title "ranting Yankee schoolmaster," of which he was quite proud. And I was proud of him, excited too, and I will admit, a little envious. I hovered over him, dosed him with cough medicines and syrups, scolded him when he forgot his muffler or his heavy coat, and followed him about to meetings with a pair of dry socks and a flask of whiskey in my bag. He was loved and hated, shaken by the hand, and jumped on by a man wielding a club. This man, a stranger with a rag tied round his face and a feather in his hat—a veritable highwayman!—was wrestled to the ground but fled before his face could be revealed. Mister Ashley was hauled up and dusted down, his spectacles retrieved. When I produced the whiskey flask, he waved it off. "No need for that." But when he got back to the office he drained the thing and went home with a defiant stagger in his walk.

Early in eighteen sixty-eight he and Abraham took the train to Raleigh, where they set about to put their mark on a constitution that would at last get North Carolina back into the Union. "You must be proud," I said to Mother Hester, "to have your son a delegate to the constitutional convention."

She tilted back her head against her chair and smiled through half-shut eyes. "My boy is going to the *Senate*."

Inside the house, Martha clattered pots onto the stove.

WEEKS went by. Abraham became frustrated. The convention had convened on January fourteen. Now it was February seventeen and the delegates had worried over railroad freights and banking, argued over how the Rebel debt had been incurred and whether or not it should be repudiated, argued the pros and cons of suspending habeas corpus in times of insurrection, pondered the threat of Northern whiskey to the local market, discussed the salubrious details of a petition for a particularly nasty divorce.

All these, except perhaps the divorce, were issues of importance, but Negro suffrage, the most important issue, the one Abraham had come here primed to conquer, had not been advanced one inch. Time after time he had tried to put it on the table, time after time it had been swept off in a wind of talk.

It was cold in the assembly room, although a fire was roaring in the grate. Truculent-faced white men who had nothing to do with the proceedings came in from the street, and without so much as taking off their hats, clattered their boots across the floor, and lifting up their coattails, turned their backsides to the flame, blocking off the heat from the delegates, laughing, calling out to friends and chattering—in short, disturbing the proceedings any way they could.

Meanwhile, the Conservatives, blue-lipped and by their own account blue-blooded, had a ripe old time adducing proofs that the Negro by his very nature could not command respect from the white race. The entire breed was lazy, feckless, degenerate, lacking in rationality or judgment. What's more they stank, they were content to live in hovels, and while their men might make black women into wives, their lust flamed after white ones.

Abraham shivered quietly through all this, and yet accustomed as he was to hear himself called ignorant, inferior in intellect, illiterate—they loved to say he was illiterate—no matter how he kept his hands loose in his lap, his face composed, he felt his umbrage rise. When Mister Marler, the gentleman from Yadkin County, stood up and announced in one breath the superiority in all things of the white race, and in the next his lack of prejudice against the colored man, Abraham's patience gave out. He leaned back casually in his chair, and thrusting out his legs and securing his thumbs inside the armholes of his vest in the manner of the Southern gentleman in his pontificating mode, he assumed a genteel drawl.

"Why, sir," he said, "my mother is so black that if I were a chicken and saw her coming down the road at midday, I would think it time to fly off to my roost. My father, though, was white. The best blood in Brunswick County flows in my veins, and if I could do it, in justice to the African race I would lance myself and let it out."

The entire room froze, even the interlopers by the fire. Then, as though a single puppet master pulled their strings, all heads turned to Abraham.

"How dare you, sir," the gentleman from Yadkin said, and it was on. The room erupted in a roar—of red-faced rage on one side, of enthusiastic hooting on the other. Delegates jumped up demanding to be heard, going at each other as if the fate of all mankind hung on the side which could shout loudest. A chair turned over, and another, a desk, another chair. Inkwells spattered and spittoons at ends of rows spilled out their sand. Someone by the fireplace let out a wild, high hog call, someone whistled, someone cursed, someone produced a knife and went for Abraham. The session broke in disarray.

Two hours later it resumed. By then everyone had calmed and the constable had turned the interlopers out and locked the doors. Abraham, eyes hooded, sparkling, dangerous, resumed his seat, his coat drawn back to show the slash of pure white shirt bleeding through his waistcoat.

Mister Rodman rose, attempting to pour oil on troubled waters. He was a Rebel converted to the Republican Party through his own reasonings. Despite this, he was respected by the Conservatives.

"Emancipation," he said, "is accepted by all as an inevitable result of war. Slavery is dead, and no one seeks or expects ever to revive it. I acquit the Conservative Party of all such purpose. But from emancipation necessarily follows suffrage, and the Conservative Party is proving on this point to be a party purely obstructive, which opposes everything and proposes nothing, which aims at a reactionary revolution incapable of success, which takes up the 'Lost Cause' after it is irretrievably lost, and prolongs without a hope of success the animosities of a rebellion which could never have admitted of any justification.

"This party professes to deprecate a war of races, but the whole declamation of its leaders is directed to inflame the antipathies of race, and to create a mutual animosity. If the people of North Carolina with a large majority of white men should, against all prejudices, elect a colored man governor, I should regard it as conclusive proof of his preeminent fitness for the place."

Everyone sat silent, perhaps because they had had enough of violence for one day. As for Abraham, the speech aroused in him a vision of the future. He had set his heart on senator and every minute saw it coming closer, but after that . . . dared he aspire so high as governor? Enough, he told himself, enough, next you will find yourself aspiring to be president. And yet, why not? Why not? Had he not advised a president, had not Mister Lincoln looked into his eyes and listened to his words, and weighing them, found them rich with possibility? *One step at a time, man, do not overreach ambition, prove yourself, let other men advance you. Be calm, be cautious, practice statesmanship.*

He looked across the aisle and saw John Graham of Orange County watching him with a cold blue gaze, and he knew that no matter what he did, no matter how securely political equality might be locked into the constitution, no matter if the Rebels were given back the right to vote, he could not convert the spite and hatred in that face to equanimity, much less cooperation. A sigh went out of him. His temper flared, and he saw in Mister Graham's eyes opposing temper.

IT was late, the night session over, and Abraham was heading for his rooming house when a voice behind him called, "Galloway!"

He turned. Mister Graham's face flickered yellow underneath the street lamp. Behind him, Plato Durham lurked in shadow like a second in a duel.

"Good evening, Graham."

Mister Graham drew himself up to his full inconsequential height, formal, portly, patronizing in the flicker of the street lamp.

Abraham looked down at him and laughed. "Have I offended your aristocratic sensibilities by not calling you 'Mister'? Have I offended your small godhead? Yes, I see I have. But why should I not? After all, your *Signal* newspaper takes *my* name in vain."

Mister Graham looked puzzled. "How so in vain?"

"In their reporting, they omit 'Mister' and put '(negro)' in a bracket after it." He made quoting movements with his fingers in the air. "And not so much as a capital *N* to give it dignity."

"But are you not a Negro? Is it not the truth?"

"I do not see '(white)' coming after *your* name, so I can only take it as an insult."

Mister Graham began to speak, but Plato Durham, who had stood behind him silently through this exchange, tugged on his sleeve, hissing in his ear.

"What is it?" Abraham said to him. "Afraid he'll get into something he cannot win? Afraid a '(negro)' will get the better of him?"

Mister Graham made a sudden movement and Plato Durham seized his arm. "Do not get into it," he hissed. "It will end up in a fight you cannot win."

"A fight?" Abraham said. "You mean a fistfight? I *do* take that as an insult. And, sir, you mistake my meaning. By something he cannot win, I mean an honest debate."

Graham fought a moment with his face, but Plato Durham's hand was on his arm and he controlled it. "Look out, Galloway, just you look out. When the bluecoats are gone . . ."

"Should I take that as a threat, Graham?"

"Take it any way you wish, boy."

"Oho, so it is 'boy' now, is it? You descend, Graham, you descend. You brag about old-fashioned Southern chivalry while you are nothing but a pack of curs following Mister Johnson to his lone impeachment. Or do you think he should not be impeached? Admit it, you do not. What you want is nothing more than what he wanted—to return the South to its old sinful ways where you could subjugate the black man and breed bastards on his wife and daughters."

Graham sputtered. "How dare you, boy, how dare you?"

"What, you do not think I speak the truth? Look at me, Graham, look at me well. I am the living evidence that what I say is true. And, Graham, think on your brothers who are pale like me, your sisters and your cousins. Does not proof live in your family too?"

Graham's face seemed to swell, its yellow color underneath the flickering street lamp turning dark and thick and mottled. "I'm done with you, boy." He spun on his heel, and then spun back, raising his cane in a clenched fist. "You will not survive, Galloway, your type will not survive."

CHAPTER EIGHTEEN

WE were sitting on his front porch when Abraham told me of his run-in with John Graham. Mother Hester was sleeping with her chin sunk on her breast. Neighbors sat on their front stoops and porches watching boys play baseball in the street. Martha was sitting on the step with little Abraham on her knee, feeding him mush with a small spoon from a large bowl, crooning to him, pretending to ignore our conversation. Or to ignore Abraham. It frustrated her that he was away so much, although she was as proud of him as any. She was young, though, and wanted her man in bed with her at night. Ignoring him when he came home was her way of playing the coquette.

"After all, you did provoke them, Abraham," I said. "To speak of lancing, of draining off white blood in favor of the African, it was a dreadful insult. Martha wept about it all day long."

"How did she hear of it?"

"It was reported in the *Journal*. Everyone here saw it. It was a scandal in the town. No doubt you made enemies."

"Pah! I do not fear them. They are cowards all."

Martha slid her eyes across her shoulder and then slid them back. A small boy slid into home base. A cheer went up and down the street.

"Perhaps for your family's sake you could be more temperate."

"I am who I am, I cannot be other. If it means I run aground, then that is how it has to be."

"Run aground? You mean . . . ?"

"It's possible. They intend to keep us down. They have been forced to make us free, but they have no intention of giving us equality. We have to fight for that. And when we have fought too much and made them angry, there'll be trouble, I can smell it coming. We must push through everything we can before it does."

"Fighting for the freedmen's rights is one thing, but provoking them for private reasons is foolhardy."

"Private reasons? What do you mean?"

"The references to your white blood. Is that not undue provocation?"

"Indeed it's not. It's time someone stood up and called a gay dog a defiler. They've got away with it for centuries and

188

still they creep about the houses of our women looking for an opportunity. After which they say, 'Why look, a white-skinned nigger, how peculiar.' We must put a stop to it, and since no one else has the courage, it seems it must be me."

"You humiliate them."

"I intend to."

"To humiliate your own father?"

"Why should I make allowances?"

"Perhaps if you went to visit him, you'd find him proud of what you have accomplished."

"My father sold me, his own blood. And went to war to keep me in my place. He was a captain in the navy, so I have been told. Now he is beyond humiliation."

"Oh. I did not know. I'm sorry for that."

"I did go back once."

"When?"

"After the war. After Wilmington fell to the Union."

He was silent for a moment, then, "It was a strange experience. As I pushed open the gate and came along the walk, it seemed to me the little boy I once had been was sitting on the porch step watching me. But then I realized that the child was white and a notion came into my head that it was my black self that my father sold. The white self he had kept and loved and treated as his son."

He stopped, running his hand across his eyes. I did not speak.

" 'Hello, there,' I said," Abraham went on. "The child cocked his head but did not greet me, and I went to stand before him, wanting to touch him, to brush him aside, to establish that he was imagination, and was about to lift my hand when he looked up. 'I am waiting for Papa,' he said. 'It's your papa I came to see,' I said. 'My name is Abraham.'

"The child shuffled aside and patted the step beside him. 'I'm John Wesley Junior. You can wait with me.' So I sat down with my elbows on my knees and my hands clasped underneath my chin. From the corner of my eye I saw the child rearrange himself into the same position. I said, 'John Wesley, where is your papa?' And he said, 'He went to see God.' 'God?' I said. 'God called for him to come,' he said.

"For a moment I did not understand, but then I did. 'When was this?' I asked him, and he shrugged, turning out his hands. 'He went off on a ship. He is the captain.' 'Is he now?' I said, 'And what ship might that be?' He bristled like a pup who has just seen a kitten. 'You can ask my mama if you don't believe me. My papa is a hero, a hero in the war.' 'Who told you that?' I said and he said, 'My mama. She said my papa went to war to keep the nigger in his place.'"

I interrupted. "Oh Abraham, that must have hurt."

"Like a ferret in the gut. And I regret what I did next. I asked if that was why God called for his papa to come. I spoke sharply and the child's face creased and flushed. Tears came to his eyes. I put my arm around his shoulders. 'I'm sorry, John Wesley, truly sorry,' I said. 'I know you miss your papa.' But then I could not help myself. 'I miss mine too,' I said, 'I wanted him to be my friend.' John Wesley sniffed and turned to look at me. 'Does your papa not love you?' And I said, 'My papa is dead.' It frightened him. I wish I had not said it. It was cruel."

We sat in silence, I pondering this information, Abraham

pondering something of his own. At last I said, "What is it you wrinkle up your forehead over now?"

"I was thinking about Mister Rodman's speech."

"What of it?"

"With all the best intentions in the world, he might get up and say that from emancipation follows suffrage, he might even believe it, and to any rational mind the proposition needs no argument, but the gentry, the Conservatives, the men who hold the reins of power, the likes of John Graham and Plato Durham—these men are not rational. They are controlled by hate, by prejudice, which of its nature is irrational."

"Not all white men are like that. For instance, you just mentioned Mister Rodman."

"Mister Rodman, I concede, is an exception. But I challenge you to name one here in Wilmington."

"Why Mister Ashley, of course. He is a good man, with nothing in his heart but love, and nothing on his mind but the advancement of the freedmen."

"He is an exception too, he is a carpetbagger."

"You call him carpetbagger, yet you would object to hear him call you nigger."

"I apologize."

"So what have you against poor Mister Ashley?"

"Nothing, I suppose. Nothing against *him*."

"Against whom then?"

"It doesn't matter."

"Come, tell me honestly."

"It's his teachers, these white girls he brings down to be his teachers."

"Aha! Then you resent them. You do not like to see these white girls teaching Negroes, you see it as noblesse oblige."

"I confess it. I prefer to see the black man teach his own. I fear that no matter what their good intentions these white girls will instill into their students the notion that their elevation can only be achieved by sitting humbly at the feet of their old enemies."

"But these girls come from the families of abolitionists."

"Abolitionists or not, they are still white. I admire them. I commend them. I would never say a public word against them. I think they are good girls. I think they have good motives. But they are white. I do not trust the motives they do not know they have any more than they trust mine."

"You think the teachers do not trust you?"

"Not a bit. They may never have owned slaves, their families may have inveighed against the institution, but in the very act of coming down to teach us these nice girls condescend. And condescension is bred out of mistrust."

"You malign them."

"Have you seen a single one come to a colored home for other than the duty of their work?"

"It's against the Mission rules."

"I rest my case."

I opened my mouth to offer him Miss Kellogg, but no, she was fuel to his flame. So what about myself? Did I too condescend? Had I no place here, no right to sit companionably on this porch and argue with this disputatious man? No right to love and tend to Mother Hester?

"Abraham, if you trust whites so little, why do you trust me with your mother?"

He turned to me surprised. "Because she loves you, and because you are the same as me."

A sound came out of my mouth, and came again. The sour taste of bile. Shiny objects dancing at the edges of my sight. The skin beneath my right eye twitching, twitching, like a palsied thing. I tried to move my hands, to hide my face, to hide my shame, to make myself entirely vanish. But they would not move. I struggled with them and they would not move, and when I looked I could not see them.

"Eugenia?" Abraham's voice was gentle, and I realized he was holding both my hands inside his own. "Eugenia, hush, be calm. There, there. If I release you, you will not jump up and run away? Ah, that's better, that's my good girl. Eugenia, I did not mean to hurt you or offend. Remember, I too am neither one thing nor the other. I too war within myself."

"You take me for . . . ?"

"A child of the South, like me."

I looked down at my knees, intent on not meeting his eye, but he bent his head, looking up at me half smiling, forcing me to look at him. "Come, come, Miss Spotswood, did you think nobody knew?"

His question hung between us like a sign hung at a crossroads, and I knew that in answering it I could set the course for the rest of my life. I took the cautious route.

"Why did you not speak of this before?"

"I thought nothing of it. No one else did either."

"No one else? *Who* no one else?" I swept out my hand to indicate the people up and down the street, most of whom I knew well since I had cared for them when they were sick. "Surely you don't mean . . ."

"They took you to be one of them. It's been so from the first."

I felt a flush creep up my neck. My head felt tight and hot. "I've been an object of discussion?"

"If you have, no one has mentioned it to me. Eugenia, look at that child there, that woman over there, that old man sitting on the fence across the street. To them mixed blood is unremarkable."

"But how can they judge me to be mixed? My skin is white. My family is white. The entire circle of my family's friends take me for white."

"To the whites your black blood is invisible because they want it so, but the black race knows its own."

"Well then, they know more than I."

"You're unsure of it?"

"I have no proof."

"What proof do you want?"

"Certainly not the opinion of a band of . . . of . . ."

"Of niggers?" He made a rueful face and laughed. "You have prejudice against us. It's to be expected."

"I do not. I do *not* have prejudice. Why, the best friend I ever had was black. I even used to fancy to myself he was my brother."

"Was he free or slave?"

"Slave at first. My father bought him for me."

"And then?"

"And then I grew to love him."

No sooner said than I wished I could suck the words back into my throat and swallow them.

"And after that?"

"I freed him. I did free him."

"And what became of him?"

"I do not know. I told him to go north to Canada. I haven't seen him since."

A small boy hit the baseball with a tremendous crack and everybody's heads turned up to watch it vanishing across a roof. Half a dozen children went shouting off to find it and the baseballers stood about smacking their fists into their palms and spitting on the ground. Abraham sat watching, saying nothing.

"I have offended you," I said.

"No, not at all." He glanced at Martha, who was busy scraping mush off her child's chin, then leaned toward me, lowering his voice. "You miss him, don't you?"

I opened my mouth to say, "Of course not, he was just a slave," but instead I said, "He was not my brother, that was just the nonsense of a silly girl. Although for years I did fancy I had a brother *somewhere* in the world."

"A Negro brother. Your father with a slave."

"Abraham, you press me hard."

"What do you think became of him, this brother?"

"I think I have no brother after all. I think . . ."

"The child was you?"

I drew my breath in hard, and let it out. "I do suspect it."

He leaned toward me. "What was that you said?"

"I said, *I do suspect it*. There, I've said it out aloud. I hope you're happy now."

"Come, come, don't cry. No need to cry. Here, have my handkerchief."

I snuffled into it. It was bright red, like his suspenders. "I'm sorry, Abraham. To carry thoughts like this inside my head is hard enough, but to speak them out aloud . . ."

"A suspicion of the truth can sometimes be more distressing than the truth itself."

"I do not know how to resolve it."

"You will, in your own time."

"It used to comfort me to think I had a brother."

"Well then, since I have no sister, or none who will acknowledge me, why not let *me* be your brother?"

"I would like that. Although it makes me feel obliged to wash your handkerchief before returning it."

He laughed. "My mother treats you like a daughter anyway. She loves you."

"And I love her."

He looked about him as if suddenly seeing the poor sagging little shacks jammed one against the other with barely enough room for a flower in a tiny patch of yard, the ragged little boys playing baseball in the street, their families sitting on their stoops like rows of birds.

"Yes, there is love here," he said simply. "There is ignorance and foolishness and selfishness and perfidy as well, but there is love. When we look at each other, we know that we are family."

"And yet I love my other family as well. Abraham, talking

to you like this makes me feel like someone pushing off into the ocean in a flimsy boat. I feel as though I am already drowning and must cling hard to what I have been all my life."

"You cling to being white because you have been raised to think that being white is superior to being black. But you must admit the white man's behavior up to now has been foul, especially what he has done to the women of our race. That you should so much as suspect your father in this way throws a cloud on his virtue. Would you not rather side with the virtuous half of you that has been wronged than the half that has done wrong?"

"But my father loved me, he loved me as his daughter. I admit that if my mother was a slave he did her wrong, and his wife also, but is that a reason to abandon half myself? Why must I choose? After all, if my mixed blood did not matter to my father—and I'm not conceding yet that I am mixed, just considering the possibility—then it should not matter to me either. I should just ignore it."

"If you ignore it, you must first admit it to be true. Otherwise you are back in the same position as at first."

"You are too clever. You confuse me. Surely when you and the other delegates are done with writing a new constitution, mulattoes will be free to be whichever half of them they please, or both."

He looked at me, a long slow look.

"So I must choose? I must be either black or white?"

"For your own happiness, I think you must."

"I don't know what to do. I don't know how to find out who my mother was."

He touched my wrist. "And you may never know. One day, though, your heart will tell you how to choose. You can depend on that."

The hooting of a distant train. Martha rose and set little Abraham on his father's lap. She went into the house and came back out with a brown cardboard suitcase in her hand. She set it on the porch.

"Kiss Papa," she said, a look of anguish on her face, "it's time for him to go on back to Raleigh."

ABRAHAM did not come home again for weeks and I began to sense in Martha a thrill of irritation toward Mother Hester. "Ah, Eugenia," she would say when I arrived, and it was as though a mantle of responsibility slipped off her shoulders. She would lean against the doorpost and watch me work, something she had never done before. She was a prickly person and we had not been close. Up till then she had regarded me with something close to toleration, and never showed resentment of my friendship with her husband. I admired her for that.

Now I felt a change in her, a sort of sympathy, a kindness. Sometimes she would walk with me to my next appointment, young Abraham slung on her hip, and talk and talk as though a lake had burst its banks inside her head. She did not speak of politics, and although I know she had overheard the conversation between Abraham and me about my birth, she did not mention it. Instead, she talked about her courtship days with Abraham. She had met him on a Sunday, so she told me, when he came to do the preaching at their church in Beaufort.

"Although his sermon wasn't real preaching, he barely mentioned God. 'We must have a voice in government! The freedmen have to have a voice in government!' He went on and on, saying it six hundred different ways and pounding on the pulpit. 'We cannot trust the whites to legislate on our behalf! We have to have the vote!' and everybody said, *Amen, amen!*

"And then he looked directly in my eyes and said, '*And women too,*' and all the women rose up from their seats and raised their hands to heaven and—I swear it—fell in love with him." She laughed, delighted with herself. "But he came home with me, and my mother and me, we ran out to the kitchen and cooked that man a slap-up dinner and my father said, 'Young man, I wish you would come every Sunday so I would get fed like this,' and we sat around the table talking about politics and he asked me what I thought and watched me when he thought I wasn't looking, and when I did look—oh, that smile of his!

"And when we'd finished eating I went to help my mother in the kitchen but she said, 'Child you got a good man there don't you let him get away,' so I went back out and asked him would he kindly like to walk with me along the beach and he said yes and it was awful windy, the sand flying and my skirt hardly would stay down and I said to him, I said bold as brass, 'Mister Galloway, I am eighteen and I would like to marry you.'

"He laughed and his hair blowing all about and he said, 'I am twenty-six and I like a woman who can make a quick decision.'

" 'But can *you*, sir?' I said, and he took me in his arms and kissed me so my hat fell off and blew into the sea."

We were both laughing now. "Oh, oh," I said, "that is a wonderful story. You must love him very much."

Her face took on a worried frown. "But I love my parents too. When we lived in New Bern, Abraham and me, we would go across to church with them every Sunday morning and afterwards go to their house for dinner. But they are growing old. My father's hands." She curled her hands up into claws. "He's had to give up fishing on account of it. He helps sell other people's catches on the wharf, but there's no money in it, just a little to get by on. And my mother's had to take up as a cleaning lady at the hotel and the hospital and her feet ache all the time. I do so wish I had some money I could send them, I wish I could be there to help. I never was afraid in Beaufort, or in New Bern either come to that, but now, because of Abraham, I feel afraid."

"What are you afraid of?"

"White people. Anytime I go about the town I feel their eyes on me. I feel . . . I feel as though they'd like to *do away* with me because I am the breeder of his children." She set her chin against the small head on her shoulder. "Until my child came, I thought I was the perfect wife for such as Abraham. I thought that I was strong. But now I have turned fearful. I fancy dreadful things when he is out of town. I panic when a knock comes on the door. I dream of blood."

"What would you like to do?"

"I'd like to go to Beaufort to visit with my parents. I think that it might calm me."

And so she went. And came. And went again. It was to be her pattern.

CHAPTER NINETEEN

MID-MARCH of eighteen sixty-eight, and the new constitution was complete. The delegates smacked each
other on the back, a few joined hands and danced, and one
man went up front and sang a song. The reporter from the
Sentinel smiled above his notepad and the next evening Tom
came out to his porch, newspaper in hand, and read aloud:

*At 12 o'clock on yesterday, the animals were turned loose
and dispersed to their native jungles. All the white women
and children in this city were kept indoors for fear of the
consequences involved by unmuzzling such a motley horde.
They can venture out this morning, as, perhaps, the last of*

the mongrels has disappeared or is only skulking around, harmless and contemptible. All are gone, the air is purer, the streets are cleaner, the community is happier.

We hear that the closing proceedings of the infamous assemblage became more discreditable, if that were possible, than any of those which preceded it and which have brought a disgrace upon the House of Commons that will render it an unfit place for decent men to assemble for some time to come. Let all the disinfectants known to the Pharmacopeia be brought into requisition at once to purify, and to cleanse the infected room. Let the windows be kept open, so that the Spring breezes can have free and gentle play through the polluted arches.

In the barbarous regions of Africa, it is the instinct, when human sacrifices are to be made and bloody rites celebrated, when bestial appetites are to be gorged and brutal lusts gratified, for the savages to form a ring and dance, in demoniac glee, around the intended victims. This African assemblage closed its session in the genuine and appropriate African style. One, looking into their Hall at midnight of Monday, and beholding the scene then and there transpiring, might well have imagined that he had been suddenly transported into the regions of which Livingstone gives us an account.

The victim was ready—The Sacred Old Constitution of our fathers, under which we have lived and prospered—and the savages gathered around it hand in hand, and danced and sung boisterous and ridiculous melodies. This is no metaphor. It is literal fact, and will bring a blush of *shame to the cheeks of every true North Carolinian, that the good and honest old State has come to such a pass, namely that a set of apes and hybrids should be holding a brutal carnival in her halls of legislature and shocking decency and propriety and civilization by their impious and drunken orgies.*

Tom finished reading with a mocking flourish and folded up the newspaper. Clyde was sprawled out with his back against the bottom step, his left leg off and his right leg stuck into the yard. He twisted his head back over his shoulder.

"What all's *that* about?"

Tom grinned. "It means they don't like that we got the vote for Negroes in our constitution and they can't do a thing about it. Now we'll have a *real* election."

IN Wilmington, at breakfast, the Colonel set his spectacles upon his nose and read the same report aloud, also with a mocking flourish, but of a different sort. "So now the coloreds have the vote," he said. "It matters not a whit. They're too ignorant to find their way down to the polls."

"You should hope and pray they do," I said, "since if the new constitution is ratified, you'll get your own vote back."

"How do you know that? We've not yet seen a copy of this so-called constitution."

"Mister Galloway has told me. It was he who pushed it through. If justice is to be done, it must be done for everyone, that is his opinion. All suspensions are to become void and every adult male will have the vote, literate or not, owner of a property or landless, on that he was categorical. Your position in the army will not be held against you any longer. You'll be a voter once again." I laughed, teasing him. "And you can thank him for the privilege by giving him your vote. Maybe we can make a notice and set it in the window of your office: *Galloway for Senator!*"

"Senator?" Christopher began, but his father interrupted. "You speak as if you know him well." And he peered at me above his spectacles like an old bull who can't quite see the matador.

"His mother is my patient. I'm often at the house."

He eyed me thoughtfully. "Is that the case? You spend too much time amongst the coloreds."

"It is my job."

"It is unhealthy."

I was coming home from work, a cold wind flattening my skirts, when Sylvie Younger passed me on the street. I spoke to her, but she was singing to herself and made as if she did not hear me. For some time now I had suspected that she came and sat with Christopher more often than I knew, that she preferred to be alone with him, a hardly ladylike desire, and yet, I told myself a little spitefully, at her age she must drive full speed before her steam runs out. The thought no sooner in my mind than guilt came tumbling after. Had Christopher not told me time and again that he would marry when he had sufficient money? Did I not want him to be happy? Of course I did, of course. So had he just proposed to Sylvie? Was that why she had passed me in a daze of happiness?

Christopher, a woolen muffler round his neck, was swinging on the porch, the chains making a cold *squeak-squeak* at their attachment to the ceiling. "There you are, late for supper again," he called, stepping down to the verandah. "Gladys left a plate for you in the oven. Chicken tonight, with spinach and dumplings, very tasty. Come on to the kitchen where it's warm and cosy and I'll keep you company."

In a minute he had me settled with my supper, he across the table with a steaming cup of broth. He said nothing while I ate, just watched me with that uninterpretable smile of his. After a while I grew impatient. "Cousin, is there something you would like to tell me?"

He seemed to shuffle through his thoughts, began a sentence, stopped.

"What is it? What?" I said, and waited for his declaration about Sylvie.

"I've been thinking about this horse and cart you say are needed at the orphanage."

"Horse and cart? What have the horse and cart to do with anything?"

"I will donate them."

"I beg your pardon? You will what?"

"Donate them."

"Christopher, I am confused."

"Then I will say it slowly. I will donate the horse and cart you say are needed at the orphanage."

"You will? How wonderful. How very kind. How unexpected. Mister Ashley will be grateful."

"And there's another thing."

I gathered spinach on my fork. "Ah. Yes. The other thing."

He gave me a strange look. "This fellow Galloway. Your association with him. It could be dangerous."

That thrust Sylvie Younger from my mind. I set my fork down. "How so, dangerous?"

"He is so . . . so very *visible*, anything could happen."

"Such as what? What are you hinting at?"

"I'm not hinting. I am warning. This Galloway has enemies. Everyone in town knows that. To be associated with him is not prudent."

"How can I help it if I am to take care of his mother?"

He tilted forward on his chair. "Eugenia, dear Eugenia, you are too full of compassion. You are too kind, too selfless and hardworking. Surely in this circumstance you should consider your own safety. This man Galloway is a troublemaker. He is an irritant, fueling unachievable ambitions in the coloreds, which can only lead them to frustration and a fall."

"So ambition is restricted to the white man?"

"Not entirely. But each person has his place in life and must be content to achieve what he can within it."

"You mean a black man must not aspire to . . . let me see . . . to senator?"

"You mock me."

"I do not. Answer my question. Must he not aspire so high?"

"Since you demand an answer, no, it is unthinkable."

"Just yesterday it was unthinkable for a black man to aspire to vote. Yet today we have it. Is not that remarkable?"

"It's a disgrace that must be remedied."

"Aha! Now we get to the stomach of the matter."

"Eugenia, dear cousin, let's not quarrel. You have an odd affection for the coloreds, which leads you to an irrational trust in their ability."

"I do trust Mister Galloway. He's an honest man."

"I concede he might be honest, but he's a troublemaker."

"He is a leader."

"He's a leader, as you say."

"And he's my friend."

"Eugenia, you go too far. It's one thing to help these people, but to claim you are his *friend*. A man like that."

"A man like what?"

He glanced around, then, lowering his voice, "Eugenia, it is delicate, I know, to speak about such matters, but surely you have heard . . . surely you know . . . how can I put this? You must understand that even though this man might have light skin, he is a Negro after all, and he has Negro inclinations."

"Inclinations toward what?"

"It is not fit for me to say."

"Thank you for the horse and cart." And with that I took myself to bed.

I came alert with the tingling fear that follows nightmare, certain there was someone in the room. I lay completely still and searched by moving just my eyes. It was my habit to draw the curtains back and raise the window a handsbreadth before I went to bed. The moon was round and brilliant, the sky around it pitch-black cloudless, so that its silver light seemed to be reflected over and over as though in a thousand mirrors. The effect inside my cottage was a sort of brilliant darkness, every object colorless but clearly seen. The room was empty, not so much as a suspicious shadow in a corner.

Reassured, I pushed the quilt back and stepped softly to the window, looking first toward the alley because if danger should be lurking I thought it would be there, then looked toward the house. Silence and no movement. I told myself it had been nothing but a dream, but no, there it was again, the slightest sound, a sort of scraping. It lasted but a second and then nothing again, except what could have been a footstep, or the thumping of my heart. I took the bellpull in my hand and waited, my senses all alert. Nothing. Not a sound. And yet it seemed to me that something furtive had just taken place, something dangerous. The Clark-Comptons murdered in their beds?

Going to my writing desk, I fumbled for my house key, then in slippers and a dressing gown crept across the yard to the back door, peered in through the sidelight, then slipped my key into the lock and with held breath turned it with the merest click. I edged the door ajar, and one cautious foot before the other, crossed into the hallway, heading for the staircase, where I was greeted by the reassuring sound of the Colonel snoring in his sleep.

I crept outside again and this time went toward the stable, circled round it to the gate, and peered across to find its doors onto the street securely shut, the street itself as silent as the sleeping town. And yet the more absence and silence I found, the more I became convinced I had heard something underhand. The horses stolen maybe? I came back to the side door of the stable, but it also was securely locked. I ran my hand along the planks in search of a space I might peer through, but although the planks were half an inch apart in several places, when I applied an eye I saw only blackness. So I applied an ear instead and to my relief was rewarded by the soft blowing of a horse. I laughed out loud and was taken over by a yawn.

However, I was doomed to sleeplessness. About to climb back into bed, I heard a rattling at the gate into the alley, and then my name called by what sounded like a child.

"Miss Eugenia, please, Miss Eugenia."

Oh no, I told myself, a baby at this hour? I pulled my clothes on, wrapped myself in a shawl, and hurried to the gate. Here, for caution's sake, I stepped up onto the crossbeam at the bottom, and taking hold of the top of the gate, raised myself on tiptoe to peer across into the alley. A small boy stood looking up at me, big-eyed in the moonlight.

"My ma," he said.

"She has been brought to bed?"

He nodded.

I glanced to left and right to assure myself it was not some sort of trap, then stepped down and fumbled for the key. Outside, I locked the gate and dropped the key into my pocket.

"Lead on," I said, and was surprised when the child took me by the hand. "You have brothers and sisters?" I asked, intending to calm him with conversation.

"Ain't none but me till now," he said, and I understood that the sight of his mother in labor had unnerved him.

"Your ma will be all right," I said. "By morning you'll have a baby brother in your house, or perhaps a sister."

He pulled my hand, an urgent movement. "It's stuck," he said, and now there was panic in his voice. So I gave up conversation and stepped lively.

The faster I went the faster he went, and so we reached his house at a run, a good thing too, for we burst in the door to find a heavy woman in the act of sitting on the unfortunate mother's belly.

I flung my shawl aside. "Get off! Get off!" I cried, and shoved her. She tumbled backwards, legs in air, and came down with a thump and a shriek on the far side of the bed. She rose up in high dudgeon and if the boy's father had not been in the room I might have come out on the wrong end of that night. As it was, it took but the smallest examination to determine that the child was coming sideways.

"Hold her down!" I snapped, and to my surprise both the heavy woman and the father jumped to obey. At the same moment, the mother clamped her mouth tight, curled her shoulders down toward her belly, and pushed with all her might.

"Don't push, don't push," I cried, although I do not think she heard me, she was in such pain. When the spasm passed, I thrust my hand inside her, and with her screaming blue murder and panting and puffing like a wheezy grandma, I succeeded in turning the slippery little body.

"Push now," I said, and the baby slid out like a hot knife through butter. "A little girl. A lovely little daughter."

I wrapped her in a towel and turned, looking for the boy. He was on his hands and knees, peering round the doorjamb.

"Come here, child, come see your little sister."

He ducked back out of sight, then one arm and a shoulder reappeared at normal height, a half head, then a whole head, and he crept into the room. He held his arms out and I set the baby in them, supporting her from underneath. I love a childbirth when it is successful, but I will never forget the look on that boy's face, as though he were looking at an angel. I think he did not breathe for a full minute, just stood there gazing, gazing. Then he looked up at me. "Our baby," he said.

I laughed and kissed him on the cheek. "We have to wash her now."

I floated out of there and headed toward home, well pleased with the evening's work. Moonlight lit the street, making the shabby houses quaint and pretty, like an artist's fantasy. Every door was closed, every window dark with sleep. But before long I turned onto a street where every house was lit and every doorway filled with frightened faces.

"What is it? What?" I asked the nearest person, an old man in his long johns leaning on a stick.

He glanced along the street. "You ain't heered it?"

"I heard nothing."

"It be a ghost."

No sooner said, than the sound of hoofbeats coming from behind.

"It be it again," the old man cried, "it comin' back." He grabbed my arm, and pulling me inside after him, slammed the door, drew the bolt across and blew the lamp out with a hissing sound. The room fell into blackness, the window a bright rectangle. The sound of slamming doors echoed up and down the street.

"Who is it?" I whispered.

"It be a ghost," the old man said again, dragging the word out in a respectful whisper.

"Rubbish," I said. "Ghosts don't ride horses."

I made as if to approach the window, but he seized my arm again. At the same moment a low moaning came from behind us. I swear my heart leaped out of my chest, hung unbeating in the air, then fell back in and beat as if to wake the dead. And the dead did seem to wake. A figure rose out of the darkness.

"This here's my wife," the old man said.

I began to laugh, and gasp, and laugh again, my heart still pounding fit to burst. "Your wife? It's just your *wife*?"

I turned back to the window, and there in the moonlight stood a horse and rider, the horse pure white, a large beast, very handsome. The rider, like a guest at a costume party, was got up as a skeleton and apparently wearing nothing but a sheet, which was flung across one shoulder and fixed about his waist.

And then an eerie monotone: "Attention! First hour! In the mist! At the flash! The Ku Klux are abroad! Retribution is impatient! The grave yawns! The scepter bones rattle! Let the doomed quake! The hour of the Avenger is at hand!"

"What nonsense is this?" I said, and breaking from the old man's grasp, I sprang toward the door, flung it back, and stepped out into the moonlight.

"You there!" I cried. "What do you think you're up to?"

The skeleton swung around and looked at me, and in the same movement dug its heels into the horse and vanished hell-for-leather up the street. As the hoofbeats faded, lights began to glow again in windows, doors opened, nervous heads appeared.

"Gone?" one doorway whispered to the next, and echoed, "Gone."

By questioning several, I gathered this apparition had claimed to be the ghost of a Confederate soldier gone to hell during the fighting at the battle of Fort Fisher. Since then he had had not one drop to drink, he claimed, and demanded water to be brought out by the bucket, of which he drank four to quench his thirst.

"Four?" I said. "Four *buckets*?"

They swore that it was so. They had seen him do it.

"It was a trick," I said. "No man can drink four buckets. He must have had a pouch hidden underneath his sheet and poured the water into that."

The old man, who had followed me outside, said, "Lordy, we been tricked."

"But what's it all about?" I asked.

He gave a wavery low laugh. "It be about the votin'. They's tryin' skeer us outa votin'."

And within seconds laughter rattled up and down the street, the angry laughter of relief, quickly followed by the muttering of heads-together scheming.

CHAPTER TWENTY

I had slept late and was alone for breakfast. Christopher had gone off to his office, the Colonel to his shipping agency, and Cousin Kate and Aunt Lavinia were nowhere to be seen. I was tired and ate little, flipping through the newspaper.

Quite an excitement, it reported, *was created on our streets Sunday morning by the discovery of a number of mysterious notices that during the previous night had been posted at several prominent points in the city. They spoke of an Avenger and are supposed to have emanated from the headquarters of the somewhat notorious "Ku Klux Klan" whatever that may be! An eyewitness who*

*refuses to be named claims to have seen a skeleton upon a
snow-white steed riding the streets in the small hours of
the morning. His bones were clad in nothing but a wind-
ing sheet and his skull not in its normal place upon his
head but supported underneath one arm, while his steed's
nostrils emitted streams of flame with a strong odor of
brimstone. Was this apparition Ku Klux? Was he risen
out of Hell? What does this mean?*

I contemplated this piece of news while sipping on a cup
of tepid coffee. Then on an impulse, set the coffee down and
went outside and crossed the yard toward the stable. The side
door was unlocked. I glanced across my shoulder at the upper
windows of the house, pulled back the door and slipped inside, the smell of herbs and garlic and hot peppers floating
down around me from the rafters where they hung to dry. I
crossed the floor and peered across into the stalls. Both horses
were there, the roan one and the white, but it was on the white
one, Christopher's, I fixed my eyes. I pulled the half door back
and went to him. He pressed his muzzle to my palm and
snorted. I ran my hand along his neck and down his flank.
Then I did the same thing to the roan. And it seemed to me the
roan was cooler. So the stallion had been ridden lately? Had
he been ridden in the night? Had I been mistaken in assuming
both horses were in the stable? I went back to the stallion and
stroked his flank again. He was the larger of the two, more
spirited, perhaps more naturally warm.

A sound behind me made me start, but it was just the stable cat come to wrap herself about my ankles. I bent and

touched her back. She purred and angled up her tail. "It's a disgrace that must be remedied"—Christopher's voice inside my head.

I attended to my cases that day in a daze of worry and fatigue, the ghostly mounted figure of the night before appearing and vanishing ahead of me. Had it been Christopher? My mind insisted that it was—the way he turned and looked at me before he fled, the way his horse was hooded, half covered by the sheet. No, not Christopher. My heart would not allow it. Yet . . . and yet . . .

By the time my cases were all seen to I was in such a state of agitation I could barely think. I went back to the Freedmen's Bureau office and sat down at my desk. I shuffled through my notes but could make no sense of them, so I set them on one side and rose and paced about the room. The market bell struck five. I paced and paced. The market bell struck six. With it, resolution entered me. I would be forthright. I would go to Christopher. I would confront him. I would demand the truth.

At his office, his clerk said he had left just minutes earlier, some business to attend to at CC Importers. So back downstairs I went and marched my indignation north along the wharf. The wind was up again and singing loudly on the waterfront. I bent my head to it and clung on to my shawl, heading for the alley staircase that led up to the CC business offices.

The alley gate was locked, but beyond it a light moved in the warehouse so I entered there and was still in shadow by the doorway when I spied Christopher, lantern in hand, conversing with two men whom I recognized as Cannerty and

Coombes. Cannerty was a stringy man with a face the color of egg custard and a tobacco-stained moustache. Coombes was of more modest height, barrel-chested with a rolling seaman's walk and a bald head eroded into ridges by the weather.

I say they were conversing, but I soon gathered the three men were deep in argument. They stood with their backs toward me on the far side of the floor, looking down at something hidden from me by the bales and crates and barrels in between. The wind shrilled underneath the eaves and their voices came to me distorted, the lantern swinging with my cousin's gestures, making shadows come and go. I stood irresolute. Should I reveal myself? Risk having them turn their argument on me? Or should I creep back out?

The wind drew in its breath and a man's voice came overloudly in the sudden hush, "It is *money*, young man, *money*. Is that not what you want? Would you have us support your greenhorn father and ask nothing of you in return?" Then once again the angry shrilling of the wind.

At last some sort of decision seemed to have been reached. Christopher set the lantern on a barrel, bent, and seemed to tug at something. Then the three men swung away and clattered one behind the other up the stairway leading to the CC offices. The door swung shut behind them.

At once I gathered up my skirts and made my way as quickly as I could to where they had been standing. To my consternation a pair of coffins sat one beside the other on the floor. They were rough made and had been well nailed down, not the way coffins are usually nailed, but with outsize nails whacked in so hard the wood around the heads was dented by the hammer blows. I nudged one with my foot, then bent and gave it a good shove. It did not move. Thumping on it gave back the impression that there were no spaces inside to produce an echo. If it had held a body, a thump would have produced a hollow sound, I knew that from the gold mine. But this held something solid and jam-packed. Thumping on the other produced a different sound and when I had shifted the lantern a little I saw it had been opened and the lid set loosely back. I glanced up at the door the men had vanished through, then bent and heaved it up. Inside were carbines—short light rifles, soldier's guns, I knew them from the war—and with them cap and powder boxes fixed to belts. A sick feeling came into my throat. I could not move. I could not think. I saw again the ghostly figure on the horse. *The grave yawns! The scepter bones rattle!* And then the lantern flickered, and above, the rattle of an opening latch.

THE next thing I remember I was at the Equal Rights League office, asking after Abraham, who came out of a meeting with a puzzled look. He had warned me not to come there. To seem to be conniving with the Radical Republicans could put me in the way of trouble.

"What is it?" he said. "My goodness, you're shaking like a stick in a storm. Has something dreadful happened? Come in here, sit down, tell me everything." And in another minute I was sitting on a box in a small storeroom pouring out my story, Abraham listening with narrowed eyes and an expression on his face like calculation.

"Abraham," I said, "what is this Ku Klux? Is it true they're trying to scare the Negroes out of voting?"

He shrugged. "It's a white man's club. I believe it started out in Tennessee, a joke of sorts, students out to entertain themselves by dressing up as ghosts and scaring superstitious country Negroes. But then it spread. It turned political and serious and organized, the Rebels' way of counteracting us."

"Us?"

"The Equal Rights League. Ambitious black men. Sympathetic whites. Do you know Colonel Roger Moore?"

"Not well, although I believe he is a client of my cousin Christopher."

"And of course you know Colonel William Sanders at the *Journal* newspaper?"

"Everyone in town does."

"Those two, or so I hear from people who should know, those two have got together and are busy hatching out a brood of Klansmen here in Wilmington."

"To scare the freedmen out of voting?"

"Terrorize them, rather. And their sympathizers too. Not just out of voting, although that would suit them well enough, but into voting for Conservatives. There will be violence, you can count on it."

"They hate you that much?"

"I think it is not hate so much as *horror*"—screwing up his face in mock disgust—"that a man of color might be sent to legislate on their behalf. And I can see their point. For centuries we were but animals. Now we presume to think that we can rule the state. To them it must be like a mule aspiring to be king."

I laughed a nervous laugh. "And what about the carbines in the warehouse?"

He took his left hand in his right and cracked his knuckles suddenly so that I jumped. "It seems your cousin and his cohorts are either Ku Klux or assisting them."

"My cousin seemed to be opposed."

"Then he is being pressured into it. Apparently in exchange for employment for his father."

"I can't believe that Christopher would do it. I can't believe that he is wicked."

"I'm sure *he* does not think he's wicked. I'm sure after a moment's contemplation he will think he's doing the right thing, that he is helping to protect the Southern way of life."

"But the Southern way of life is over. It was over with the war. Everyone knows that."

"There's a difference between knowing and accepting." Abraham nodded, his gaze inward as though collecting a new thought. "Eugenia," he said, "the mind is an odd thing, full of sealed containers and dark alleys and dead ends. It can be good and pure and full of violence both at once. It can believe that God holds sway on earth and that the Devil does, and it can love and hate in the same thought. If it were not so we would all go mad." He turned to look at me. "Do you understand what I am saying? Your cousin is a man like all the rest, he can be both good and wicked performing the same act."

"But perhaps I was mistaken. A high wind was up. It made a lot of noise. Or perhaps I mistook where they were standing. Perhaps they were talking about something completely innocent. Perhaps . . ."

"You heard him say, 'It's *money*,' did you not? There's plenty to be made in gunrunning."

"Gunrunning? Do not say that."

"It's a way of making money in a pinch, and God knows, everyone is in a pinch these days."

"I don't know what to think. Abraham, what should I think?"

He surprised me then. "You love your cousin, don't you?"

"I love him very much. He is my family. I don't want to malign him. I don't want to accuse."

"Then don't," Abraham said gently. "Just believe in him and go on loving him. We all need to love our own."

"But what about . . . ?"

"Forget it, just forget it, erase it from your mind."

"But Abraham."

"I will take care of it."

"But how?"

He reached across and set two fingers on my mouth. "Hush, now, hush. If you know nothing, it won't hurt you. And Eugenia, do not go out after dark between now and the election. No matter the emergency, do not go wandering the streets."

I was stupid with fatigue by then and so made no objection, but retired early to my bed and slept heavily until the small hours, when I awoke to gunfire somewhere close at hand, and twice heard shouting and more gunfire in the distance.

I woke to daylight and a kerfuffle going on outside, the Colonel shouting in the yard—at Christopher, I discovered, running out into the yard with the buttons on my blouse in the wrong holes. The Colonel had him by the shirtfront and was spraying spittle in his face, such was the strength of his emotion.

"What have you got me into?" he bellowed, shaking Christopher so that his head bobbed on his neck. "I will not be responsible. I'll have no part of it." He shoved suddenly, at the same time letting go the shirtfront so that Christopher fell hard onto his backside.

Up till now Christopher had been making soothing *Now now, Father* noises, but at this indignity his temper flared. "Is it *my* fault they were stolen? Is it *my* fault CC Importers secures its warehouse with a lock a child could pick?"

The Colonel advanced toward him one fist raised and he scooted on his backside, flipped onto his knees and rose hastily, backing up against a rosebush. At the same moment he spied me standing with my mouth agape.

"Go away!" he cried.

But I had sensed the hand of Abraham. "What's been stolen, Christopher? What's been stolen, Colonel?"

The Colonel looked down at his clenched fist as though surprised, then back at me, a sheepish half smile coming on his face. "Nothing. Never mind. Just a little tiff between my son and me. Go on in the house."

THE second night was like the first. I retired early, slept for several hours, and was once more awakened by the firing off of guns. I heard shouts, a woman screaming, but followed Abraham's instructions and did not leave my bed.

The morning newspaper described patrolling bands of

Negroes on the streets, a good many with guns, and those without armed with broomsticks, branches, fence rails, whatever came to hand. Aunt Lavinia did not come down for breakfast. Cousin Kate, grim-faced, reported that the terrors of the last two nights had induced in the poor thing a fit of vapors. Please would I come upstairs and see what I could do?

The poor thing lay like a wilted flower against her pillow, moaning gently with the back of one hand thrown dramatically against her forehead. I assured her she would live to see another day and prescribed a cup of strong black coffee.

We had not yet finished breakfast when she appeared perky as a sparrow with a letter in her hand. It had arrived by early post and its effect on her was better than a cup of coffee, no matter how strong it had been brewed. This letter was from her old lover Doctor Wilkins, that much she would tell us, nothing more. She blushed and simpered reading it, then turned back to the start and read it through again, and went on doing so even while the Colonel read aloud about the night's "Negro terror and intimidation."

"Where did they get the guns?" I said, but he turned lugubrious eyes on me and did not answer.

THE day of the election turned out quiet, the Conservatives clinging firmly to the view that the coloreds would have neither wit nor courage enough to show their noses at the polls. But when all was said and done, the citizens of Wilmington were disgusted and amazed to learn that not only did they have Mister Holden back as governor, but the ranting schoolmaster Mister Ashley had been made superintendent of education for the state, seventeen Negroes and the hairy *caah*petbagger Gizzard French had been elected to the House, and three other Negroes to the Senate, one of whom was Abraham.

Stories of corruption in the ranks of the Republicans circulated from the first, beginning before any of the unfortunate accused could possibly have got his hands around a bag of money or a piece of legislation, much less have bent his mind on how to use it for what the Raleigh *Sentinel* delighted to call depraved and venal ends. *Fraud! Greed!* It trumpeted. *Inability to keep the state's finances in control.* Those wicked men were padding their expense accounts, funneling fat railroad contracts to their friends, coming drunk to work and brawling in the House and Senate chambers, filling their own pockets to the ruin of the common man.

One day when Abraham was home for the weekend, I questioned him about it and he laughed. "Anytime politics and money come together, there is bound to be finagling. But of everything that is reported and averred, you might believe one word in a thousand and still hold to an exaggeration."

As for the Ku Kluxers, he stood up boldly in the Senate and announced their names. "I say here," he said, "for the benefit of Mister William A. Graham, Joseph Turner, and the other Ku Klux, that if I go to Orange County and get killed or Ku-Kluxed, some of them will suffer for it. Sam Morphis, how long have you belonged to the Klan?" At which the session broke into a hubbub.

Martha was pregnant with another child by then. She wept

a lot and seemed daily to become more volatile. She took to meeting me at her front door, newspaper in hand. "He has called the senator from Alamance a bullhead," she would cry. "He has called the senator from Craven County infamous." "He has called the railroad president a liar, coward, scoundrel, and poltroon." "He has refused to drink the governor's health and the governor has had him kicked out of his office. What possesses him to do such things, Eugenia? They call him pugilistic. They say he is a pugilistic Indian. I do not understand why they would call him Indian."

"Come now, Martha, think. Everywhere he goes he stands up boldly and proclaims his father was a member of the gentry. And the gentry cannot stand for that. So they excuse themselves by putting out the story that some passing Indian is responsible for this thorn in their side."

"But they say he stinks of Tangle Foot and Pop Skull. Eugenia, he does not stink. He is a clean man, clean."

I laughed. "If accusing him of being a drunk Indian is the worst they can do, I would advise you not to worry. And they do say good things too. Why just last week they called him muscular, majestic, of colossal, marvelous proportions. They said he had imposing dignity."

"They did not. They said those things of Gizzard French."

"But they said Mister French was outshone only by your husband, so the compliments apply to him as well."

She sniffed. "That was the other paper, not this one."

"Then read the other paper. It gets closer to the truth."

Her eyes teared up. She let the paper drop onto the floor. "I do not want to learn the truth about my husband from a newspaper. I want him here with me. I am always waiting, waiting for him to come home."

She drooped toward me and I took her in my arms. "Come, come, be strong. Your husband loves you very much, I know it for a fact, but he has work to do, important work. He's out to change the world, to make of it a better place for your children to grow up in."

"And I never know if he'll come home alive or carried on a board. Eugenia, I love him so much that sometimes when I lie awake at night alone I think I hate him." And she wept stormily into my neck while I murmured reassurances, wondering, perhaps with envy, what it would be like to love a man so much.

ONE night Abraham was waylaid by four robed men on the way back to his rooming house. They would have done him in with clubs if he had not pulled his pistol out and made them dance. He was arrested for it, charged with brawling, and tossed into a cell for two days and a night despite his plea of self-defense. It was not the first time he had been arrested, although it was the first in Raleigh, and he had taken to avoiding dark streets on account of it. When he came home that weekend, Martha went for him with all the fervor of a hanging judge.

"It's not the going to jail," she cried, "it's not that you are forced to fight, that you have become a brawler in back alleys, dragging yourself home bruised and bleeding, a fine example to your children. It's that one day there will be too many of them, or you will be taken unawares. It's knowing any day my babies might be left without a father. *That* is what I cannot bear." And she burst out in explosive weeping, Abraham's voice soft, consoling, pleading, although I could not hear his words. I had stepped up to the porch and was about to knock, but backed away again and turned for home.

The next morning Martha took the train to her parents' house in Beaufort, where she stayed until her child was born. During that time, Abraham went to be with her on his free weekends and came only twice to Wilmington, to check up on his mother, who told him she could take care of herself, go off and see about your wife. When the child was born he sent a message, and two weeks later brought Martha back to Wilmington and placed the baby in his mother's arms.

"His name is John," he said.

Mother Hester stiffened. "It be your father's name."

"I know. You must forgive me."

CHAPTER TWENTY-ONE

MEANWHILE Tom prospered. From time to time he drove the mule cart into Raleigh with a load to sell into the stores. He had regular clients now, and while the citizens of Chapel Hill were still too poor to do much buying, or too miffed to patronize an upstart Negro, the shopkeepers of Raleigh cared for nothing but to make a profit from his wares. When everything had been disposed of and payments taken in for last month's sales, he paid a boy to take care of the horses and spent the night at Missus Ingle's Negro Rooming House.

This rooming house was where Abraham stayed in Raleigh and the two men would get together for a meal or a walk about the town and tell each other what was happening. Abraham was fascinated by Tom's enterprise and once spoke about it in a speech before the Senate.

"You say the Negro is a lazy creature because in all his years of slavery he would not work except under the whip, but I tell you the Negro is not lazy, he is just too smart to be a slave." And when the mocking laughter had died down, "If there is no gain in it for him, why should he work? There is no gain in working for a master without pay, or for an employer for a wage that will not keep his family. But give a Negro a good wage, or let him buy a piece of land, and then stand back and watch him work. It is my contention that the Negro on a little piece of land can do better than the planter ever did on his.

"When the Union army came to Beaufort," he went on, "thousands of the poor and destitute came flooding in because they wanted freedom. They had no money, no way to support themselves, and at first they lived on handouts from the commissary. But they worked hard. They made themselves houses and they planted gardens and put themselves to work. And I am here to tell you that just two years later, while eight hundred whites lived on the commissary, only four colored men were still dependent on its charity, three of whom were cripples and the fourth was blind."

Which speech fell into a disbelieving silence on one side of the chamber and was hailed by a raucous chorus of *Hear, hear!* and *Tell it!* on the other.

SOMETIMES, coming home from Raleigh, Tom would pull the wagon up outside the gate and sweep his eyes across his growing property. Pickets interweaved with brushwood marked off kitchen gardens where cabbages and squash, string beans and collard greens grew fat and ripe and juicy. Beside each doorstep a dozen tobacco plants grew strong and tall, with nearby a bush or two of red hot peppers used for dosing people who had got themselves the stomach gas or making poultices for headaches, toothaches, and arthritis. Chickens gazed with broody eyes from rows of nests inside fowl hutches or squawked and squatted on their roofs.

The old hound dog Clyde grew up with had been buried in the woods and a new one, still a puppy, was intent on hunting Rebel Cat, who tormented him by waiting for the crouch before the charge, then sprang in one sight-blurring movement to the porch rail. Transportation ate his heart out in the barn beside the brand-new chestnut mare, and half a dozen pigs were always sprawled at length beside the road. Cotton plants in full white fluffy blossom, cornfields of an almost rank luxuriousness of leaf and stalk, the ears fat and heavy. And the sound of human voices calling to each other, the sound of singing mixing with the song of birds. It was a place of industry and cheerfulness, and in those days, hope.

And yet, although Tom loved the place and felt his soul expand each time he looked at it, he felt a hollow in his heart. His mother said he should get married and there were pretty girls aplenty he could choose from, but when he thought of marriage he could only think about Miss Genie, and so he pushed it from his mind.

Meanwhile, the size and population of the farm grew larger. Folks took to calling it "the Maryson place," then

"Maryson's," and then just "Maryson." Letters came addressed to Maryson, N.C. "We folks from Maryson," its inhabitants would say and Tom's heart would swell to hear it. Enfield took a board and burned the name on it and fixed it to the crosspiece over the main gate. Then, one eye on Clyde's reaction, he burned a pair of boards with *Bricket Lane* and set them up on posts at each end of the property, and moved them further down each time it expanded.

Clyde took little interest in the name above the gate, but the periodic moving of the street signs gave him enormous satisfaction. It was like an announcement to the world that he was worth a lick. He went about with a proprietary, paternal air, checking up on everything, calling out encouragement, making sure that everybody earned their keep. And no one seemed to mind this squirty, skinny little jar-eared hobbler coming by to pass the time of day and cast an eye on what was going on.

What bothered Clyde was that the watcher in the woods was back. He came each evening with the gathering of dusk. One minute he would not be there, and then he would, as though materialized out of the trees, reins in one hand, rifle in the other, and his head turned slightly to one side, an air of questioning about him. Clyde would come across to Tom's front porch and keep an eye on him while listening to Tom read the newspapers, which he did to the scrape-scrape of his whittling, the snap-click of Uncle Benjamin's caning, the tock-tock of his mother rocking with Baby Gold or Glory curled up in her lap, and Ma pretending not to listen through the kitchen window.

Since Tom took both the newspapers from Raleigh, the *Standard* and the *Signal,* and the *National Freedman* too, which cost a dollar for a year, it was a lot of reading to be got through.

Clyde said, "What for you want with reading all them newspapers?"

"We need to know what's happening in the world."

"I got enough to know on this here property. Don't need knowing what-all else. Ain't one enough?"

"They all have different opinions."

Clyde looked fiercely down toward the shadowy woods. "So long as they don't start bringing their opinions here."

Tom laughed. "They won't."

But it bothered Tom as well, this solitary watcher. Back when first he used to come he had seemed ghostlike, as though he might have been imagination. These days he was bold and visible and obviously solid flesh. And yet when Tom went striding down to challenge him, or Clyde went swinging on his wooden leg, he pulled his horse around and vanished back into the woods as if he really were a ghost.

One day on his way to Raleigh a pair of horsemen followed Tom along, one on each side of the wagon. "Don't like to see a nigger get too big," one called, and the other, like an echo, "Don't like to see a nigger get too big."

Tom ignored them and they fell behind, and after a while when he turned his head to see, they both had vanished. That evening, sitting with Abraham on a bench outside the Capitol, he said, "There's a man sits on a horse down by our gate and watches us. He started up with it when Clyde and I first set up together on the farm and then he quit. But now he's back."

"The same man?"

Tom shrugged. "Same or not, it makes no nevermind."

Abraham nodded, looking thoughtful. "Be careful, Tom, be careful."

ONE evening, before the afterlight had faded into shadow, in that brief time of stillness when the sounds of day have ceased and the cry of insects and the call of night birds not begun, they came trotting into Maryson, four of them, casual and easy in the saddle, as though they had been riding by and on a whim swung off the road to greet a friend. They were not robed or hooded, but wore Confederate uniforms, their hats pulled low down on their foreheads and their faces shadowed. They did not shout or call, just came ambling up the track and pulled up in the yard.

Tom's mother had been rocking on the porch, waiting to feed him when he came home from a meeting at the Preacher House. When she saw the riders start to come, she rose and went to greet them at the rail, "How do, neighbors," although she knew what they were and anger thumped against her ribs. "Come on in a while and set, there's coffee on the stove and cornbread in the oven."

One of the riders tilted his hat. These men were not white trash, but gentlemen, although they did not answer her, just looked about, murmuring among themselves.

"How do," she said again, and this time it was a challenge,

spoken loud enough to bring Clyde and Uncle Benjamin clattering out onto their porch.

"What-all you fellers want?" Clyde said.

Still they did not speak, just sat there looking from one porch to the other and continuing their murmuring.

"Go on, get outa here, get outa here."

One of the men laughed and spoke softly to the man beside him. A prayer began inside Tom's mother's head, and then Ma Bricket came out with Clyde's rifle in her hands and sighted at the riders down the barrel.

"You heered what my boy said. Get outa here. Go on along."

The lead rider swung his horse around. "And who are you?"

Ma drew herself up straight. "I'm Missus Bricket, that's who. And over there, that's Missus Maryson. We family, and peaceable, don't need no trouble outa you. Go on along."

They sat there looking up at her and one man spat into the dirt, his eyes still on her face. She braced herself, the rifle steady in her hands. At that moment Baby Gold appeared out of the corn on the far side of the yard. She was four years old by now, with gold dust skin and hair of molten gold standing out around her head like a halo on a saint. The riders did not notice her, a tiny golden figure against golden corn, but their horses grew skittish and the one closest to her shied and slid its rider off into the dust. He cursed picking himself up, and climbed back on his horse and cursed again. Baby Gold vanished back into the corn as silently as she had appeared, and as though an order had been given, all four men swung their horses round, and with a flourish and a thundering of hooves, took off back along the track, like a band of small boys caught out in a mischief.

When Tom got back home from his meeting and stepped up on his porch, he was startled to find Clyde, rifle at the ready, watching him approach, and all the others gathered in the kitchen. Clyde, ashen-faced and shaking, followed him inside.

"It were the night riders," he said. "The Kluxers. They have got us in their sights."

THAT night someone tore down the Bricket Road signs and the Maryson sign above the gate. Enfield put them up again. Two days later they were down again, and a stretch of fence down to the bargain, cows straying on the road, and somebody had slit the puppy's throat and strung it up beside the gate.

Ma fumed. She cursed. She stomped out with Clyde's rifle and shot toward the woods, reloaded and then shot again. She came inside and then came out and shot another time. She took to chopping wood as though it were an enemy and did not cook or wash or do a thing of use all day.

As evening started to come down, she began to peer toward the woods beyond the gate. "Where is that feller now? Where is that feller now?" But there was nothing but the shifting of the light.

Next morning, Clyde came hopping in a panic, his left leg in his hand. "Tom, Tom, you Tom!"

Tom came, pulling on his pants. "What is it?"

"It's Ma, she has entirely vanished and my gun is gone."

When they found her three days later in the far-off woods, she was approaching death. She was black and blue all over and could hardly bear to let them touch her, like a rabbit who'd been skinned. All her hair had been burned off, and her privates slashed with a straight razor, the cuts purposeful and clean.

It was Clyde who found her. "Who did this to you, Ma? Who did this?"

She did not answer, only moaned, and when Tom and Enfield heard Clyde shouting out for them and came crashing through the undergrowth, they found him naked to the waist, his blood-soaked shirt wadded in between his mother's legs.

Eight days it was before she told her story. She had resolved to have it out with the watcher in the woods, but had been sprung on the minute she had crossed the road. They stripped her clothes off, beat her with a branch, and marched her, bruised and shivering, all that night until they seemed to tire of her. Someone produced matches and made her burn her own hair off her head, and when that was done, someone laughed and said, "Now down below," and when she wouldn't do it, whacked her so hard on her fried and frizzled skull she felt her brain jolt back and forth. No reason to be dead, she told herself, and held her hand out for the match.

It was after that the cutting had begun, first one man, then a second, and a third, passing the razor hand to hand.

CONSTABLE Pike came clopping on his horse. "How many altogether, Missus Bricket?"

"Maybe fifty or a hunnert. A good big crowd. I figure they was coming after us again and I surprised them." She grinned awkwardly, setting a hand against her jaw. "I figure if I hain't gone out huntin' for that feller on the horse, they might have shot us all, or burned the barn, or the *en*tire place. It were a mercy, that it were."

"You recognize anyone?"

"They were dressed up in robes, the lot of them, and wore hoods with faces painted on, and horns. Some had long moustaches stuck on too, and beards."

"You recognize a voice?"

"They made them strange."

"A horse?"

"It were too dark, and once they beat me blood was in my eyes."

"Damn!" Clyde said, and smacked his fist into his palm. "They will get clean away."

That night the Preacher House burned down and no one knew a thing about it. In the morning, Clyde went the rounds of every cabin in Maryson. By evening he was captain of a night patrol.

CHAPTER TWENTY-TWO

I missed Abraham while he was off in Raleigh, and pondered on his words about the black half of me being the more virtuous. His arguments had moved me, but like a train that must be shunted back and forth before it can be turned, I fell into a double life. In one life I was white, and in the other black, and yet in both I was the same person called Eugenia Mae. It was as though, when I was with the colored race, my own skin became colored, and I would work all day among the freedmen, comfortably accepted as their own. But when I went back home and the front gate closed behind me and I stood looking at the house, newly painted with new chandeliers gleaming in the windows, all color drained away. The notion of a black self became abhorrent and I hid even the thought of it in case it showed. I felt like a pretender, an actor on a stage. I did not know who I was or who I ought to be.

At the same time, on my visits to the freedmen's schools, I would find myself examining the children, not just for sores or coughs and colds and fevers, but for the color of their skin. The ones who occupied me were the pale ones, some a brownish gold, some the color of milk coffee, or like honey, almonds, buttered toast. And some so white I could have taken them back home with me and claimed they were my cousins. I could not but think about the violent wrongs that had produced them.

And then one morning I woke with a strong desire to visit Mama's grave. I do not know what inspired this, perhaps the fact it was my birthday, that I was twenty-eight years old, had been in Wilmington upwards of four years and not one thing about my parentage had I resolved.

I told no one I was going, just left the house as though heading out for work. Instead, I headed north along the river. It was a warm day, but I was used to walking distances. I had comfortable shoes, a shady hat with a wet sponge underneath the crown, a couple of ham biscuits I had saved from breakfast in my pocket, and a military drum canteen of water slung across my shoulder on a canvas strap. This last had been given to me by the Colonel to carry with me in the summer, although he'd made me promise I would give it back if things should "come to a bad pass," by which he meant if he should need to go to war again.

I walked all morning and found the farm deserted. For a

long time I stood staring at the house. It smelled of rot and rats and mildew and was overgrown with weeds, half the roof caved in and the front door hanging from its upper hinge as though somebody had kicked it. I stepped up carefully and with one hand took it by the edge and pulled. It did not budge so I took it in both hands and heaved. It came completely off the hinge and I had to dodge aside to let it fall, which it did with an amazing crash. Peering in, I found the walls all tipsy and the floor gone rotten from the damp. Spiderwebs were everywhere, fat spiders crouching in them, eyeing me, and I was sure I heard the rustling of snakes. I backed away and went to hunt for Mama's grave.

I was sure it was a long way off—the perception of a child—and searched for a long time before I stumbled on it overgrown with clumpy grasses very near the house. The headstone had fallen flat and when I knelt and pulled the grasses back, Mama's name *Hester* was overgrown with moss. It seemed significant in some unfathomable way that she should share a name with Mother Hester, whom I loved so much. Had I ever loved Mama? I must have, but could not remember. And could not remember her, not her face or figure, just that one sentence spoken in a peevish voice, "Such curl, it is unnatural." And then the wrench of hairbrush through resistant hair.

I blew my nose on Abraham's red handkerchief. A child of the South, he had called me, by which he meant a half-breed like himself. "I am a half-breed," he would say, "a bastard," and the whites would draw offended heads into their shoulders like turtles who had seen a fox.

"Half-breed," I said softly, and then louder, "half-breed."

I had said the word "mulatto" to myself a thousand times, but not this word. Indeed, I had refused to think it. Now, with it on my tongue, I did not like the taste. And it struck me forcibly again how many of the children in the freedmen's schools were not quite black, or only hinting black, or almost purely white. "A fancy girl," that's what they called the light-skinned pretty ones. A fancy girl. Fancy for what? For sin? For wickedness? For the breeding of black babies who looked white? For breeding me? I thought about Cousin Kate, the way the bristles on her back went up the other night at supper. "Born white by accident," someone had said. "By accident?" she said. "What accident?" And then the slipping of the eyes, the discreetly nuanced silence. It was not the first time Cousin Kate had charged that fence and I wondered if the Colonel had once had a fancy girl grazing in his field as my father had in his.

As my father had in his.

I had not meant to think it, but somehow in that moment I came to know, without a doubt, with utmost certainty, with such conviction that my entire body shivered like a tree shaken by wind, that I was Tilda's child.

"Half-breed," I said again, and found it to be just a word like any other. It was a peculiar sensation, like stepping into someone else's mind and discovering it vacant.

Just then an owl gave its opinion on the gloominess of life and I realized I had stayed too long. I scrambled to my feet and turned for home. Too late. Already dark was coming down and soon the sandy trail was lost, the trees and bushes huddled into unseen masses. I stood there blinking, widening my eyes, then looked up at the sky. For one brave moment I thought of going back and taking shelter in the house, but then I thought about that rustling and the spiders smiling in their webs. Nothing for it but to wait until the moon came up. And so I spread my shawl and sat down on it to wait, slapping at mosquitoes now and then.

The night was warm, the sky a fine high blackness. "Black as Africa," I said aloud, and immediately thought of Tom, how, when we were living at the gold mine, he would creep out at night and stretch out in the open with the mules to sleep. I thought about the morning I had gone to warn him he must run, Papa was set on selling him, and how he stood there with his gentle big hands hanging at his sides. "I got no place to be but here with you," he said, but I insisted, and later on he came behind me in the cabin where I was packing food for him into a knapsack. "Miss Genie," he said. And now I heard his voice again and felt a softening in my bones. I fell asleep like that, Tom's voice a deep protective presence at my back.

If there was a moon that night, or if the sky stayed black or filled with stars, I do not know. I was woken by the morning call of birds and lay there half inside a dream in which I turned and kissed him. Then a crow called rudely from a branch, a late mosquito buzzed around my head, and a painful itching started in the palm of my right hand. I licked and blew on it, then rose and stretched and shook the sand out of my shawl.

I had not expected to be missed since I often came home after the family had retired. But as I approached the house, expecting nothing but an early morning hush of sleepiness, I saw activity out in the street and in the yard and on the front verandah, the front door of the house thrown open and a crowd of people making such a commotion that no one noticed me until I was upon them.

"What is it? What's the matter? Has there been an accident?"

A shout went up and Cousin Kate came fairly flying down the path, Aunt Lavinia in a flurry after her, crying, "I knew it! I knew it all along, that it would happen, something dreadful!" That was when I realized I had been discovered missing and—*embarrassment!*—a search party was being formed.

Even Mister Ashley was there, standing underneath a live oak in the center of the road, face pale and spectacles askew, awkward as a Yankee in a sack. He was home from Raleigh on a visit, and judging from the relief which streamed off him like water down a waterfall, I had no doubt he had been blamed. He came across and took me in his arms, then drew back suddenly, as though he would be criticized for that as well.

Then here came Christopher, shoving him and Cousin Kate and Aunt Lavinia aside, me half laughing now, half crying, frightened by the general fright, and by Christopher as well, the fierceness with which he questioned me.

"Who was it? Who did this to you? Who was it?" (I am sure if I had pointed an accusing finger someone would have died within the hour.) And then his disbelief and anger when I said, "No one. It was no one, I was just lost, lost in the dark and fell asleep."

He seized me by the shoulders. "Don't try to protect him.

It was that fellow Gall—" But I clapped my hand across his mouth.

"Do not say it, it is not true. I went to Mama's grave and night caught up with me. I am quite safe, I am not harmed," and breaking down, "Oh dear, I'm sorry, very sorry for the trouble I have caused."

At which Christopher's mood changed suddenly, the way it would, from murderous anger in a flash to jollity, and now what was this—endearments? whispered protestations?

"There, there," I said, patting his arm. "There, there. Do not upset yourself."

Behind him I saw Sylvie Younger watching us from the verandah, decked out in a pair of bright green leather gloves of a shade so bright it hurt the eyes. Bright gloves were the style that year.

CHAPTER TWENTY-THREE

Since Ma was Ku-Kluxed, Tom had not been across to Raleigh, but business needed to be done, and with Clyde's patrol proving an efficient deterrent, he resumed his trips. He was cautious, though, traveling by day and staying home on what promised to be moonlit nights because these were the nights the Kluxers came out to do their dirty work.

One day he and Abraham were sitting on a wall, watching the passersby. "Why are you not married, Tom?" Abraham asked. "A farmer needs a wife."

Tom said, "I have to take care of my mother." And went on to tell how every evening she went out to the porch to watch for her husband to come home, how every night she went to bed a little sadder than before. "I think," he said, "that if my father doesn't come she might just die of sorrow."

"You could advertise for him."

"I asked her to do that, but she said, 'He know where to come.'"

"What about her other children? You could advertise for them."

"She will not hear of it. I don't know why. Perhaps she is afraid that by advertising and having them not come she would lose hope."

The two men sat in silence, then Abraham said, "My mother has grown strange in her old age. She mourns for me as if I never had come home. She knows I am her Abraham, and yet she mourns."

"Who cares for her while you're here in Raleigh?"

"My wife Martha when she is in town, neighbors, a nurse who comes by from the Freedmen's Bureau, a fine woman who's become a family friend. Miss Spotswood is her name."

"What was that you said?"

"I said a fine nurse from the Freedmen's Bureau."

"No, her name. What was her name?"

"Spotswood. Eugenia Spotswood."

"Eugenia *Mae* Spotswood?"

"That I do not know."

"What is her appearance?"

"Dark hair considerably more curly than my own, skin considerably lighter, her features hinting so lightly of mulatto she passes easily for white."

"Mulatto? Then it is not her. The Miss Spotswood I knew

was white. For a moment I . . . But no, she went off with her father to Australia early in the war. Strange, though, that you should know a person of that name in Wilmington, since that's where she was from." He ruminated, chewing on his lip. "No doubt your friend is of the dark side of the family, you know how that can be."

"Are you quite sure *your* friend was white?"

"As sure as I am sitting here."

Abraham glanced sideways at Tom quizzically, began to speak, then let his breath out bit by bit, like a man coming to a time-enough-for-that conclusion. "Then it's a strange coincidence indeed," he said.

Tom carried the coincidence back home with him, puzzling and puzzling over it, one half of his mind telling him Miss Genie was in Australia, the other half telling him she was entirely somewhere else. And all of him whispering, "Mulatto, mulatto, surely she is not mulatto, and yet she had that hair . . . ," arguing with himself and dreaming of her in a way he had not dared before, so preoccupied that he went about with a faraway look and sometimes did not hear when asked a question, or only half heard and answered the wrong question.

The day the new constitution was published in the paper he had spread it on the kitchen table and read the whole thing carefully, but could not figure if marriage between blacks and whites had been made legal. Clyde had stuck his head inside the window. "What you reading now?" And when Tom told him, set his elbows on the windowsill. So Tom had drawn the candle closer and read the whole thing through again, this time aloud. But still he couldn't figure out about the marrying and when he asked Clyde what he thought Clyde just looked at him and sucked his teeth. But then he turned the page and read about the white girl down in Chatham County whipped naked with a board for bringing forth a Negro baby, and he pushed back on his stool and blew his breath out hard.

But if Miss Genie turned out to be mulatto . . . Each time Tom thought of it his breath stopped and his eyes went glassy from imagining. The notion that Miss Genie might be persuaded to become another Missus Maryson became wedged inside his head like a bird's nest in a tree. This, he told himself, was what everything had been about, the buying up of land, the gathering of people, the hard work of developing the property. It had all been for Miss Genie, everything had been for her. *Dear God, please let it be.*

"What's that?" Clyde said.

"Nothing. Just talking to myself."

"You grinnin' big enough to split your face for nothin'?" Clyde cocked his head and smirked. "What-all you up to, Tom?"

A few days later when Tom came and sat beside his mother on the porch with his feet up on the rail, she said, "What's the matter with you these days, son?" and Clyde, who was whittling on his steps, called out, "I figure your Tom's got a lady on his mind. He is in love."

Tom ignored him. His mother looked across at Clyde.

"I knows the signs, I been in love myself," he said defensively. "Although she would not look at me. She were above me." He set one hand against his heart and gave a great dramatic sigh. "Miss Genie were her name."

Tom swung his feet down from the rail and his body upright in his chair. "Have I lost my mind?"

And Clyde, with all the wisdom of a worldly man, said, "It takes you that way, don't it?"

Uncle Benjamin, who was caning behind him on the porch, said, "Son, you do not know the half of it. I pined after your ma for nigh on twenty years."

Clyde fell into a respectful silence. Then he said, "I pine after Miss Genie. I do not understand why she went runnin' off. She coulda stayed. In spite o' Ma she coulda stayed. Tom, she were the nurse I told you of. She brought me home and coulda stayed right here with us. She mighta been above me, but at least she coulda stayed. It were wrong of Ma to chase her off."

Tom said, "This Miss Genie. What was her full name?"

"Miss Eugenia Mae Spotswood. Why?"

"Nothing. Never mind."

But Clyde was not a man for never mind. "I knows all about her," he said importantly. "She were from Wilmington, she were, and before the war she were working in a gold mine down along the Charlotte road. She learned how to be a nurse there and when the war come, she took off working in this secret hospital, the one where I were took to when I snuck out of the Salisbury prison on the dead cart. We had all sorts in that hospital, fellas running off to keep out of the army. Some were real sick, sick to die. Once we had—"

"You did say Spotswood, didn't you? Eugenia Mae?"

Clyde said peevishly, "She shoulda stayed. Ma had no right to chase her off."

Tom's mother, who had been looking off toward the gate

seeming to pay no attention, said as though speaking to herself, "She *had* to go."

"What's that?" Tom said.

"She *had* to go."

Clyde called, "What's that you say, Missus Maryson?"

"I said none of your business, Clyde."

But Clyde had sensed a story. With a half-made doll in one hand and his whittling knife in the other, he came across and plumped down on Tom's steps.

Tom's mother looked at him. "It ain't your business, Clyde."

Clyde looked injured. "Tom and me, we're partners. We have to tell each other everything, that's what he said when we set up together. He said as how keeping secrets from each other would get us into trouble."

Tom said, "I don't mind."

And so his mother told about how, back when the war was ended and Eugenia brought Clyde home, Eugenia had come to her cabin asking after Tom. At first she had refused to tell her anything and went off into the woods, but when she came back Eugenia was still there, weeping on the step, and so she had relented and let the sobbing girl pour into her ear the story of her father and a slave called Tilda.

"She weren't sure of it, you understand. She weren't sure this Tilda was her ma, she could of been mistook. And that was why she had to go to Wilmington. She had to find the truth."

She turned to Tom. "She were a good girl, Tom. And she loved you, I'm certain sure of it."

"She told you that?"

"She did."

"Then I must find her."

"But if she was mistook . . ."

"Mistaken," Tom said patiently.

"Mistaken. If she was mistaken. If she's white."

"She's mulatto." And he told them of his conversation with Abraham.

When everyone had told each other what they knew, and Ma had been hauled out and made to say her piece, Uncle Benjamin set out praying loudly to the Lord, "Thy will be done and bring Tom's father back home safe, and bring Miss Genie too, so Missus Maryson and Tom can have a double wedding."

"Double wedding?" Clyde said. "But . . ."

And Uncle Benjamin said, "Son, you said yourself she would not have you, and anyway she is a nigra, she is going to marry Tom."

"Miss Genie a nigra. I'll be dogged." Clyde screwed his face up, sucking on his teeth, then hoisted himself upright and started out across the yard.

"Where you going, son?" Uncle Benjamin called after him.

Clyde half glanced across his shoulder, stumbled, and continued on.

"You! Clyde!" Ma called, but Uncle Benjamin reached and set his hand hushingly against her ankle. "Let him be, just let him be."

Clyde went up the slope behind the house and sat down in the grass. He sat a long time thinking on Miss Genie, not in any systematic way, just letting memories of her filter through his mind. He tried to reconstruct her face, but it was blurry with the mist-edged quality of time. And yet she had remained with him for almost five years now, a tersely gentle presence glimpsed sometimes from the corner of an eye, a voice heard but not quite heard in the rattling of a cornfield in the wind or in the roar of rain, the sensation of a hand, practical and comforting, upon his stump.

A cloud peeled off the sun. He lay back in the grass and pulled his hat to shade his eyes. So Miss Genie was a nigra. The notion stood inside his head inquiring what he thought of it. He tried to concentrate, but the wild emotion he had felt when first he heard it had now drained away. He felt, without acknowledging he felt, relief. If Miss Genie was a nigra he was not obliged to be in love with her. He was not obliged to dream of what had always been impossible, or fret because he could not be a man. Tom would go to Wilmington and bring her back to Maryson and here she would remain.

He bent one knee and set his other leg across it, wiggling the foot and making up the scene of homecoming. "Clyde," Miss Genie would exclaim stepping down out of the wagon, "why Clyde, just look at you, old friend." And she would bend and kiss him on the cheek and he would blush and turn his head aside and grin. He would not feel broken anymore.

BY next morning Tom had fallen down the other side of fantasy. It was too much to hope for. Miss Genie was an educated woman. She could read anything, she did not have to spell out words and struggle over them, and she could write fast and still write pretty, her tongue not flicking back and forth to help her get it right.

His mind went back to that day at the gold mine when she had told him she was going to set him free. How she had said, "Don't look at me like that, you break my heart," and tucked his freedom paper in the pocket of his shirt. How she had turned away and then turned back, tears welling in her eyes. "Tom, I love you. There, I've said it now."

He had clung to that *I love you* all these years and dreamed of it at night. Thinking of it now he found he could not breathe. Still and all, he told himself, although she might have loved him well enough to set him free, that had been years ago when she had no one else to love. Abraham had said she was not married, but surely she had fixed on someone else, someone who had been to university, an educated man. He sat a long time pondering that thought, and then went off to look for Enfield and Elijah.

A week later a brand-new cabin stood beside the gate. One week after that, Tom came walking with a young white man at his side. Both carried bundles and the young man had a shotgun slung across his back. They went into the cabin and after a few minutes came back out without the gun or bundles and came together up the track. It was a little after noon and hot and everyone was flat out snoozing on their beds.

"You want cold tea?" Tom said and the two of them sat together on his porch and drank it and the young man talked and Tom talked back and they nodded to each other, and then Clyde came outside rubbing sleep out of his eyes.

"That's Clyde Bricket," Tom said. "He's my partner in this place. Hey Clyde, come here! Meet Everett Miles. He's a student from the university. He's going to turn us into educated men."

CHAPTER TWENTY-FOUR

IN those days I was much consumed with paperwork. Mister Ashley rarely came back home from Raleigh and his absence had left a vacancy filled only sporadically by a military clerk. This meant I often was obliged to sit up late at night getting things in order. The missing families ledger had fallen out of use since by now it was assumed that whoever could be reunited through its pages had already been so. Few requests came in and mostly they were hopeless so I knew that if I ever were to find this woman Tilda it would not be by going down that path.

I considered an advertisement, but that would mean exposing my request to all of Wilmington. Then it occurred to me that perhaps a midwife had been present at my birth. If I could find out who that was . . .

I thought of asking Cousin Kate, but quailed before the thought. Aunt Lavinia, though, might be sympathetic. After all, she was no saint. Since that first letter from Doctor Wilkins she had been a regular customer at Gizzard French's store. Here she bought boxes of pretty writing paper and phials of scented oil. Back home, she cut up squares of fabric, soaked them in the oil, slipped them in between the sheets of paper, and then closed the box and set it on her bedroom mantelshelf a day or two. At the end of this time she had a box of delicately scented paper—rose, lavender, hibiscus, lemon, strawberry—on which she wrote long secret letters to her lover. When he sent letters in return she stored them in the empty boxes with petals from the garden strewn on top. She was a sentimentalist. Perhaps she would be sympathetic.

But then I thought about the way she and Doctor Wilkins used to whisper in the garden. Were they gossiping or making love? I loved Aunt Lavinia, but could I trust her? I knew I could trust Cousin Kate.

One day I saw Cousin Kate working in the garden. She wore a yellow sunbonnet and was busy with a pair of pruning scissors. Screwing up my courage, I went across to question her.

She looked thoughtfully at me beneath the brim of her sunbonnet. "A midwife? Why do you ask?"

I was ready for that question, and managed a casual response, but she pursued it.

"I do not know if there was any midwife, but there were

complications. Your papa confided that in me after your poor mother died."

"What sort of complications?"

"He did not say. I suppose it was a hard birth, or perhaps she had milk fever. She was not the same again."

I pressed her, but she said, "Eugenia, dear, you've had enough trouble in your life."

"You must tell me. Please."

"I do not know particulars. After you were born, Hester rarely came to town. She changed, she became . . . peculiar. When a child is born, a woman sometimes becomes . . . how shall I say this? . . . deranged. It is a common thing. I think it might have happened to your poor mama. Most women come through it in time."

"But she did not? Is that what killed her? Papa said she died of an illness of the brain."

"I suppose that would explain it. I don't really know. She was dead and buried before the family knew she had succumbed."

I hesitated, and then blurted out a question that for years had bothered me. "Did my mother kill herself?"

Cousin Kate stiffened. "Why would she do that?"

For having had her husband's half-breed bastard foisted on her when she could not have a child. "Tell me, Cousin Kate, did my mother kill herself?"

Cousin Kate looked down at her garden scissors as though they had developed an affliction. "One did not inquire." And she nipped the dead head off a rose.

. . .

MOTHER Hester's feet were playing up again and I treated them morning and evening with compresses. It calmed my mind to be with her, although more and more she was in what I thought of as her other world, a world in which she spent hours whispering secrets to her darling Joel. If I intruded on the conversation, she looked furtive and Joel retreated back into the wall. Sometimes when I came she knew me, and when I left she wept and called me daughter. Other days she asked my name a dozen times and seemed relieved to see me go. These episodes upset me, but I was used to them and each time expected that tomorrow she would be back inside my world again.

She had aged since Abraham went off to Raleigh, not with the steady daily aging of a woman growing through her years, but in staccato spurts, her progress toward the grave arrested each time he came back into town, released with a sharp sigh like a train leaving a station when he left. More and more she would complain of heavy legs, of tingling in the feet, or numbness, complained she could not sleep, although she spent hours in her rocking chair out on the porch sunk so deeply into sleep, with her mouth hung open and her body tilted at a crazy angle, that sometimes when I came to visit her I thought she was already gone. A dozen times I climbed the steps with a telegram to Abraham composing in my head. But then she would rouse, and holding out her arms, begin to weep. "At last, you've come at last."

Then Martha, if she was in town, would come out in her

apron, the baby on her hip, and reprimand her for drooling on her clothes or letting something, a teacup maybe, fall onto the floor. "Mother *Hes*ter," she would say. And she would go to the front gate, calling out for little Abraham and blaming the old woman who had been told to watch him and had forgotten he was there. By this time he was five years old, a handsome little fellow, dark-skinned like his mother and with her tightly curling hair, but independent like his father and with his seductive smile.

These days Mother Hester regarded both the children with a sort of nervous admiration, constantly astonished at them, throwing up her hands whenever they were brought to her, as though she had just this minute seen them and was not sure who they were, but never touching, never reaching out her arms to them. When little John was set onto her lap and her arms positioned to contain him, she would sometimes forget that he was there and must be watched in case she let him fall. Or she would squeeze him tightly so he cried for his mama, and when Martha came to rescue him, she would grip a little arm or leg convulsively, rocking back and forth, then just as suddenly release her grip, lapsing into vagueness. Or she would cry, "My child! My child! They have come to take my child!"

Martha, shrill-voiced, would cry back at her, "He is not your child! He is not your Abraham! He is my John." And go off muttering, "That old woman, that old *woman*." And the next day, or perhaps the next, she would pack her bags and take her children off to Beaufort, because, she said, her parents needed her. And when Abraham came home she would come back.

Mother Hester grew more sprightly when Martha was out of town. Her feet hurt less and she spent less time sunk in torpor on the porch. Often, when I paid my visit, I found her broom in hand, or flicking with a duster, or making her slow way up the street, shopping bag in hand. Once or twice I thought of asking her advice about Tilda. I did intend to look for her, I still did, and yet the time I might have put into that enterprise I spent with Mother Hester. And understood why I was doing it, I was no fool. If I should find this Tilda, I would be obliged to her. Not obliged to acknowledge her before the world, not obliged to acknowledge her at all, but in my heart I would be obliged to think of her as Mother, I would be obliged to love her, even if I did not find her lovable. And right here was the nub of my procrastination. I did not want her for my mother, I wanted Mother Hester, whom I loved. And so I did not speak to her of Tilda. Instead, I went to Gizzard French's store and bought a peony and planted it beside the rosebush in her tiny square of yard, and the rose bloomed yellow and the peony sagged heavily with pale pink blooms.

CHAPTER TWENTY-FIVE

ABRAHAM was coming home. He had been two years in the Senate and it was time to run for reelection. Martha had come back from Beaufort and was inside making supper, all athrill. Mother Hester and I were out front sipping tea. It had been a lucid day for her and we chatted back and forth like two ordinary women sitting on a porch.

Nervousness was in the air, restlessness was in the street. Since the evening of the so-called Negro terror and intimidation, the Ku Klux had not reared its head in Wilmington, at least not visibly, but reports of violence filtered in from all across the state. Reports turned into rumors, rumors to assertions, assertions into categorical pronouncements, which, in turn, turned into newspaper reports: *The Kluxers. The Ku Klux. The Klan.*

In outlandish garb they came by night to shoot into the Negro cabins, and the cabins of the Freedmen's Bureau teachers too. They burned down meetinghouses, churches, cabins, barns and fences, dragged entire families off into the woods, beat them with boards and branches, cowhides, shot them and their little children, outraged women, cut off ears, slit nostrils, hung them up from trees and gateposts and the rafters of their barns, tossed people into ponds to drown, then hauled them out and did such vile things to their bodies a decent person should not speak of them. A farmer who had signed for the Republicans woke to find all his geese and chickens with their necks wrung, his pigs bloated up with poisoned corn.

The *Campaign Anti-Radical* reported, unperturbed, *To us a Ku Klux is a perfect myth, whose existence is known only to radical newspapers. There may be such a creature as a Ku Klux, as there might have been such a nymph as Egeria in the days of Romulus and Remus, but we have just as much knowledge of one as the other.*

No one knew what to be afraid of and what not. No one doubted, though, that whatever was going on out in the countryside, the cause of it was the election.

What bothered me as much as anything was that every low-down man jack seemed easily supplied with guns. That Christopher might be involved was like a demon from Pandora's box which from time to time would angle up the lid and peer at me with a grotesque yellow eye. Surely there is something I can do, I told myself, surely if I went to someone in authority and told them my suspicions, the flow of arms to Klansmen through Wilmington could be curtailed. But who to tell? Should I make report at the Conservative headquarters, where Cannerty and Coombes could often be discovered going in and out? And of the Republicans, who better to report to than the man who had already told me to erase the matter from my mind?

So then, should I go to Christopher and plead with him? This man who these days strutted in the finest of fine linens, whose coattails swung behind him with an air of manly unassailability, who carried gifts home to his family, this man who had achieved his dream? Should I accuse him to his father? Since their argument out in the yard, I had sensed a coldness between the Colonel and my cousin. A kind of wariness. They were civil to each other and neither Cousin Kate nor Aunt Lavinia seemed to notice any rift, so after all perhaps there was none, just my keenly sensitive awareness of every shifting smile or frown or subtlety of tone. If I made my accusation to the Colonel, I would hurt him very much, of that I could be sure, and as for Cousin Kate and Aunt Lavinia, how could I inform them that their comfortable situation—the hats and gowns, the pretty drapes and cushions and the double damask tablecloth—was at the cost of other people's lives? Should I tell them their donations to charities about the town were born of wickedness? Could good be done as a result of wickedness? Starving children's lives had been preserved. Was that sufficient counter to the lives the Klan had damaged or destroyed?

I have never been a woman much inclined to talk with God, but sometimes I would argue out aloud with someone not myself. It did not bring me peace. I was convinced that Christopher was guilty, and yet I could not think my cousin was my enemy, indeed I think I loved him more, as though by loving him still more I could save him from himself.

Out on the street, neighbor children were once more playing baseball. One of the onlookers, a girl of nine or so, had little John perched on her hip. He was laughing, and from time to time she leaned down to his fist inside her own and kissed it. The ball was hit. She jounced his arm and shouted, "Go, go, go," and he shouted with her, "Go, go, go."

"Is he not the dearest little thing?" I said to Mother Hester.

She turned to me with anguish on her face. "They will come soon, they will come and take my child."

I had become accustomed to her bursts of grief, but still they took me by the heart. To grieve so hard and for so long and never to be comforted. I reached across and set my hand on hers. "He has come back to you," I said, "you must not grieve," although I knew that she would grieve forever for the son she had not known for more than twenty years. We sat in silence, nothing but the rocking, rocking of her chair. I thought of Tilda. Did she grieve every day for me? Had she grown old and strange with longing for her daughter? The thought made my insides curl up on themselves.

A commotion started somewhere down the street, voices and the sound of cheering. Abraham was home. By the time he reached the house a crowd had gathered, agog for news of what was going on. Martha, dishcloth in hand, came running to fling herself upon him. By the time she reached him, he was already on the gatepost and leaned to kiss her before taking off on his oration. Young Abraham scrambled up beside him and stood clinging to his father's leg, gazing solemnly about him at the crowd.

The sky was growing dim by the time everybody's questions had been asked and answered and they started drifting back to their own houses. Martha ran inside in a panic that the supper might be burning. Abraham swung his son down off the gatepost, then stepped down himself and came to kiss his mother, and me too, as naturally as if I really were his sister. At that moment it occurred to me that I had never felt so easy in my skin.

Reluctantly I rose to leave and was almost at the gate when Abraham called, "Wait, Eugenia. I have something for you."

I turned and found him holding out a letter. "From a common friend."

Martha was calling, "Supper!" at the door and I had only time to thank him. Thinking it was from Mister Ashley, I slipped it in my pocket, planning to read it at my leisure after supper. When that was done, I went back to the garden house, lit the lamp, and, pulling out the letter, opened it.

The writing was not Mister Ashley's, which had a fast-paced look, as though he could not get his thoughts down on the page as quickly as they came to him. This writing was studied, careful, very neat, as though the writer had taken pains with it, thinking out each sentence before it was put down.

Dear Miss Genie. I turned the page and ran my eye down to the bottom. *Yours with affection, Tom.*

My breath went out of me. I sat down on the bed, staring at the window, where I saw myself reflected darkly.

Dear Miss Genie,

For a long time I have wanted to tell you that your Tom is not a simpleton as everybody said, but I thought you had gone with your father to Australia to work in a copper mine. I have often thought about you there and wished I could come across the ocean on a ship to knock on your front door.

Now I have discovered you are in Wilmington, which is a surprise. Abraham Galloway, the senator, gave me this information. You see, I did not go to Canada as you directed me. I became lost because I was very ignorant back then, and did not know north from east. I worked for some time on a turpentine plantation and then ran off to New Bern, where I took up working for the Union army. Abraham taught me to be a scout and now he is my friend and tells me you are well, for which I am thankful.

In New Bern I learned to read and write and read a map and now I know which way is north, although I do not mean to go there since I have a farm near Chapel Hill. I own it with Clyde Bricket, who tells me that you were his nurse in Salisbury. He says to tell you he is very sorry that you went away while he was having his leg cut off again, but he forgives you.

Miss Genie, we have taken in a student from the university. His name is Everett Miles, and instead of rent he has been giving us a proper education. We made him a new cabin by the gate where he studies all night with his rifle propped beside him. If he hears suspicious noises, he fires into the air, and twice so far has saved us from the Kluxers. Clyde does not take so well to books but I have now read fifty-four and these days I am reading poems by a gentleman called Mister Milton. They are sometimes frightening because they speak of Hell, but Everett tells me I must read such things if I am to be a truly educated man, which is my strong desire.

I have also laid my hand upon a fairytale called The Water Babies written by a Mister Kingsley. It is a strange book about children living underwater, although Everett assures me it is famous. I like it because the boy in the story is called Tom, the same as me. Also, he has a hard life as a chimney sweep and finds a better life, which is the way my life has also been. I have never been a chimney sweep but I think perhaps that climbing down a chimney would be like climbing down a mine shaft, which is something I have done.

Abraham is famous now, but he has enemies who hate him. As you know, I am a big man, very strong, and I have sworn to help him if he should ever need me. You were kind to me when I was nothing but a slave and I would help you too. Send me a telegram and I will come.

My mother has told me something about you that surprised me. I have many questions I would like to ask and hope one day to see you face to face. May God bless and keep you in his care.

Yours with affection,

Tom

I do not know how to tell you my emotions as I read this letter. I can only tell you that I folded it and set it on my writing desk. Then I took myself to bed, where I lay looking at the darkness. Six, seven times since I had come back to Wilmington I had sat down to write to Clyde and ask how he was faring and if his leg had healed—I would have liked to know—intending to ask casually after Tom. But I found when I put pen to paper that I was overwhelmed by fear that Tom was dead, or that Clyde would run to him and speak of me and then write back and say Tom did not remember who I was. I had attempted to set thoughts of him aside, but his memory kept tapping at my door. Now I imagined opening it to find him standing there, smiling down at me in that gentle way of his.

I've come to tell you your Tom's not a simpleton.

I slept, and woke.

Now I know which way is north, although I do not mean to go there.

And slept again, and woke.

My mother has told me something about you that surprised me.

After that I did not sleep.

OUR letters were polite and formal. I told Tom what was happening in Wilmington, he told me what was happening near him. He had become an official recorder of abuses and passed on to me some things that made me nervous for his safety. In Chapel Hill, he told me, groups of forty-fifty Ku Klux rowdied up and down the streets at all hours of the night. They galloped round the campus of the university, beat up Negroes, and drove white Republicans out of their homes. A man they took to be a state detective was hauled from his hotel by a party of perhaps a hundred and given a sound whipping, the poor man left bleeding on the road. All this they got away with until a poor white woman whacked a Klansman with an axe, which prompted Governor Holden to beg a company of federal troops to guard the town.

Tom did not question me about my mother and I did not volunteer. And yet it seemed to me that I was on a journey toward him, a long slow journey, soft sand sucking at my feet with every step, but sometimes with a hardness underneath so that I seemed to skate, my arms flung out for balance and my mind dizzy with the thrill of it.

For all these years the thought of love, or falling into it, had been secured inside another of the boxes in my head. But now the lock was broken and the lid was off. I was amazingly, undoubtedly, ecstatically in love with Tom. His presence was around me every day, his face as clear as if it had been yesterday I kissed him at the gold mine and sent him on his way. Each morning when I woke I told myself it was a dream and every night before I slept I prayed to dream again.

I have observed across the course of life that when a woman falls in love the air around her seems to glow. She becomes magnetic, enigmatic, disconcerting. It is a mystery of the body, I believe, an enchantment of a sort, a magic emanation. One evening while we were drinking coffee on the front verandah, Christopher said, "Eugenia Mae, you seem to be a different person these days."

"Different from when?"

"Oh, I don't know. From back before."

"But everyone is different now. The war changed all of us."

"I don't mean that. I mean . . . Eugenia, you live among us every day and yet I feel I do not know you."

"Come now, don't be silly. It's imagination."

"You act . . . I do not know how to say it . . . you act as though you have a secret."

I laughed, setting my hands against my cheeks. "A secret? Why, you make me sound exciting."

"You go off every morning early and do not come home till suppertime, or after, or come home for supper and then vanish off into the night unchaperoned and undefended. And sometimes do not come back home until the small hours of the morning. Who knows what you get up to?"

His voice had taken on an edge. I looked across at him, but could not see his face, just his outline against the evening sky.

"What is it you think I might be getting up to?"

"Nothing, nothing. It was just a way of expressing my concern for you. Wilmington may seem to be a big town, but in reality it's very small. You understand how that is. Everyone knows everything. It's difficult to keep a secret. No matter how you try to hide it, it will eventually come out."

"Nonsense. I'm a nurse. I visit the sick in their houses. I help the teachers in the freedmen's schools and do my best to get orphans off the streets. I deliver babies and teach poor mothers how to care for them. I sit beside the dying and try to comfort the bereft. I work hard, Christopher, to earn a living, and am available to any of my patients day or night. I am offended, cousin, that you should complain of me."

I was considerably stirred up now, and jumped up from my chair, facing him hot-cheeked. He raised his hands as though surrendering.

"Hush, hush, calm down, I did not mean offense. Sit down and drink your coffee. There, that's better." And when I had calmed a little, he went on, "Eugenia Mae, we all love you and admire you, every one of us. You are a good woman and to help the poor is only right for someone of your station."

"My station? What can you mean—my *station*? Have you forgotten I have nothing, not a penny to my name? That I left this place disgraced, my poor papa bankrupt? Do you not remember that? Since then I have labored on a gold field like any slave or Irishman, and in hospitals as well. I have never told you this before, but since you accuse me of a secret, I will tell you this. When the war broke out, I took work in a secret Union hospital in Salisbury. It was in the cellar of a house out in the countryside. We cared for men who did not want to join the Southern Cause—"

Christopher cut me off. "Don't tell me this. I do not want to know."

"But it's a fact."

"Dear cousin, all that is swept under the carpet now, forgotten. And besides, it is not that, it's something else I feel you hide from me, some other secret. I think it has to do with Mister Galloway."

"So we are back to *that* old chestnut."

"I have heard he is for votes for women."

"I am myself."

"If you could vote, I suppose you would align yourself with him?"

"Since I cannot, what point arguing the matter?"

"Let me put it this way. If you are this man's friend, then you are obliged to look out for his safety. And if *I* am *your* friend, then I am obliged to look out for his safety too."

"What are you saying, Christopher?"

"That I care about you. That I do not want to see you suffer. That all the world knows Mister Galloway steps along the line of danger every day, and that if he steps too far, if his enemies should . . . surely you have heard the rumors of a plot to do him in?"

"I know he has been several times attacked. And slung in jail because he put his fists up to protect himself."

"It may be nothing more than gossip, and if it were not for your peculiar . . . attachment, I would not concern myself with it. Your friend, Eugenia, needs a guard."

"His friend Mister Eagles talked to him about it once. He said at his height he is so conspicuous a target that a guard could do no good."

"Nonsense."

"He will not do it, I can guarantee you that."

"A guard could be arranged he would not know about. Someone to follow at a distance and watch out for assassins."

"Who?"

"You forget I am a lawyer. I know all sorts of people. I'll look around for someone we can trust."

"But who would pay him?"

"Don't worry your head about a little thing like that."

"I can't believe you would do this for him."

"Not for him, Eugenia. I thought I'd made that clear."

"I don't want you to do it."

"And why not?"

"It is an interference."

"It's a kindness. Your friend is reckless. He needs taking care of."

"And there you have it, Christopher, a white man's attitude. The poor nigger does not know how to take care of himself, and so the massa has to do it."

"I did not intend—"

"I know. You cannot help yourself."

He made a shifting motion with his neck. "I've offended you. I'm sorry."

"Then let me go to bed. I am fatigued."

CHAPTER TWENTY-SIX

THE Republicans held their nominating convention at City Hall. A battle raged between the two factions of a split party, one side of which had been convinced that the Yankee carpetbaggers had been using them for their own ends and ought to be thrown out. The other faction did not hold with this. Some thought the carpetbaggers were entirely in their corner, while others thought the only people they could trust were Negroes like themselves.

From the Bureau office I could hear them going at each other with an ardor that inspired the *Journal* to report on what it called "the big local radical show featuring greasy negroes in a ludicrous, disgusting farce." Abraham supported

Mister Eagles, his good friend and neighbor who was running for reelection to the House. A pleasant fellow, he had been a medic in the Union army and sometimes helped me with my patients. Abraham was to make a speech on his behalf.

On the day he was to make it, the convention turned even more unruly. It was hot. The hall was packed. All the doors and windows stood wide open and shouting, hissing, laughing, and booing echoed up and down the passageways and out onto the street. I managed to ignore it long enough to organize myself before I went out on my visits. When I came back that afternoon, the uproar was unabated, so I set down my black bag and went to spy on what was happening.

Abraham was on his feet just finishing his speech. "Friends," he said, "there is something rotten in Denmark, something wrong with the Party here. Defunct Northern men trying to creep into Southern society are at the bottom of it, and are trying to gain popularity by splitting the Republican Party. At the first ward meeting on Monday night, certain bolting politicians talked about having all the intelligence on their side, but I would wager that there was more intelligence at that ward meeting in those thick woolly heads than the white men on the other side could boast of. And yet one of you sells out for a ham, another for a pint of whiskey. I tell you, if you colored people fail to vote for Eagles, then if there is a hell on earth and you don't fall into it and be damned, I'll eat potatoes before they are grown."

And he went to his seat at the back of the room accompanied by loud stamping and hallooing.

I touched his shoulder and he turned and smiled at me. No

sooner done than the man standing beside me—and he a Negro too!—leaned in between us, addressing me but making sure that Abraham could hear.

"Fancy a big nigger do you, Miss Eugenia?"

I pulled away. "How do you know my name?"

At the same moment, Abraham swung out of his chair to tower over him. "Avant, you are a goddamned mischief maker!"

I must admit the little man had spunk. He shoved his face up into Abraham's. "And you a goddamned whitey fancier!"

At which Abraham reached back and slapped the fellow's face with all his force. Avant stood a moment, swaying, blinking, half fell onto the floor, sprang up again, and went for Abraham with flailing fists. Abraham reached out a long arm and took him by the throat and held him off while two policemen came shoving through the crowd. A reporter for the *Journal* scuttled after them, furiously taking notes.

Despite temptation, Abraham had applied no pressure to Avant's miserable throat, although in court Avant would look aggrieved and put on a hoarse voice and claim that devil Galloway tried to strangle him. Inspection of his throat and the testimony of the two policemen showed him to be a liar. At which the magistrate sighed in his beard, begged the Honorable Senator to please behave himself, and threw the matter out.

ABRAHAM'S valiant support would help get Mister Eagles re-elected, but it also set the poor fellow in the way of the grim reaper. Mister Eagles was poisoned that same night. He and

Abraham and some others went to a saloon to reconstitute themselves after all the shouting and excitement of the day. They sat around a table, ordered a shot of whiskey each, and fell into discussion. Abraham had not yet touched his glass when Mister Eagles, who had tossed his back, stiffened in his chair, rolled his eyes up, and collapsed across the table. Fortunately the saloon owner knew what should be done. He poured salted water down his throat and made him vomit. Quite a rumpus went on, so I heard, everyone accusing everyone and fighting, even the saloon owner thumped twice in the head. By next morning, he was weak but well enough recovered for the *Journal* to report the poisoning was nothing but a rumor. Mister Eagles, it claimed, "was only attacked by a complaint to which he has been subject for a week or two past." Which everyone knew to be a lie. They had all seen him hale at the convention.

I was mixing a compress at the kitchen table, Martha perched beside me reading pieces from the newspaper aloud. When she read of Mister Eagles's poisoning, her voice went flat and anxious, but when she turned the page and read of Abraham's scrap with Mister Avant, she flew into a rage. She rushed into the bedroom and came flying with her suitcase and the baby on her hip, crying, "Abraham? Where are you, Abraham?"

Both Abrahams came running and she went striding off along the road, her son clinging to her skirt, her husband calling after her. He ran behind her, begging her to stay, to not be foolish, to have courage, but she would not heed him, and eventually he was obliged to take her suitcase and put her and

277

the children on the train. "Which," he said ruefully when he got back, "is not such a bad thing. Since it now seems I have enemies in both camps, I'd rather she not be here if I am to be done to death."

"Don't be silly," I said. "No one's going to kill you."

He tipped his head toward the street. "Come walk with me," and when we were along a way, "I don't know how much my mother understands, she's in and out so much, but I do not want her frightened. I'm a target, you know that. If somebody must die before all this is done, I will not be surprised if it is me."

"So you believe Mister Eagles was poisoned? It was not a sudden illness?"

"I know he was, and no doubt I would have been as well, except I had drunk nothing. Now both glasses have been emptied out and washed, so there can be no investigation."

"I wish I could have examined him when he was ill."

"You are involved enough."

"That man Avant knew my name."

"I know. It worries me. Perhaps you should go to Beaufort too."

"Nonsense. I'll do no such thing. I'll stay right here and watch you win reelection."

Which he did. And when the votes were counted, kept his seat with unscathed popularity. In fact, all three black senators were reelected, and although the black assemblymen were not all the same people, the count of them remained at seventeen. Gizzard French was handily returned, and Mister Ashley also, ready to continue driving the Rebels wild with his insistence on free education for the poor. But all across the state Republicans had been ousted in favor of Conservatives.

Two days later, the Colonel came home with the news that he had been made a partner, that CC Importers was now CCC Importers. A workman had that very day painted the extra C above the door. A wagon followed on behind him. On it was a brand-new red velvet studded couch and a pair of matching chairs with ornate curling legs. He had them placed opposite each other in the parlor, although I never saw him sit on any one of them.

CHAPTER TWENTY-SEVEN

IT was the evening of the Great Conservative Celebration, mid-August hot and breathless, the sky a violent blue. Since three o'clock guests had been pouring into Wilmington, the trains jam-packed with red-faced gentlemen, ladies flapping feathered fans, children flop-necked and grizzling for a glass of water, please, another glass of water. All the hotels in town were full. Owners of rooming houses were busy spreading mattresses on floors and tables and verandahs. Every Conservative had his house filled up with guests.

Major Hughes, an important orator from New Bern, came to spend the night with us, bouncing in the door full of declamatory triumph. We also had the Carroltons from up the river, a roundly pleasant couple, soft around the edges, and bony Mister Pender with his pinch-mouthed wife, this pair from Smithville. Sherry was served. Major Hughes proposed a toast to "our glorious victory" and then another, and another, so that by the time the crystal bell was rung to say the soup was served, even the ladies were a little tipsy.

Gladys had labored all day in the kitchen. She was allowed inside the house by now, and her husband Jacob often served as waiter. That day he had come down on the three o'clock from New Bern, and when his shift was over came in uniform directly to the kitchen, where I overheard him regaling Gladys with an account of the idiosyncracies in food and drink of the incoming passengers. Supper announced, he slid about with bowls and plates and platters, silent as a wraith, a white napkin folded on one arm, interpreting the raised finger, the slight turn of the head, as precise, definable instructions. When he was not needed, he stood mutely at attention just inside the door, never seeming to look at anyone, never seeming to hear a word of what was said around the table, although I knew he was inhaling every word and sentence, every nuance, every hint and innuendo, every inhalation and expulsion of breath. He was the perfect deaf-mute Negro, once worth perhaps two thousand dollars, more.

Major Hughes dominated the discussion. He had a big, solid-looking head, with a red-veined nose, a formidable moustache, and a beard that seemed to have been trimmed, in a fit of pique perhaps, to an abrupt jut of a thing, stiff and taut and out of balance with the luxuriant excess of his upper lip. If he had a wife he had not brought her with him and from the moment of his arrival set about to flatter me, appearing not to notice that I did not take his silk-eyed ogling and outrageous compliments as flattery. He was a man of self-importance, flatulent of mind, and as it turned out to my great disgust, of body too.

"Before the election," he declaimed after yet another toast, "the Radicals were wreathed in smiles, and they chuckled over the great victory in store for them. In this they reminded me of the anecdote I once heard of an Irishman and a bull. An Irishman was walking along the road one day, and observed in an adjoining field a bull wrought up almost to frenzy, pawing the ground and digging it up with his horns, and doing many other unreasonable things. The Irishman thought it would be rare fun to catch him by the horns and rub his nose in the dirt, and the more he thought of it the funnier it got until he rolled over with laughter and glee. Finally he could resist the temptation no longer, so he jumped over the fence, seized the bull by the horns and just as he was about to execute his plan of rubbing its nose in the dirt, he found himself tossed back over the fence, very much hurt and bruised. As he limped sadly away he remarked, 'Bejabbers, it's a mighty fine thing that I had my laugh first.'

"And so it is with the Radicals. It is well they had their laugh before the election, for if one of them has smiled since I have not seen it. The Negroes have at last come to their senses, I am glad to say. Only three or four carpetbaggers returned to the legislature! That is something to celebrate indeed."

He made a booming sound like a roll of drums inside his chest, then drained his glass, and by an inclination of his shoulder, drew Jacob to him, wine carafe in hand. Another full glass poured, Major Hughes glanced around the table with a look of whimsical regret. "I'm sorry to see, though, that our sister city Wilmington did not succeed in ousting that warlike fellow Galloway."

"No matter what sense you think the Negroes may have come to elsewhere," Mister Pender said in his sour voice, "those in this part of the state have not."

Major Hughes turned his head and looked at him as though sizing him up and finding him to be nothing but a little man.

Christopher, with a quick sideways glance at me, said, "He's very popular in Wilmington. Even with some whites who should know better."

"Nonsense." Mister Pender spoke emphatically. "It's the Negroes who hoist him into office, and despite our best efforts, hoist him back again."

"You can't blame Wilmington for Galloway," the Colonel said. "He's from New Bern. Major Hughes must take the blame."

Major Hughes set his fists against the table and tipped back in his chair, a ponderous, condescending movement. "My dear Colonel," he said heartily, "we refuse to let you pass the blame to us. After all, when it comes down to it, the fellow is from Smithville, so Mister Pender is responsible."

"That's not entirely true," Mister Pender said. "His father may have fetched him down to Smithville for a time before he sold him, to a railroad engineer, I believe, but he was bred upriver on the Galloway plantation."

"Do you mind, sir? Do you mind?" the Colonel said. "There are ladies present."

Until now I had not said a word, but this I could not resist. "Oh, yes," I said airily. "Mister Galloway's quite frank about it. A child of the South, he calls himself." I looked around. Everyone was staring and I made my face look innocent. "By which he means a half-breed."

Mister Pender flushed. "John Wesley Galloway was a good and honorable man."

"A man who sold his son," I said, "his blood. A man who went to war and died to keep his son a slave."

For a moment I thought I'd gone too far, but Mister Carrolton interrupted. "He did not *go* to war, young lady. He was impressed. The recruiters had a time of it, I tell you. I was one of them. Chased him up and down the coast, he slippery as the devil. And as for dying to keep his son a slave, he died of yellow fever off in the Bahamas."

"Oh," I said. "I thought . . . I heard . . . I thought I heard . . ."

"Yes, dear, we understand," Cousin Kate said. She swung her gaze around her guests. "You must excuse Eugenia. She does not mean . . ." She leaned in, lowering her voice. "It is her *work*, you see. She is out among the coloreds all the time, and such a *blessing* to them too, but she is acquainted with a side of life less *charitable* young ladies never see or hear. She tends to pick up *notions*."

I started to be angry, but when I saw her wrinkle up her nose and smile winsomely around the table, I realized that by embarrassing me she had saved me from embarrassing myself.

She looked up at the clock. "But now, gentlemen, off with you to the Colonel's study. We have a fine cognac for you and some superb cigars he himself imported. And then we must *decamp*. The parade is due to start in half an hour."

THE half hour up, we ladies arrived downstairs with our noses powdered and our hair in place. The Colonel's study door was still tight closed, the rumble of men's voices going on behind it, and so we gathered in the parlor.

"Do you think we should disturb them?" Cousin Kate said. She was a woman of great spirit, but interrupt her husband in his study? Never.

And so I volunteered. I tapped and pushed the door aside and entered, almost in one motion. Mister Carrolton and Mister Pender were standing with Christopher and the Colonel by the window, deep in smoke-wreathed conversation. The Colonel broke off in the middle of a sentence and all four turned accusing-faced toward me, glasses and cigars in hand, as though the sacred temple of cognac and tobacco had just been profaned.

"I'm sorry, gentlemen," I said. "It's getting late."

I had not seen Major Hughes yet, but soon discovered he had so enjoyed the cognac that he had fallen off to sleep in the Colonel's leather armchair, his jaw dropped and his heavy thighs spread wide. No amount of shaking or shouting in his ear would rouse him, so we left him there, apparently to no one's chagrin, and set off along the road toward the Conservative headquarters building at the corner of Market Street and Second.

It was now eight o'clock, the sky turned puce against the

blaze of torches, flaming tar barrels, rockets shot into the air. The Conservative headquarters was an imposing building, brick, with brass lanterns mounted on each side of the front door. Its windows sported patriotic buntings and glowed with gaily colored lanterns, the houses all around lit up with lamps and lanterns set on windowsills, in doorways, slung under verandahs, from fences and gazebos. And the shouting, laughing, someone weeping with emotion, shrieking children running in and out with dogs lolloping behind, the din punctuated now and then by the resonant deep boom of cannon coming from the waterfront.

Negroes were there too, some of whom I recognized as having gone with the Conservatives, for that haunch of ham, perhaps, or in peril of ejection from a job, maybe even from conviction. Others I knew to be passionate Republicans, and as I had no option but to be there, I hoped they would not notice me, or if they did, forgive me. If Abraham had been there I would have truly been embarrassed, but he had left town with Martha, who had surprised us all by coming down for the election. Indeed, she had been quite the heroine, standing beside her husband at the polls "to watch out for assassins."

The minute Abraham had made his winner's speech, she became intent on once more getting out of town, and making him come too because "Who knows what will happen now?" She even begged Mother Hester to come with them, but Mother Hester was as fixed to her front porch as if she were part of its construction. When Martha discovered Abraham intended to stay in Beaufort only long enough to see her safely settled with her parents, she burst into accusing tears. "You have a yen for martyrdom."

"Sweetheart," he said, "if they will set assassins on me, they can set them anywhere, but I do not think the mood against me is that violent, truly I do not. The Conservatives may not be happy with my reelection, but they have put up with me for two years now and I think their joy at having ousted so many Republicans will counter their dismay at having me for two years more. At least they know I'm honest."

"You have a duty to your family."

"I have a duty to my people. Come, come, don't cry. You married a politician, after all. Come, sweetheart, if it will make you happy I'll stay with you until things settle down. A week or two maybe."

At the time I had agreed with his decision, but now, full of the revelation about his father, I could not wait for his return. Could John Wesley Galloway's resistance to the draft mean that he had loved his son? And I plunged into an imaginary conversation in which Abraham came to understand he had.

Christopher bent and set his mouth against my ear. "What are you thinking on so deeply?"

I looked up at him and smiled. He was my walking partner for the night and kept a firm grip on my arm, perhaps from sympathy because he knew I did not want to be there, or because he feared I might run off, or perhaps he thought that by making me participate he might transform me into a Conservative.

I admit there was a fascination to the evening. No, I lie, there was a grand excitement. If I had been a Conservative, I would have been transported, as everyone around me seemed to be. Celebration is too weak a word. It was like a moving gala, an ecstasy of vindication, an ancient Roman triumph. Not before or since have I been witness to such a hedonistic feast of exultation—see how I run out of words? And yet I sensed an underlay of something not pure joy, relief perhaps, and yet with malice in it—no, more than that, malevolence. With half my soul, the white half, I sympathized because I understood, but the black half of me shivered.

It was to be a night of speeches. Colonel Cowan came out to the balcony and raised his hands for silence. "We have accomplished an absolute world's wonder," he told us. "North Carolina is redeemed." And he went on to speak about "our cause," at which I sensed a sort of wincing in the crowd, as though this expression reminded them too painfully of their Lost Cause. Colonel Cowan seemed to sense it too, and quickly changed "our cause" to "our purpose," which, he said, had been misrepresented.

Heckling started on the edges of the crowd and I hoped the night would not slide into fisticuffs. Colonel Cowan stretched his neck and turned his gaze toward the culprits.

"On the day of the election," he said in his outraged politician's voice, "circulars were issued, and since the election, reports have been industriously circulated to the effect that it is the intention of the Conservatives to put the Negroes back into slavery."

A murmur ran through the people down below him, a good many of whom would have liked to do just that.

"You have ruled us," he said, still speaking to the Negroes, "with a rod of iron ever since you had the vote—you have ruled us improperly—and we do not intend you should rule us any longer if we can help it. We do not admit that Negro equality means Negro supremacy, and we never shall admit it, but we have no idea of interfering with any of your civil rights. And as for reducing you to slavery again, I tell you here in the face of this assemblage, if it is ever attempted, I will take your side and help you to resist it."

A scuffle broke out at the back—someone threw a stone and someone's face was cut—and Colonel Cowan's speech came abruptly to an end. It had been a spirit dampener and the crowd was not so wild with joy as it advanced down Front Street, where the lightwood torches were discarded and spirit lamps and spirit-soaked balls of cotton on the ends of poles taken up instead. This lit up the procession with a wilder, brighter light, and seemed to have the same effect on people's spirits. The cheering started up again, a band struck up, and the crowd swung into a march, waving handkerchiefs and roaring its approval outside each illuminated house, groaning its way past houses where dark windows announced the lair of a Republican.

A handsome trading vessel done up as the Old Ship of State rocked beside the wharf, banners and streamers pendant from its mast, and manned by youthful seamen in full marine costume. These were responsible for the firing of the cannon, which we heard later could be heard as far away as New Bern, almost thirty miles!

In all the jostling, Christopher and I became separated from the rest of our party. We were casting about to find them when I spotted Sylvie Younger sailing through the crowd with full sails set toward us.

"Here comes your Sylvie," I said teasingly. "I'd best find Aunt Lavinia and the others so you two can be alone."

"Sylvie? Not tonight!"

"Why, Christopher!"

But he grabbed my hand and we went scuttling off together like a pair of wicked children, giggling a little, embarrassed at ourselves, with the intimacy of conspirators.

The procession moved to Mister Waddell's house at Third and Orange. He came out to the balcony with the air of a man accustomed to being listened to. He was, I think, the most ebullient person in the whole parade, having just been elected to the U.S. Congress, where he would be put in charge of post roads and post offices. He assured the Negroes that the Conservatives were their true friends while at the same time setting the gentry back into their rightful ruling place, with underneath the merest hint of threat. He was a man beloved in the town. I did not trust him one iota.

I grew tired of speeches, irritated by the accusations of corruption, the exclamations about dear old Carolina and our glorious victory, the sentimental blather about honored names and the proud bearing of the Southern nobleman, the tearful *Thank God*s that the Old North State was now back in the hands of her true sons. And as for the meal-mouthed adulation of the Southern woman! I do not think I ever met a woman as noble, virtuous, or of such a sensitive and shrinking nature as we have been made out to be. Certainly I am not so myself, and Cousin Kate was hardly shrinking. Maybe Aunt

Lavinia fit the bill for sensitive, although her affair with Doctor Wilkins ruled out virtuous.

Now it was Colonel McClammy's turn to get up and say his piece. My irritation turned to anger as he swung into another highfalutin rant against the fallen Radicals. "Viciousness," he said, "venality" (as if we had not heard both ad nauseam), "outraging every sentiment of virtue, decency, and Southern pride."

Like the other speakers, he offered neither proof nor evidence, nor even anecdotes spun out of gossip (Abraham would have driven his point home with a good joke), and I wanted to leap out and answer him. I wanted to demand an accounting for all the poison spewed these last few years because of a few black faces in the legislature. I wanted to weep, to hit out at someone very hard. I wanted to shout, "Liar! Distorter! Bigot! Smug-faced, presumptuous prig! What about the good done? What about the good?"

Of course I didn't, just ceased to pay attention, and heard nothing of the rest of the McClammy speech except one phrase which leaped into my ear: *De mortuis nil nisi bonum*—Of the dead, nothing but good. It would come back to haunt me.

We moved on to Mister Heyer's residence at the corner of Fourth and Red Cross, just south of the railroad. This was a poorer section of town, and Mister Heyer, perhaps because he was the county treasurer, gave a dry, cataloguing sort of speech, abrasive in its tone and without a single decorative flourish. It was an odd stop on the route, uncomfortable, but I understood it, and when Christopher's grip grew firmer on my arm, I knew that he did too.

Across the railroad, just a stone's throw off, was Abraham's house. It could not be seen. The brilliance of the procession, with its lamps and torches, turned everything beyond it deepest black. I peered, squinting up my eyes, but not a light could I discern, not so much as the outline of the roof. It was as though the house, with my beloved Mother Hester and her beloved Joel, had been swallowed up. This stop had been intended as a challenge, the throw-down of a gauntlet, I was sure of it. I shuddered with foreboding.

What happened after that I don't remember. I was swept along unseeing and unhearing. There were other speeches, I suppose, but all I can remember is the pressure of the crowd, its deafening loudness, and its waves of exultation and depression, like a giant breathing. And through it all, Christopher's exigent, sympathetic hand upon my arm.

On the way home, he had us fall behind. "I'm sorry about that," he said, "it was in bad taste, making speeches within earshot of your friend's house."

I shrugged it off.

"I felt you were upset."

"I found it rude."

"Will you tell him I apologize?"

"Apologize? You did not make the speech."

"I feel responsible."

I turned to look at him. "What has got into you, Christopher? Abraham is a Republican, a Radical. He's on the other side."

"So are you. And yet I love you."

"You would apologize to him for my sake?"

"Eugenia, sweetheart, will you marry me?"

I stopped dead in my tracks. "Marry you? Good heavens! And you in love with Sylvie Younger!"

"Sylvie Younger? What fantasy is this?"

"I thought you were in love with her."

"My foolish sweet, it's you I love. Have I not said the same a thousand times?"

And I had responded lightly that I loved him too, knowing but not acknowledging that there was something more to it on his side than the affection of a cousin.

"Have I not told you I intended to marry as soon as I was on my feet? Have I not also told you *that* a thousand times?"

"You did not indicate to whom."

"It seems to me I made it very clear." He was laughing now, pressing my arm in quite a different way as he drew me into the shadow of an overhanging tree. "Come, come, what do you think? Do we not make a handsome pair?"

"But what of Sylvie Younger?"

"I am kind to her for your sake, because she is your friend. Sweetheart, I have loved you from the minute I first saw you on the train. No, long before. Since that morning when we saw the fog bow at the beach."

"Christopher, I cannot marry you."

He made a sound of disbelief. "Come, Eugenia, it does not suit you to be coy."

An alarm of pity went through me. I wanted to reassure, to warn, to reprimand, but most of all to keep all revelation of myself inside. How clumsy I had been. I had misled him. How could I now confess to loving Tom? Blood rushed and rushed into my head and blossomed through my skin in hot red guilty flowers. I could not speak. I could not breathe. My cousin's face grew large and small and large again, and all my bones dissolved. He took me in his arms murmuring endearments, *sweet* and *dear* and *oh, my love*, and I leaned into him, helpless to resist.

I do not know how long we stood there melded to each other, I lost consciousness I think, but eventually I became aware of his hands moving on my body and his mouth against my neck. I pulled away, began to speak, but there was no way to explain. A man asks you to marry him, you swoon into his arms, what explanation can you give?

"You do love me, do you not?"

"I do, of course I do, but I cannot love you as a wife."

"Because of *him*? Eugenia, how could you? He's a *Negro*."

I had never mentioned Tom to Christopher, not one word, one hint, one innuendo. Had he been spying on my letters? Had he steamed them open, reading them before they got to me? Or crept into my cottage when I was away and sat down at my desk?

"I must go home," I said. "I am unwell. Christopher, let go my arm. You're hurting me."

He stiffened and then backed away, both hands behind his back. "I'm sorry, oh Eugenia, I'm so sorry. Have I injured you?"

I rubbed my arm. "A slight bruise, maybe. Nothing."

"I'm very, very sorry. I did not mean . . . It was emotion." He fairly bounced with agitation, one eye glinting in the dark mass of his head. "Eugenia, you must marry me, you must marry me and save yourself."

"Save myself? Christopher, you frighten me. Whatever can you mean?"

"The shame, Eugenia, the shame. You would become an outcast in society. A *Negro* and a *married man.*"

"Married? Oh, I see. You speak of Mister Galloway."

"Who else? You have another lover?"

"Don't be foolish. Abraham is not my lover. You know that. He is my friend."

"Then marry me."

"I cannot."

"And I cannot guarantee his safety."

"Surely you would not have me choose—my cousin or my friend?"

"Life is full of choices. You've had it both ways ever since you came back here to Wilmington. But you cannot go on like this. You must declare allegiance to one side or the other." He snatched my hand. "Eugenia, for God's sake, and for your so-called friend's as well, please say you'll marry me."

"You will protect him?"

"I will see to it."

I thought of my dear Tom.

Of Abraham dead on the ground.

I said, "I will."

CHAPTER TWENTY-EIGHT

SOME days of misery went by. I do not know how many. And now I faced another sleepless night. Worry about the promise I had made to Christopher made such a clangor in my brain I knew there was no point in going to bed. So without bothering to get into my nightgown, I lit the lamp and propped myself on the couch with my feet up on a pillow and lay there all night trying to figure out solutions.

I fell into a doze as dawn was breaking, but a bull alligator bellowed in the swamp, and another and another, the sound carried on the dead-still air. A cock crowed, birds began their morning agitation, and up and down the street cows lowed, impatient for the cowherd to come ringing his bell and take them out to pasture. I gave up then and went to draw the curtains back. As I did so, I saw Aunt Lavinia, in a pale mauve dressing gown and slippers, stepping stealthily along the path toward me. I ran to let her in.

"What is it? Is someone ill?"

Her eyes were ringed with shadows, her hair disheveled, her sleeping net tipsily across one ear. "Eugenia Mae," she said the minute she had entered, "I have lain awake all night in a fit of indecision."

"About what?"

"About whether I should tell you."

"Tell me what?"

"That you cannot marry Christopher."

"Who told you he had asked me?"

"Why, Christopher of course. He wanted my advice on how to break it to his parents."

"Break? You sound as though they might be disapproving."

"My dear, these things are delicate. It's not as though you . . . never mind."

"Not as though I brought with me a fortune? Not as though I'd not disgraced myself by working with the poor?"

"Now, now, don't get upset. Nothing like that matters in the face of . . . of . . . my dear, I know the mulattoes of this town, especially the white ones, like to feel themselves our equals, and to some extent, for the purpose of not stirring up contention, we must let them think it. Some of their fathers openly acknowledge them, and there is a place for them in civilized society, a certain type of place. But when it comes to marriage, it simply cannot be allowed, it cannot be done."

"What are you telling me?"

"My dear, surely you know, surely your papa . . . no, perhaps he did not. It was unwise of him, he should have told you. Still, you are fortunate I have come to you like this, in kindness, you understand, in perfect kindness, because Eugenia, I'm very fond of you and do not wish to see you suffer. If you had married unawares and the evidence came in the first child, or the second, Christopher's law practice would be ruined and the family shamed as well."

My heart was thudding in my throat. "Please speak plain."

"Come sit with me, my dear." She went to the couch and sat, patting the seat beside her. "There, that's better. Your father . . ." She stopped, looking intently at the wallpaper as though its stripes and roses might inspire the proper words. "Your father . . . oh dear, this is very difficult."

"Are you telling me I am mulatto, that my father had me of a slave?"

She set her hand against her breast. "There, it has been said and I am grateful not to have the sentence pass my lips."

"Who was this slave? What is her name?"

"That I cannot tell you."

"But if she is my mother I must know. Is her name Tilda? Is it?"

"I do not know."

"Look at me, Aunt Lavinia. Look into my eyes and tell me you don't know."

She looked into my eyes. "I do not know. But it's quite impossible for you to marry Christopher."

"Who told you I'm mulatto? Your Doctor Wilkins?"

"Eugenia, you must not blame me."

My breath came rapid and my head grew faint. So Aunt Lavinia's lover had told her after all. And now did everybody know? Had the family's social set been practicing discretion? Had there been whispers behind hands, winks and nods in coffee shops and murmurs in masonic lodges? Nothing gauche, of course, nothing blatant, boorish, or indelicate. A hint, a lowering of the eyes, a pinching of the lips, a sort of social nudging. I had thought I had been unhindered in my work because it was an evidence of virtue in the gentry, a natural condescension to a lower caste. Now it seemed as if a crowd of people shouted in my face: I had been left alone because I was mulatto. And yet, because I was so white, and because the Clark-Comptons were the Clark-Comptons after all, the whole business had been ignored, a semiblind aristocratic eye turned decorously toward it and then turned away.

"And so the whole town knows?" My voice came high-pitched, vanishing.

"Come now, dear, no need for hysterics. Doctor Wilkins I immediately swore to secrecy, and I myself have spoken not one word. No one knows, of that I am completely certain. A secret between two can be held tight, a secret held by more is not a secret. You know how gossip goes."

"You did not confide in Cousin Kate?"

"I did not. Eugenia, I may seem to you a fribbling woman, but I do know how to keep my mouth shut. And I know the ways of men. Southern women have always been supposed to be sweet innocents, to close our eyes to our men's wicked recreations. I may gripe and rail because the slaves are free, which goes against the grain, but I am glad, too, for their freedom. Why? Because it cuts our men off from their women, it forces them along the path of righteousness. Eugenia"—she took me in her arms and held me tight against her—"Eugenia, I have suffered as your mother must have suffered, Cousin Kate as well. We were not obliged to raise a child not our own, but we have had to watch them running on our properties and smile and make no comment on their lightness or that they wear our husband's faces. Do not blame your father. He was just a man, with the weakness of a man, and he did love you, you must admit that. He was cruel to his wife, but he did love his daughter. Eugenia dear, you must not blame me."

"I do not blame you, Aunt Lavinia."

"You will tell Christopher you cannot marry him? I can trust you to do that? Of course no need to tell him why. A general excuse will do. Just say you've changed your mind, you only love him as a cousin, anything you like. You'll find him in his office. I did not come to you until he'd gone off for the day because I wanted you calm before you spoke to him. He plans to make a great announcement once he has his parents' blessing and we would not want him embarrassed . . . wait, don't go rushing off. My dear, do sit . . ."

But I was already out the door, her voice plaintive behind me.

CHAPTER TWENTY-NINE

THE market bell rang six as I headed for the waterfront, my thoughts racing every which way. I had barely reached it when a little boy came gasping to plant himself in front of me, his eyes standing in his head and his hair straight up like a figure of a child in fright.

"Come quick, Miss Eugenia, please come quick."

"What is it? What?"

"Mister Galloway, Miss Eugenia."

"Oh, dear God! What is it? Tell me!"

"I been told to say come quick."

I pulled a coin out of my pocket. "Run to the post office. Send a telegram to Tom Maryson, of Maryson near Chapel

Hill. Have it say 'Come now,' and sign it 'Eugenia'." I grabbed him by the shoulders and looked into his face. "Can you remember that?"

He nodded.

"Then run, *run*! As fast as you can!"

I ran myself then, already knowing, that dizzying certainty that teeters on the edge of doubt, the word spreading silently around me as I went, shoving from my path the people streaming from their houses, their throats a wordless questioning, so that the streets I ran through seemed already draped in loss.

The door stood open and I ran in without stopping to the bedside. Mister Eagles was already there. "It is the shivering season, it is the shivering season," he whispered, like an incantation.

Abraham was shaking violently, hot sweat running onto sheets already slick with it, and a convulsion coming, his eyes rolling, his back arching with such ferocious strength it took both of us to hold him on the bed. Mother Hester, who had snapped into full clarity, clutched a basin of cold water and a rag and was sluicing water on his almost naked body.

The convulsion eased and he lay exhausted, his only movement a continuous surface shivering of skin, and the sweat still running as though the hands of God had reached down out of heaven to wring him dry.

"Drink this, drink this, sweet boy," his mother crooned, but although I held his head up, his jaw was shut so tight we could not get a drop of water into him.

Mister Eagles fumbled in his pocket and produced a bottle of Hostetter's Stomach Bitters.

"I think it will not help," I said, "but we can try."

This time we managed to open his mouth a little and Mister Eagles dripped some medicine between his teeth while I rubbed his throat to help it down, but the liquid ran out from the corners of his mouth. A new convulsion started. It came and went without developing.

"You should have called me earlier," I said. "He has been sick for hours."

Mother Hester set the bowl down on the bed and wrung the cloth out into it. "He been sick not yet an hour. Walked in on his own two feet and said he had a headache from the rockin' of the train. I set about to make some tea, but he took to vomitin' and shakin' and his legs collapsin' under him."

Mister Eagles said, "I've never seen the yellow fever work so fast."

"The yellow fever?" Mother Hester said. "Don't you know nothin' a-tall?"

"It's the shivering season, what else could it be?"

"Ain't you got no ears on your head? Ain't you heered the things they says agin him? Ain't you heered the whispers and the threats? And weren't it *you* they got to last time with their poison?"

"Last time they went for Abraham it was with a knife. The time before, with sticks."

"They have poisoned him this time."

"I recovered when they poisoned me. He will recover too."

Mother Hester made a spitting sound. "They done learned from you. They done give him a good dose."

"More emetic then."

"He already brought up everythin' inside hisself."

Outside the house a rustling like the wind in trees and the murmuring of voices. The market bell rang seven.

Mister Eagles drew his hand across his forehead. "There's nothing more to do but pray. Where are Martha and the children?" He looked about as though he had just realized they were missing.

"In Beaufort still, and we can thank the Lord for it," Mother Hester said.

"We must send her a telegram. And call a preacher."

"Don't want no preacher tellin' his good lies. God ain't agreed to this. He raised my boy up like he done that Moses, to lead his people through the wilderness." She laughed harshly, her voice rising. "He raised him up and then he plumb forgot him, let them fellers in big houses get to him. He shoulda done better for my boy. Shoulda done better for my people. We suffered hard as Moses's people, suffered all these years, us women there just for the usin', and then they takes away our children, our own children, and give them to their wives."

"What did you say?" I said.

"I said they stoled our little babes." Tears dripped off her chin.

"But Abraham came back to you," Mister Eagles said. "God gave you his freedom years."

Mother Hester looked fiercely at him, her fists bunched as though she would do battle. "They done stole my little babe what I had not a minute held. I never seed that babe again, did not know what they even called her for a name to look for her."

304

"*Her?*" I said. "Did you say *her?*"

"Sit down, Mother Hester," Mister Eagles said. "You must not exhaust yourself."

Mother Hester gave a great sigh and sat down heavily. "Tilda, they says to me, you is no good to us now, we is going to sell you off." She wiped the back of her hand across her chin and set her fists beneath her breasts. "They done hurt me *here*. And now they have done this."

"There is still hope," Mister Eagles said, but I brushed him aside.

"Mother Hester, did you say your name was Tilda?"

"That were what they called me. Hester is my name, I said to them, but the missus's name were Hester too. She were too proud for a slave to have her name."

"*Who* was too proud? What was the missus's name?"

"I done told you—Hester."

"But who took your baby girl? Was it Hester's husband?"

"Don't matter now, don't matter. They gone off now, my babe with them, don't know nothin' what became them."

"What was his name? Tell me his name."

She shook her head. "Don't matter, it don't matter."

"Was his name Spotswood? Tell me, was it Spotswood?"

"It were, the same as yourn. It were why I took you to my heart so, child. I say to myself, here this sweet girl what coulda been my own."

"Why did you not say something? Why did you not question me?"

"How could I, child? How could I?"

With one hand on Abraham's breast, I leaned and kissed

him on the mouth. *Oh, my brother. Oh, my brother.* His lips were soft and giving, no response.

I straightened, my hand still on his breast, which rose and fell so faintly the movement was almost imperceptible. His sweating had stopped, he did not shiver, but lay limp.

"Kiss him, Mother Hester. Kiss him while he lives."

With a heavy movement, she leaned and kissed him, then sat back in her chair, her eyes going from Abraham's face to mine and back again, recognition kindling in her eyes. I took her in my arms. I could not speak. *My mother. Oh, my mother.*

The market bell rang eight. Outside, the silence of a breathing crowd.

Mister Eagles whispered, "It's best that I go out and tell them."

He went. I heard his voice, but could not hear the words. I had expected grief and shock to form itself in noise, but there was silence still, nothing but that breathing, and with it now a sort of distant unbelief, like the echo of a long and solitary journey just begun.

CHAPTER THIRTY

THE newspaper next day announced his death. A plain
announcement, and a lie:

*Abraham H. Galloway, a prominent colored politician of
this section, died at his house in this city yesterday morning. He had been suffering for some time under an illness
combined of bilious fever and jaundice, which resulted
in his death yesterday. The funeral will take place from
his residence in this city, then to St. Paul's (Episcopal)
Church, tomorrow (Saturday) morning, at 10 o'clock.* De
mortuis nil nisi bonum.

De mortuis nil nisi bonum—of the dead nothing but good. "As if there is something wicked they could tell, but in their great benevolence refrain. How *dare* they!"

"How dare they what? And where on earth have you been? Mother has been worried half to death." Christopher stood looking at me from the doorway of the morning room. "What is it? What's the matter?"

I shook the *Journal* at him. "Surely you have seen this? Surely you must know."

He came into the room and took it from me, folded it, and set it on the window seat. "Eugenia, my dear wife . . ."

He moved as though he would embrace me, but I stepped away. "You promised me," I said. "You promised."

A shadow came behind his eyes. "I did my best. I did. But who am I to stay the hand of God?"

"The hand of God, my eye!"

"Eugenia, sweetheart, you're taking this too hard."

"Get out of here! Go on, get out!" I flung away, suddenly exhausted, and afraid, too, of my emotions, which until now had been steady, purposeful, directed, in the way of a nurse in an emergency. A shadowy light fell on the newspaper folded on the window seat, making the small square of Abraham's obituary appear distorted, huge. A draft of air, a dropping of the blood, a clatter in my head, a rapping sound like someone beating on a drum, a black figure out on the back porch, swaying and dissolving—it was the waiter Jacob—and Christopher's blond head dissolving into it, a hard whisper coming at me through the window, ricocheting back and forth, the sensation of a fall begun.

I woke to the wrench of smelling salts and Cousin Kate's face above me, a pink fan frantic in her hand, a small green bottle in the other. Beside her, Aunt Lavinia with a glass of water and an expression of disaster. Christopher, pale, apologetic, hovered just above her shoulder. I spoke to him.

"If you will help me to my room, I will get some sleep."

NEXT morning I did not go to breakfast, could not bear to eat, could barely dress myself or comb my hair. At eight I dragged myself across the garden to the house, intending to slip out and go to Mother Hester's. As I went along the passageway, the Colonel called out from his study, "Eugenia? Is that you, Eugenia Mae?"

I ignored him but he called again, at the same moment appearing in the door, his face white and the collar of his shirt askew. Christopher came behind him, his eyes shifting from his father to me and back again.

The Colonel said, "Where are you going?"

"To Mister Galloway's funeral, of course."

"You are doing no such thing. There will be trouble in this town today." His beard worked below his moustache. "It is a . . . a disgrace," he said at last, the word coming from him like a small explosion. "It is . . . irresponsible. An invitation to an insurrection."

He peered toward the sidelight by the front door as if expecting a crowd of dark-faced retribution to appear. "Wife!" he called and Cousin Kate came running down the stairs with Aunt Lavinia at her back. "Wife, see that all the servants are dismissed. We want no servants on our property today. And stay inside, everybody stay inside, do not so much as show your noses."

He reached up and seized his head in his hands, clinging to it as though he feared it might fall off. "There will be blood today, there will be blood, I sense it coming."

"Sir," I said, "when I was working at the gold mine, rumors came flying every day of runaways gathering their forces in the woods, marching down the road to cut our throats. But nothing ever came of it. The Negroes are a peaceful race. They are used to evil being done them. They have learned to turn their eyes to God and wait."

"To wait? For what? What are they waiting for?"

Heat came inside my head. "Sir, if I should suspect you of complicity, if I should discover evidence you are involved . . ."

His mouth fell open, his pink lips working under his moustache. "I swear," he said. "Eugenia Mae, I swear . . ." He swung on Christopher. "Is this your doing? Is it?"

Christopher drew himself up haughtily, as though insulted by the question. "I have inquired. There is no evidence of foul play."

"And so they triumph," I said bitterly.

"Eugenia, you must take care," the Colonel said. "You must not go to the funeral. You must stay here with us. We must lock the doors and bolt the shutters."

"Oh no," I said, "you will not shut me in. I will attend his funeral."

"No," the Colonel said, "you will not. You are family, I'll not let you into danger's path."

"These people are my friends, many are my patients, they know me well. They are my family too, and Abraham my brother."

Aunt Lavinia made a little mewing sound, but the Colonel did not seem to notice. "That's as may be," he said, "and you're a kind, good woman, the way you have taken these people to your heart. But we are your true family and I beg you, in our hour of fear, to stand beside us."

"I assure you, there's nothing to fear. There will be no insurrection."

"Eugenia Mae, I beg you. Consider your Cousin Kate's sensibilities, and Lavinia is frail in her emotions. Do not add the burden of anxiety for you."

"But what about Abraham's mother? She has lost a son. She needs to be supported through the ordeal of this day by those who loved him."

Christopher sniffed. "Are you not taking sympathy a little far?"

"Be quiet, Christopher," the Colonel said. "Eugenia, did we not take you in and love you when you were bereft? Did we not care for you when you were deathly ill? Provide you luxuries that you could not afford? Turn a blind eye to your politics? Tolerate you mixing every day with people of low caste? Do you not owe us loyalty for that? I have lost a son and daughter in my life. I do not want to lose another daughter."

"Sir, I love you, you know that."

His eyes teared up. "Then you will stay with us?"

"For today only," Aunt Lavinia interrupted. Her voice was

firm and everybody turned to her, surprised. "But tomorrow you may go anywhere you wish. Eugenia, I have not spoken of my losses to you, but when my husband died I thought I would die with him. When my son went too, I thought I would never rise again. But then I came to stay here with my brother and his dear, good wife, and their love and kindness lifted me. So, my dear, you must go to this poor woman who has also lost a son, you must love and comfort her, but you must also give your love and comfort to the family who took you in as they took me. Do not think of it as a choice, think of it as sharing. You have a big heart, dear, and a spirit full of generosity. You have enough for all."

I bowed my head. "You must let me watch the cortege from the upper balcony."

FROM the balcony I heard the bells ring in St. Paul's. I waited, telling myself I should go down and mourn, telling myself I was obliged to stay away, that it was better so, that I should let Abraham's people mourn for him alone. Telling myself I was his people too. If only I had got to him in time to tell him that his father loved him. If only he had lived long enough to know I was the sister of his blood.

And then I thought of Christopher, who did not yet know he would not be my husband. I thought about when I had met him coming on the train to Wilmington, how there had been a shadow in his eyes, an almost furtiveness, an almost lack, a hint of violence, which I had put down to the horrors he had seen at war. I thought of how that shadow faded as time

312

passed, and how, for a moment when we argued yesterday, it had come back.

My mind cleared to the scene when I had fainted, saw again the sharp rectangle of window and felt the flow of air, heard the clattering of boots, the rap-rap-rap at the back door. I saw Jacob with his hand held out, and Christopher low-voiced and urgent, "Later. Get out of here before she sees you."

Before she sees you? Who would Christopher not want to see Jacob? Had he got himself in trouble of some sort? Gambling perhaps? No, for that he would not come to Christopher. Was Gladys ill, then? She had been in fine health when Cousin Kate sent her off this morning. And what did *Later* mean?

I looked out across the trees toward the steeple of St. Paul's. Everything was quiet. It was a lovely day, no wind, not even breeze, just perfect stillness and blue sky above, and it seemed to me that I had joined Mother Hester in her other world, where everything was something else. Once I remarked to myself that the service went on very long, once an image of a coffin set upon a covered table came to me, once I felt my throat constrict and then release.

Across the street a dog was dozing on the sidewalk. Behind it, yellow jessamine tumbled through the fence. Yellow jessamine. I thought of Gladys's poor child, dead from chewing at its roots. Of the way she had accepted her child's death without bitterness or blame. Of Jacob, cat-footed in his waiter's uniform. Jacob, a waiter on the New Bern line. Cat-footed Jacob stepping up to the back porch, holding out his hand to

Christopher. And then the Colonel's voice, "Is this your doing? Is it?" His son's evasive answer.

My elbows gave way under me and I half fell against the
brick wall of the balustrade. It was my fault, my fault alone.
My obstinate insistence on brandishing my intimacy with
Abraham as though it were a weapon. My mad insistence that
Christopher should know, should *know*. I had rubbed his face
in something which to him was vile. Black blood. Black blood.
I had spattered him and soiled him. And this after my stern
preachment to Miss Kellogg to be moderate, discreet, to creep
up on old Southern attitudes tiptoed and diplomatic. I had
warned her, but I had not warned myself. Instead I had become her. I had crusaded. I had *stood by Abraham*. And I had
killed him. And had not yet wept. If I could only weep.

With the mild sun on my head, I felt a gathering inside me,
a strange force traveling along a multitude of tiny narrow tun-
nels toward a place low down in my belly, as if a goblin child
bred on me by grief was bundling itself together piece by
spiteful piece, an evil thing, malign and vengeful, made of dis-
embodied sound.

And then the tolling of the church bell at St. Paul's and a
sensation in the air of a mass of people moving.

NEWSPAPERS both North and South reported on that day, some
terse, ascerbic, condescending, some with generosity, which
I suppose they could afford now Abraham was dead. The
Christian Recorder out of Philadelphia was kind, calling him
an acknowledged leader, bold, brave, defiant, patriotic, a

guiding star amongst his host of friends. *Abraham H. Galloway's funeral,* it reported, *was the largest ever known in this State, over six thousand people following him to the cemetery. The flags in all the public buildings were half-masted, and everything possible done to honor the distinguished deceased.*

What no newspaper reported was that his funeral was silent. None of the usual howling and wailing and singing, the blowing of trumpets, the ringing of bells. Can't you see it? That procession. Six thousand Negroes weeping soundless through the white sand streets of Wilmington. Even the gulls are mute and no dog barks. The air smells sulphurous, rising off the swamps, and all the flags hang limp. No sound but the creak of springs, the grind of wheels, the pad-pad-pad of hooves and feet.

Here the firemen marching with their fire trucks polished up and gleaming, drawn by horses with black ribbons twisted in their manes and tails. Here the traps and buggies of prosperous mulattoes, the mule carts of the striving, the broken shoes and no shoes of the poor. Children from the freedmen's schools led by Yankee schoolma'ams, children from the orphanage, children from the slums and alleys and the makeshift shacks and cabins on the edge of town. Watermen and stevedores come up from the docks, turpentiners come out of the forests, farmhands from the fields. Switchmen, flagmen, brakemen, waiters, freight inspectors from the railroad yards, an entire platoon of uniformed police.

Here are barrel makers, blacksmiths, carpenters, mechanics, saddlers, cooks, St. Paul's choir with prayer books in their hands, the black-robed reverend from St. John's, the town band shouldering mute instruments, newspaper reporters, solemn-faced assemblymen and senators. Officials of the city government, officials of the county, officials of the customs house, carriages at large. Masons in black armbands marching by their lodges—the Giblem Lodge, the Sons of Lavender, Good Templars, Grand Army of the Republic, Union Brothers, Veterans of the Union in dark blue double-breasted coats, bronze buttons gleaming in the sun, black hats across their hearts.

Before them all, drawn by a horse blacker than any of the mourners, the flag-draped hearse, its high spoked wheels turning, slowly turning, carrying the senator for Brunswick and New Hanover Counties (negro) off the page of history. And that weeping, that dreadful silent weeping, like an accusation.

As they move up Market Street, with its tightly shuttered windows and nervous blank-faced doors, a man steps from the crowd and comes ahead. He pushes our gate open and stands inside it on the path, just stands there looking at the house, his gentle big hands hanging at his sides. My heart, which has been wilting, starts to pound.

But now a movement back behind me and I turn. Christopher is standing in the doorway to the balcony. "Eugenia, dear?" he says. His voice is soft and kind and hesitant. Below us, on the street, the mourners pass and pass.

"I cannot marry you," I say.

Again that shadow in his eyes. He steps toward me, grabs my arms and backs me up against the balustrade. "What is this? What?" His fingers press into my flesh, and in that moment I realize I fear him. I cannot see Tom now, but I can sense him down below. If Christopher should see him . . . if he should demand an explanation for his presence here . . .

"Christopher, you're hurting me."

Again that sudden backing off, that leap into apology. "My dear, my sweet, I did not mean . . ."

I step around him, step inside.

"Eugenia? Dear?"

Step, panic in my throat, downstairs.

"Eugenia, come back! Come back here this minute!"

The front door swings behind me. Tom still stands inside the gate. I come toward him down the path.

AFTERWORD

Abraham has been forgotten now, and my dear Tom is dead.
He was a quiet man who harbored his thoughts and let them
calm before he sent them out onto the sea. If it had been up to
him, I would have known little of his story except what I was
witness to. Clyde was my raconteur. "Tell me about . . . ," I
used to say when we sat rocking our old bodies on the porch.
And he would clear his throat, and stretch his neck, and make
a settling movement with his shoulders. "It were early in the
morning," he would say, or, "That were the day I come out
in the yard and saw," and I would fall into the tale with him as
if I had been present and could see into everybody's minds.

Sometimes, in a pause of his confabulation, I would marvel at the way life works. When first I met Clyde in the Red String hospital in Salisbury, half frozen with a rotten leg and scurvy, I had taken him for no more than a toothless cracker tossed up on our doorstep by the war. But now here we were, unlikely soul mates, living our lives out together in this house Tom built for me on the hill above the two old cabins.

And then one morning Clyde came hopping to the porch as usual, his wooden leg swinging in his hand, and plonked himself down in his chair beside me. Between us rose the smell of coffee and fresh muffins—I am not too old to cook.

"Good morning, Clyde," I said. "It's going to be a lovely day. Look at that sky."

He did not look at it, of course. His first concern each morning had always been the examination of his stump for rot. That day I said, as I had said a thousand times, "Don't do that, don't do it anymore. You've lived a long, long life and you will die of cussedness, not rot."

He ignored me, as he always had, swinging his leg across his knee and twisting his head around to look. Usually he would grunt a bit and let his breath out in a sound like disappointment, but that day he said, "Uh huh, uh-huh," a disgusted and triumphant sound.

"Uh-huh what?" Although I knew, and was almost angry with him for it, the way he had expected and expected. The Bible says, "As your faith, so be it unto you," and if anyone I ever knew had faith in something happening, it was Clyde.

He turned a pair of doglike eyes on me. "I ain't goin' to be about the place to care for you no more."

I felt an urge to whack him, just reach across and whack

him. "Don't be foolish. Put your leg on and drink your coffee before it turns stone cold."

"Look here at this."

"It's nothing. Just a bruise. You've knocked it against something."

"No I ain't. It is the rot."

"Don't say that, do not say it. You'll wish it on yourself. Here, behave yourself and drink this coffee." But inside I was crying, cursing him and crying.

He let his stump slip off his knee and the two of us sat there, raising and lowering our cups, staring off into a brand-new day that smelled of fresh-turned soil and the sharp sweet smell of pine. And it seemed to me the stink of gangrene was already in the air.

At last I set my coffee down. "Have a muffin. They're blueberry, your favorite."

He ate, obedient as a child, and like a child, dropping crumbs across his shirtfront, not bothering to brush them off.

"I'm sorry, Clyde."

He finished the muffin, washed it down with coffee, and set his cup back on the cane-topped table in between us. From the corner of my eye I saw him tilt his head from side to side, pushing out his bottom dentures in that way of his, the gums bright pink, the teeth bright white, a macabre sight which had horrified and fascinated the Maryson children and their children down the years. I turned and looked at him, a small man, skinny, unbeautiful as he had always been, and now hung with age, his eyes washed out, his hair a few unruly wisps, and his skin shrunk on his skull so that his chin, which never had been strong, was hardly there at all. His ears stood out like wings. Stiff hair grew out of them. He was about as ugly an old man as I had ever seen.

"Will you have another amputation?" Although I knew he was too old to bear it.

He knew it too and made no answer.

Next morning he did not come out to the porch, and when I went to him I found him still in bed, his face turned to the wall, stone dead, not of rot, it was too soon, but of an obstinate resolve to get death over with.

How do you know that? you ask.

I shrug. Because I knew him.

I buried him beside his ma and Uncle Benjamin, and told myself I would give up and follow him. But here I am, a daft old woman, ninety-six years old, still rocking on my porch. And here you sit, questioning upon your face, and will do so, I suppose, until you have wrung out of me the last drop of my story.

You wonder what became of my dear Tom, and I will tell you. They got him in the end. They could not bear to see a Negro so successful. He was arrested on a pretext and set to working on the railroad through the mountains into Tennessee. They came early in the morning, churning through the puddles from a night of rain. The last I saw him he was shackled at the wrists and chained to the back end of a cart. He turned and looked at me across his shoulder, then the cart jerked and he went running off with mud flying up behind his feet like wings.

By then he was no longer a young man, still strong but not

enough for railroad work. They worked him hatless through the summer and it baked his brain. They buried him beside the track without a marker or so much as a message to his wife to tell me where he lay. I heard this from a man who worked with him and managed to survive, and have gone forty years, three months and seven days without him.

Our children? Gone up north in search of an improvement in their lives. No, they do not visit. Why? Because they fear the South. I pray for them.

Christopher married Sylvie Younger, so I heard. I have forgiven him, what point in doing otherwise? A grudge erodes the soul. His fault was general to our time, although particular to him as well. A man in love is either a wise fool or a fool, and Christopher turned out to be a fool. He had no option but to murder Abraham, and would no doubt have done the same to Tom if he had seen him coming. And, who knows, perhaps his hand was behind Tom's death in the end. I must not think of that.

Aunt Lavinia had a letter from her surgeon to say that he had lost his wife, and she picked up her skirts and went off to him in Boston, never to be heard from by anyone in Wilmington again. Cousin Kate was taken in a yellow fever epidemic and the Colonel died a year later, of what I do not know, lack of tenderness perhaps. Abraham's wife Martha went to live in Beaufort with her parents. She remarried there, a man called Mister Little. Tom's father never did come home, and of his six brothers and sisters, not a one returned.

Mother Hester came to live with us, but she fretted for her Joel. An old voodoo woman provided us with a solution. She could trap a spirit in a purple bottle, so she said, and charged us nine dollars fifty-five, because, she said, Joel was not the sort to be caught easily. He was the most expensive ghost I ever knew, but he was worth it. Mother Hester lived five years with us, and when no one was about he came out of his new hiding place inside the kitchen wall and kept her company. He lives there still, I swear it, and Mother Hester too. When I go down to the old cabin I hear them whispering, and sometimes in the night I see what seems to be a candle flickering and figures passing back and forth.

As for me, I went on nursing. I never was a teacher as the fashion was for women then. If anyone learned anything from me, it was from following me about and watching, asking questions, which several women did, and young girls too, one of them my eldest daughter and another Baby Gold, both of whom are in Chicago. Glory, that sweet child, married a local man and died in childbirth. I did all I could to help her but it did no good.

You ask how Tom's relations were with me, and I know you mean how was it to be married to the woman who had once been his owner. I cannot speak for others, since I knew no others of our case, but Tom and I loved each other deeply, never a fight or squabble, not so much as a cross word. Indeed, he was so respectful I could hardly bring him to bed me at the first. I had to jump on him myself. But after that . . . suffice to say I had five babies one upon the other.

Your eyes grow round. But why? After all, it was you who asked the question. Did you not expect an answer? Or did you expect prevarication, tactfulness, a sly nod and a wink? I was a nurse, remember, and spent a lifetime wrestling with the body's functions. Winking is not in me.

No, I do not mean to reprimand. I'm glad you're here, although I'm sorry that I didn't catch your name. When you are gone, I will sit alone and rock and maybe weep a little. Then I will pray for strength and follow the three best men I ever knew—a friend, a brother, and a husband—into the next life. Perhaps it will be fairer and more peaceable.

READERS GUIDE TO

CHILD OF THE SOUTH

by Joanna Catherine Scott

DISCUSSION QUESTIONS

1. When we meet Eugenia Mae Spotswood, her race is not clear right away. Then we discover that she too is uncertain of her heritage. Did you have an impression of whether she was black, white, or of mixed race? Why?

2. Literacy and lack thereof is a major theme in *Child of the South*. The power of Genie's pen liberated Tom with "freedom papers." In what ways does literacy translate to empowerment for Tom and his community? By the same token, how does illiteracy keep communities oppressed?

3. The treatment of Conservative Southerners by the Yankees brings up issues of humiliation and retribution. We learn that just after the war, Yankee soldiers occupy the Clark-Compton main house while the family lives in the slaves' quarters. The

Clark-Comptons gripe about Wilmington being guarded by black soldiers. On a judicial level, Confederates have to be pardoned in Washington before rejoining the union. How does this tension play out in the book?

4. Clyde Bricket says the decision to sell the farm was easy because he no longer considers himself a man. What does he mean by this, and what are the implications for Tom?

5. Tom goes from being a slave who is "terrified by life into stupidity" to becoming a literate, successful farmer and preacher. What makes his transformation possible?

6. How does the Maryson name come into existence? What purpose does it serve?

7. Eugenia trusts the Yankee surgeon Dr. Wilkins enough to relay much of her past, including her family's slave-owning history and her father's suicide, but when she discloses her true quest—to find out whether she is the daughter of a slave—he reacts with coldness. If he's so sympathetic, why is her confession so sensational?

8. Compare the treatment of women to the treatment of freedmen by Conservative Southerners. How did they keep women and freedmen in their so-called "place"?

9. By prevailing social standards it's acceptable for Eugenia to extend charity to the black community, but unacceptable to

"consort" with blacks. Do you think she copes with this rule effectively? How?

10. In chapter fifteen, Uncle Benjamin expresses his desire to start preaching, but Tom and the others discourage him, citing Uncle Benjamin's history as a slave catcher. Uncle Benjamin quotes scripture: "Be sure your sins will find you out." What does he mean? Was the situation handled justly by Tom and the family?

11. Discuss the moral evolution of Clyde Bricket. How are he and the Maryson/Bricket farm a model for social change?

12. Tom criticizes one of Abraham's petitions to the Convention for its "groveling" tone, and for neglecting to include the right to vote among its requests. Abraham explains by saying, "Increments, Tom, increments." When Miss Kellogg wants Eugenia's support in opposing the prohibition of a black teacher from boarding with the whites, Eugenia objects, telling her she's trying to move faster than the so called "Southern mind" can tolerate. How does activism express itself in Tom, Eugenia, Abraham, and Mr. Ashley, the superintendent of schools?

13. Does Christopher Clark-Compton's proposal come as a surprise? How about Aunt Lavinia's reaction?

14. In the final chapter, ninety-six-year-old Eugenia has forgiven Christopher for his actions, saying, "His fault was general

to our time, although particular to him as well." She goes on to say he had no option but to murder Abraham. Do you agree with these statements?

15. Are our times both "fairer and more peaceable" than Eugenia's? What might surprise her most about race relations in modern America?